"I'm attracted to you," Cole admitted. **"And when I saw you last night...I hoped we'd have another chance."**

"We're an unlikely combination."

"Plaintiff's attorney and defendant?"

"Cocktail waitress and attorney." Among other things, she silently added.

"I'm asking you out for pie. Not proposing marriage."

"You're not?" Brenna teased, laughing at his absurd statement.

"No," he said. "I mean, yes. I take it back. You're beautiful when you laugh. I love the way it sounds. Will you marry me?"

Another jolt of awareness sizzled through Brenna's stomach. "Maybe. Let me think about it over pie...."

Dear Reader,

It's month two of our special fifteenth anniversary celebration, and that means more great reading for you. Just look what's in store.

Amnesia! It's one of the most popular plot twists around, and well it should be. All of us have probably wished, just for a minute, that we could start over again, be somebody else…fall in love all over again as if it were the first time. For three of our heroines this month, whether they want it or not, the chance is theirs. Start with Sharon Sala's *Roman's Heart*, the latest in her fabulous trilogy, THE JUSTICE WAY. Then check out *The Mercenary and the Marriage Vow* by Doreen Roberts. This book carries our new TRY TO REMEMBER flash—just so you won't forget about it! And then, sporting our MEN IN BLUE flash (because the hero's the kind of cop we could all fall in love with), there's *While She Was Sleeping* by Diane Pershing.

Of course, we have three other great books this month, too. Be sure to pick up Beverly Barton's *Emily and the Stranger*, and don't worry. Though this book isn't one of them, Beverly's extremely popular heroes, THE PROTECTORS, will be coming your way again soon. Kylie Brant is back with *Friday's Child*, a FAMILIES ARE FOREVER title. Not only will the hero and heroine win your heart, wait 'til you meet little Chloe. Finally, welcome new author Sharon Mignerey, who makes her debut with *Cassidy's Courtship*.

And, of course, don't forget to come back next month for more of the best and most excitingly romantic reading around, right here in Silhouette Intimate Moments.

Leslie Wainger
Senior Editor and Editorial Coordinator

Please address questions and book requests to:
Silhouette Reader Service
U.S.: 3010 Walden Ave., P.O. Box 1325, Buffalo, NY 14269
Canadian: P.O. Box 609, Fort Erie, Ont. L2A 5X3

CASSIDY'S COURTSHIP

SHARON MIGNEREY

Silhouette® INTIMATE™ MOMENTS®

Published by Silhouette Books

America's Publisher of Contemporary Romance

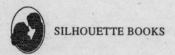

SILHOUETTE BOOKS

ISBN 0-373-07864-1

CASSIDY'S COURTSHIP

Printed in U.S.A.

SHARON MIGNEREY

lives in Colorado, with her husband and two dogs, Angel and Squirt. From the time she figured out that spelling words could be turned into stories, she knew being a writer was how she wanted to spend her life. She won RWA's Golden Heart Award in 1995, validation that she was on the right path.

When she's not writing, she loves puttering around in her garden, walking her dogs along the South Platte River, and spending time at the family cabin in Colorado's four-corners region.

Sharon loves hearing from readers, and you can write to her in care of Silhouette Books, 300 East 42nd Street, 6th floor, New York, NY 10017.

Heroes, each one…
My dad, Dan
My husband, Les
My friend Richard

Prologue

"Stand up straight when I'm talking to you, Brenna James," her father ordered. "And stop looking at your feet. Look at me. Explain these grades." He waved her school papers in her face.

Brenna stole a glance at her older brother, Michael, who stood with her in front of their father, then back at her father. Her eyes lit on the shiny insignia on his shoulders, then on the rows of colorful ribbons above his pocket.

"Answer me."

Her eyes jerked to his, and her chin quivered.

"I don't understand this, Brenna. Look at how well your brother is doing in school. You know what the difference is between you and Michael? He tries. You *don't* try, do you?"

"I try." A single tear slid down each cheek.

"I try, what?"

She swallowed and her gaze fell to her shoes. "I try, sir."

"Look at me, Brenna."

She raised her eyes to meet her father's. She hated looking at his eyes. They made her hurt clear down inside her tummy.

"You don't try." He lifted her chin with hard fingers. "You'll never make it to second grade like your brother unless you pay attention to your studies. You want me to be proud of you, don't you? The way I'm proud of Michael?''

"Yes, sir."

"Then you have to bring home papers with good marks. Now, stop crying. You're not a baby anymore, are you?"

"No, sir." She tightened her lips to keep them from quivering. "Daddy?"

"Yes, Brenna."

"It's hard for me." She dropped her head, then, peeking a glance at him, added, "Sir."

"The things that matter are always hard. You have the potential to have perfect papers, just like Michael. I expect you to practice. Do you understand me?"

"Yes, sir," she said. And because he expected it, she added, "I'll practice, sir."

Brenna sat down at the kitchen table, her legs dangling from the chair, and watched her brother hand his papers to their father. His papers were *excellent*, that's what the teacher said. "Michael's work is always excellent, Captain. He's such a bright boy."

Michael smiled and her father smiled. All because Michael had perfect papers.

She picked up a pencil and began tracing the letters. Out of the corner of her eye, she watched her father tousle Michael's hair.

She knew who was perfect. And she knew who her father loved. Michael. Tears splashed on her tablet. She couldn't be perfect like Michael. She tried so hard, but it was never good enough. Not perfect. So why even try?

Gripping the pencil, she drew bold, black lines across her paper, over her carefully formed letters.

Chapter 1

"Am I understanding you correctly, Ms. James? You didn't *know* you had violated your lease when you began storing dangerous chemicals on the premises?" Cole Cassidy moved toward the witness stand, his inner turmoil at odds with the steady, aggressive tone of his questions. Grudge matches were not—never had been—his thing. He regretted he had allowed himself to become embroiled in this one.

"I don't know what dangerous chemicals you mean."

Brenna James's eyes, clear and bright as a sunny day, never left his face. Cole's experience had taught him that liars and cheats couldn't look you straight in the eye. Her unwavering gaze hadn't fallen beneath his intense stare even once.

"Fifty-five-gallon drums of—"

"Soap," she finished, her gaze straying to Cole's client, Harvey Bates. "Biodegradable soap."

"You've also stated in your deposition that you kept ammonia, naphthalene and other solvents in your shop."

"Not in fifty-five-gallon drums."

"What kind of quantities?" Cole believed that, whatever she had stored in her shop, it was insignificant compared to that used by the automotive custom paint shop, a tenant in the same industrial complex.

"A gallon or two at a time, at the most." Her gaze drifted from his a moment, then returned. "Once I filled out an order for supplies incorrectly, and for about two weeks there was a drum of ammonia in the shop." She paused. "The kind used for commercial refrigeration."

Cole was stunned at her admission. There was always hope that someone would slip and volunteer information, but it never happened. Never. Cases were built on evasions, omission and deception. A good attorney coached his clients never to answer questions that weren't asked.

Cole cleared his throat. "You were aware of the potential hazard?"

"Yes. As soon as we knew it would be several days before it could be picked up, I called Harvey."

Yes, the woman answered. No evasion, no omission, no deception. Like so much else with this case, Brenna James's testimony didn't fit Bates's accusations that she had intended to defraud him. Cole studied her face for a moment. He believed her. He turned around to stare at his client, who shrugged his shoulders.

His client, hell. Bates and a senior partner, Roger Markham, were close friends. The case, too insignificant for a partner, had been assigned to Cole.

Bates's civil case against Brenna James had two charges, neither of which should be taking up the court's time. He accused her of storing "dangerous chemicals" on the premises and of writing bad checks. The clause in her lease that described dangerous chemicals was so ambiguous it could have included tap water. As for the check, that should have been handled by a collection service.

Cole stalked back to his table and picked up the only real piece of evidence he had in the case—a check she had written for two months' rent that had bounced higher than a spiked football. Triple jeopardy, Cole thought, recalling Colorado's stiff penalties for writing bad checks. If the woman didn't have seventeen hundred dollars, it was a sure bet she didn't have the five thousand that she would owe Bates under the state statutes.

Cole's research during his discovery revealed James Cleaning Service had held its own for a little more than three years, and the clients

Cole had talked to had been universally enthusiastic about Brenna James and her staff. However, shortly after the bookkeeper quit to have a baby, the business took a downhill slide. The whole thing perplexed Cole. He knew he hadn't asked the right questions, but damned if he could figure out what the right questions were.

Cole handed her the check. "This is a check from James Cleaning Service, signed by you, and made payable to Harvey Bates, isn't it?"

"Yes."

He took the check back. "Did it ever clear your bank?"

"I thought it had."

"Ms. James, I find it inconceivable that you expect the court to believe—"

"Is there a question in that statement, Mr. Cassidy?" the judge interrupted.

Cole glanced at the judge, then back at Brenna's attorney. He deserved to be admonished by the judge, but he would have preferred an objection from John Miller. Cole had become more aggressive, trying to goad the man into actively defending his client. Miller had not asked for a pre-trial deposition from Harvey Bates, had not issued a subpoena for Bates to testify, had not adequately defended his client in any way at all—another puzzle.

Cole returned to the table where Harvey Bates sat. Unlike the woman on the stand, Bates avoided Cole's eyes.

Cole picked up a copy of a bank statement and handed it to Brenna. "Recognize this?"

He watched her as she studied the sheet.

A full minute passed before she answered, "It's a bank statement from my business account."

"For what month, Ms. James?"

Another long pause followed.

Come on, Brenna, he silently urged. Let's get this over with.

"February."

Cole held the check back up. "Did this check clear, Ms. James? Check number eighteen fifty-three?"

He waited patiently as one slim finger slid slowly down the column of figures. She gave the task her complete concentration, just as she had with every other exhibit he had asked her to examine. He caught the bored expression of her attorney and the look of lazy indolence from Harvey Bates. Both men angered Cole. There was no sense in litigating a seventeen-hundred-dollar dispute. This was exactly the petty kind of civil suit that kept the courts clogged.

And keeps you employed, came a nagging thought.

Bates had told Cole he wanted to be paid in full. "Where does she have the money?" Cole had wanted to know. The credit report he ran on her indicated she was twenty-six years old and broke, with no property that could be attached. Her cleaning service had closed, and she had a mountain of debt. Bates insisted her family had money—her father was a retired colonel who had a fat-cat consulting contract with his old Pentagon cronies. If Brenna's father had given a single thin dime to her, Cole hadn't been able to find it.

Cole longed for the case to be finished. He backed across the floor until he could see them all—the judge, the court recorder, the clerk, the bailiff, his client, Brenna James and her attorney.

How did you get into this mess, Brenna James? he wondered for the thousandth time. Despite the evidence, he believed she was telling the truth. From the beginning he felt a primal recognition that had little to do with time or space. They had never had a personal conversation. That didn't matter. He had been attracted to more sophisticated women, perhaps even more beautiful. He had been engaged to one. But no one—*no one*—had ever hit him in the gut the way Brenna James did.

Realist that he was, he didn't entertain a single notion of pursuing her when this was over. He was Bates's tool of retribution. End of fantasy.

Today that made him angry.

"I'm waiting, Ms. James." His strident voice broke through the quiet courtroom, his hand slapping the varnished wood of the rail with a resounding whack.

"It isn't listed here," she answered, her calm reply stretching the limits of his temper.

He pushed himself away from the rail, picked up another bank statement from the table. "Did the check clear in March?"

This time she didn't glance at the sheet. "I don't believe so."

"In April, Ms. James? Did it clear in April?"

She shook her head, and her eyes never left him.

"I can't hear you." When in hell was her attorney going to object?

"No."

"Did this check clear your back during any month that you know of, Ms. James?"

For the first time, her voice faltered. "No."

Her whisper knifed through him. "I can't hear you, Ms. James."

Cole was surprised how hard it was to keep from averting his own gaze when she looked up.

"No," she repeated. "It didn't clear."

Cole handed the papers to the bailiff. "Enter these as exhibits eight through ten." He stalked back to the plaintiff's table and thought about the questions he had intended to ask, about the points of law he considered important. He faced Brenna, assessing the inexpensive gray suit she had worn both times he had seen her, her dark hair pulled into a bun at her nape. Her expression and unwavering gaze gave him no clue to her thoughts.

He sat down. "I have no further questions, Your Honor."

"Your witness," the judge told her attorney.

John Miller stood, fastening the button of his jacket in an automatic gesture. "I have no questions, Your Honor." He sat back down.

The flat statement stunned Cole.

His attention shifted to Brenna, and he wondered if her attorney's actions came as a surprise. Her expression had not changed. Cole might have thought she was prepared for her attorney's statement had he not noticed her clasped hands—so tight her knuckles were white with tension.

"Do you want to address the court, Ms. James?" the judge asked.

She stared at her attorney. The courtroom was quiet except for a muffled cough and the scrape of a chair across the hardwood floor. When John Miller dropped his gaze to the table, she answered, "No, sir."

Cole wanted to leap out of his chair, wanted to demand an explanation, wanted to yell at John Miller, wanted to rant at Brenna for not speaking out to defend herself.

Instead he sat and waited for the judge to speak.

Judge McCauley reviewed the contents of the file in front of him, then said, "Ms. James, I had not planned to announce my decision today. However, as you have not presented any evidence in your favor, you leave me with no other choice. This court finds in favor of the plaintiff. This judgment includes all moneys owed to Mr. Bates as stated in his complaint, all penalties due him under the statutes of the State of Colorado, court costs and any and all attorneys' fees he is entitled to collect. Mr. Cassidy, would you prepare the order?''

''Bailiff, please note that. Mr. Cassidy, Mr. Miller, I want to see both of you in my chambers. *Now.*''

He slammed the gavel down.

''Court dismissed,'' the bailiff said before following the judge out of the courtroom.

Cole stood and began gathering the papers on the table. Next to him, Bates also stood, hung the ivory-and-brass handle of his cane over his forearm, and made a show of unwrapping a cigar. He clipped off the end, which he let drop on the floor.

''Good work, Cassidy.'' He slapped Cole on the back. ''Roger Markham will be proud of you, boy.''

Cole stuffed the folders into his briefcase without speaking. He snapped the lid shut and looked at his client. Bates's attention was fastened on a picture of the President of the United States hanging on the far wall. Cole was suddenly reminded of the previous two cases he had won and how hollow those victories had also felt. Neither of those clients reminded him of Harvey Bates, but they, too, had said, ''Good work.'' And Cole had won largely because his clients could afford the legal trappings that came with the huge retainer his firm required. Not because justice or the law had been served.

Cole frowned, disliking the turn of his thoughts. He wanted to believe he fought for justice. He wanted to believe he represented cases that were right in the abstract, not necessarily right because they were profitable for the firm.

''I want an airtight agreement, complete with a confession that she knew that check was fraudulent,'' Bates said.

Cole's gaze followed Brenna James as she walked out of the courtroom alone. Her back was straight under the conservative suit, the line of her body feminine and elegant as royalty.

Cole's eyes narrowed when his gaze returned to Bates.

''I suppose you'd like a pound of flesh, too,'' Cole said, his temper not quite in check.

Bates smiled, all teeth and no humor. ''You've got it.''

''Her attorney will recommend she sign the minimum agreement required to comply with the judgment." Damn Roger Markham's friendship with Harvey Bates, Cole thought. As cases went, this one was the dregs—vindictive if profitable.

Bates pulled an engraved gold lighter out of his vest pocket. "Her attorney doesn't know squat. She'll sign whatever you put in front of her."

"My secretary will call you as soon as we have the terms worked out and she's signed—"

"No terms. Cash. And you call me. I want to be there when she signs."

"She doesn't have the cash, Bates. If she did, you would have seen it by now."

"All she has to do is ask her rich daddy." Bates lit the cigar, ignoring the No Smoking signs posted on the wall. He inhaled deeply and walked away, leaning heavily on the cane, his limp more pronounced than usual.

"I want to know what the hell is going on," Judge McCauley said. He sat down behind his desk and loosened his tie. "I've never in fifteen years seen such a poor defense, John Miller. I will not tolerate such indifference in my court again. Do I make myself clear?"

Miller pulled at his mustache. "Yes."

His gaze shifted from Miller to Cole, who resisted squirming under the judge's pointed finger. "And you came this close," he said holding his thumb and forefinger an inch apart, "to overplay this case. You didn't have a single valid reason to badger the defendant. I allowed you to continue your examination because of my friendship with David Simmons. I expect better from an associate of his firm than what you presented here today."

Cole's eyes didn't waver from the judge's. "I understand, sir."

The judge gave his head a sharp nod. "I expect to see the order for this judgment on my desk before the end of the week. And I expect the two of you to hammer out an agreement for the method of payment." He closed the folder and swiveled his chair around to face the window. "That will be all."

Miller followed Cole out of the judge's office. "Let me know when you've got the order drafted," he said. "Brenna and I will come by your office."

"Will that be before or after you review it?"

Miller raised an eyebrow. "For being on the winning side, you're a little testy, don't you think?"

"And you act like you don't give a damn," Cole said.

"Spare me the bleeding heart act," Miller said walking away from Cole. "You were only in this for the money—what happened to Brenna James didn't matter a bit."

Cole stopped cold. The other attorney walked down the middle of the corridor, his footsteps echoing against the tile floor. At the door leading outside, he turned, gave Cole a mocking salute, and went outside.

Damn John Miller for being right.

Chapter 2

"Here's the revised settlement agreement on the Bates case," said Cole's secretary, Myra, from the doorway of Cole's office. She glanced at her watch. "With ten minutes to spare."

"I appreciate your making those last-minute changes. Thanks." Like everything else in this case, the last week had been filled with tension and demands from Harvey Bates.

Myra set the documents on the corner of his desk. "Spare me the thanks. I know the lovely Mr. Bates is to blame, not you." She moved toward the big window behind Cole's desk.

He followed her gaze outside to the gray expanse of Cherry Creek Reservoir. The bleak windswept water suited his mood perfectly. He wished he was out there in his boat despite the weather. Even a storm would be preferable to the meeting in a few minutes with Harvey Bates and Brenna James.

"Do you think she's guilty?" Myra asked a moment later.

Cole didn't have to ask if she meant Brenna James. "Guilty or not guilty doesn't apply in a civil case."

"Don't get all technical on me," Myra returned, "or I'll start straightening your tie and treating you like the son you're young enough to be."

"Yes, ma'am."

Over her shoulder, she threw him a mocking dark glance at his tone. He grinned, then stood and put his hands in his pockets.

"The settlement makes her sound like a terrible person," Myra continued.

"It does," he agreed.

"Is she?"

"In the eyes of the law, it doesn't matter."

"You're still not telling me what *you* really think," Myra chided.

He didn't dare confess to his secretary that Brenna James haunted his dreams, that if he had a way to change the outcome of the case, he would do it.

"I think she's in a lot of trouble," he said, finally.

In the street below, a bus pulled to a stop, and a single rider emerged, absently catching his attention. Brenna James.

She gazed at the building a long moment as if assuring herself she was at the right place, then turned up the collar on her coat and thrust her hands into her pockets. Her hair was pulled into a bun; he wondered if she ever wore it loose.

She brought her hands out of her pockets, and carefully pulled a hot-pink knit hat over her hair, a flare of color for the gloomy day. Again, her hands disappeared into her pockets as she meandered down the tree-lined sidewalk away from the office building and toward the lake. If the chill bothered her, from this distance Cole couldn't tell. The bright color of her hat was a beacon that held his attention.

"That's her, isn't it?" Myra asked. "When she was here earlier for the depositions, I remember thinking she was pretty. A little on the quiet side, but then, in her situation, who wouldn't be."

Cole nodded.

"Most of the time, I think we're doing the right things. I read the agreements, and they make sense." Myra shook her head. "This time, I know what Harvey Bates—what we're doing for him—is wrong." She glanced at Cole. "It might be legal—"

"It's legal," Cole assured her.

"That doesn't make it right." Myra looked again at her watch, then crossed the room. "Back to work before my grumpy boss fires me."

Cole grinned at her. "So now I'm grumpy."

"Grumpy as a toddler cutting teeth," was Myra's parting shot as she left the office.

Alone, Cole thought about Miller's accusation that he was in this only for the money. The idea nagged at him. His gaze strayed back to the woman on the street.

Victory, and it wasn't sweet at all.

An interminable twenty minutes later, Myra knocked, then pushed open the door. "Everybody's here, Cole."

"Thanks." He rose from his chair, stretched a kink out of his back, and put on his jacket.

"Expecting trouble?" Myra asked, picking up the folder.

"No."

"You've got that worried look again."

"Hell, what could I be worried about? We won the case. Bates gets his pound of flesh, and—"

"If you tell me 'life is good,' I'll smack you," Myra said.

"Wouldn't dream of it." Cole took the folder from her and strode down the hall.

He walked through the conference-room door and in an instant assessed the small changes that had taken place in Brenna during the last week. Her skin was translucent. The blue, almost bruised-looking shadows under her eyes told him too much about her state of mind. She looked as though she hadn't had a good night's sleep in weeks. He didn't like knowing that his actions had contributed.

She looked up, her features tightly schooled into an expression of calm he almost believed. Almost.

Instead of the gray suit he had been expecting her to wear, she was dressed with almost military precision in navy slacks, a matching jacket and a white tailored shirt.

What had she been doing the last few days, he wondered. Who had she confided in? Her composure was light-years away from the turmoil he felt, and he envied her self-possession. Calm detachment had never been one of his strengths, and his temper got him into trouble more regularly than he cared to admit.

"Miss James, Mr. Miller," Cole said, extending his hand to Brenna.

He remembered her handshake from prior meetings—warm and

firm, her fingers long and her hand slim inside his own broad palm. He wanted to raise her wrist to his face and inhale the scent of her skin.

As always, the gaze from her clear gray eyes was direct. This close, freckles and the fine grain of her skin drew his attention, as did a single larger freckle at the corner of her eye. Whatever her thoughts, they were well hidden. At that moment he would have given all of Harvey Bates's retainer to know what she was thinking.

She pulled back, and reluctantly Cole let go of her hand, hoping his expression betrayed no more of his thoughts than hers did.

Cole shook John Miller's hand and turned to Harvey Bates. As usual, Cole's client was impeccably dressed, his charcoal suit, custom-made shirt, and conservative tie the epitome of the power suit. Bates's attention was on Brenna, his dislike of her evident.

"Have you had a chance to review the agreement, Miss James?" Cole asked when everyone was seated around the table.

"Yes."

"Do you have any questions?"

"No," she said with a slight shake to her head, looking briefly at John Miller, who was sitting beside her. "I just want this to be done with."

This was the most emotion Cole had heard in her voice since her anguished whisper in the courtroom. His gaze slid across the room to his client, then came back to Brenna. "You understand the language in this order goes beyond what the court required in its judgment?"

"Is this true?" she asked, turning to her attorney. When he didn't look at her, she repeated, "Is it?"

He stared a moment at his hands folded on the table, then sighed and met her gaze. "Technically, it could be."

Cole extended his hand across the table. "Mr. Miller, did you explain to your client this agreement amounts to a confession of a felony?" His eyes never left Brenna's face though his question was not directed to her.

Her attention, however, was focused solely on her attorney.

Bates slammed his palm on the walnut table. "She says she's ready to sign. So let's get on with it."

"Did you?" Studying Brenna, Cole waited for Miller's answer and ignored his client. The seconds ticked by, her mouth tightened, the first stirring of anger cracking through her calm expression.

Bates fired a gold Cross pen down the length of the table. "She said she's ready to sign."

Brenna's fingers closed around the pen, then she slid it away from her.

"In a minute," Cole said quietly. "She has the right to understand the possible consequences of this."

"What consequences?" she asked, her voice little more than a whisper.

Her query was lost under Bates's imperative tone. "There's only one that matters, boy! She doesn't have the money. No money, no release. If she's got a problem, let *her* lawyer handle it."

Cole's gaze blistered over Harvey Bates, his patience with the man gone, before he turned to John Miller. "So handle it. She asked. Tell her."

Miller pushed his chair away from the table, gave Brenna a frowning glance, and turned to Cole. "It's the agreement you said you had to have, Cassidy. My client—"

"I want to know what consequences Mr. Cassidy is talking about, John," Brenna interrupted, all traces of her earlier huskiness gone.

"Are you changing your mind?" Miller asked her. The question might have been solicitous. Instead it was belligerent. "When we met yesterday, you just wanted—"

"What is he talking about? Specifically?"

Miller scratched his nose. "He's referring to a clause that protects Bates in the event you have trouble paying off the settlement."

Brenna cut her lawyer off with a small wave of her hand and focused her attention on Cole. "Protects Mr. Bates how?"

"Paragraph six is a confession that you intended to commit fraud when that check was written," Cole said, giving her the stark truth that her attorney refused to spell out for her.

A tiny muscle twitched at the corner of her mouth. "You mean as in going-to-jail fraud?"

Cole nodded. He felt like a bully picking on the smallest kid on the block for even having drafted the language in the agreement.

"It's not just the money, is it, Harvey?" she asked, her voice devoid of emotion, almost as though she already knew the answer.

"I'm the example, right? To make sure everyone knows you don't mess with Harvey Bates."

"Damn right," Bates drawled, his lips curved into a cruel smile. He pushed the pen back toward her. "Sign."

"Take out that paragraph," Brenna said.

"I want it in!" Bates shouted. "It's—"

"No," she interrupted, her voice calm, a stark contrast to his outburst. Turning her attention back to her attorney, she asked, "Why didn't you explain this to me?"

He shrugged. "I assumed you'd point out anything that bothered you."

"And I *assumed* you were looking out for me." She stood up suddenly. "I *assumed* you were giving me the best advice you had! I assumed—" She stopped speaking, her voice shaking with anger.

Her distress flowed over Cole like a cold November wind. Other people had lost control in this room, but it had never made his stomach tighten so painfully; he hadn't wanted to protect and comfort them as he did her. But he couldn't shield Brenna from the consequences of her actions. He could do even less to protect her from Harvey Bates's twisted need for revenge or John Miller's incompetence.

Her eyes shimmered with sudden tears. With a poise that Cole admired, she raised her head and blinked the tears away. "I assumed you were doing the job I hired you to do. I couldn't figure out why you didn't—oh! Never mind! I trusted you!" Her hands balled into fists that she held rigidly at her sides. She closed her eyes and sighed. Her shoulders slumped. With all the fight gone from her voice, she repeated, "I trusted you."

Cole felt the defeat in her as though it were his own.

When her eyes opened, they were bleak as a bitter winter day on a Nebraska prairie. "You're fired, John."

She unclenched her fingers and dropped her gaze to her hands. An instant later, she lifted her head and smiled, but her expression remained brittle—no softening or lightening of her features.

"I made a mistake, Harvey. I wrote you a check that I didn't have the funds to cover. And then I make another mistake. I thought you were a reasonable man who understood that I had gotten myself into a mess, and with a little time I could get out. But patience isn't your strong suit, is it, Harvey? And, as for sympathy or understanding or a little human decency—those would never have entered into a business decision, would they?'' She paused and stared at him, clearly waiting for him to look up. ''You can't look me in the eye, even today, can you? You've won! Collect your damn money any way you can.''

''Ask your daddy,'' Bates said, raising his head. ''Then you can pick up the pieces and get on with your life.''

''Go to hell, Harvey,'' she said.

She picked up her small clutch, paused at the door, and turned to look at Cole. He met her gaze squarely, more pleased than he should have been that she had taken matters into her own hands. He doubted another attorney could salvage anything out of the case for her, but she couldn't do worse than John Miller.

Seconds ticked by.

Cole wondered again what she'd look like smiling. Really smiling. *Ah, Brenna, why couldn't I have met you some other way?*

Her attention shifted to Miller, who squirmed under her scrutiny. When her stare shifted to Bates, his color rose within the beat of a second, he dropped his gaze. She looked at him a long moment before her eyes returned to Cole.

He sensed just how betrayed she felt, knew he had been a part of it, and he hated the association. Without a word, she walked through the door and shut it behind her with a firm click.

One instant, then two beat by without a sound.

''Well. You're fired, Cassidy,'' Bates said, mimicking her tone.

''Too late,'' Cole replied. ''In case you hadn't noticed, I already quit.''

Back in his office, Cole felt as though a hundred-pound pack had been taken off his back. Representing Harvey Bates was only the most recent in a series of cases that considered only the letter, not the spirit, of the law. The time had come to make a change.

Cole stared through the window, mentally wording his resignation to Jones, Markham and Simmons. No more representing clients simply because they were assigned.

He scowled, turning that over in his mind. The overload he had accepted from Peter Jones and David Simmons had been fine. So what was it with Roger's clients? Cole hadn't wanted to represent

Bates. Even less had he wanted to represent the latest client Roger had sent him, a man accused of sexual harassment. He had an arrogant, misogynistic attitude—the man had probably done everything he was accused of and more.

Cole sat down and pulled a yellow pad out of the lap drawer.

Walking out is cutting off my nose to spite my face. He had been drawn to Jones, Markham and Simmons because of the reputation the firm had in the legal community. Harder to admit, but just as true, was that Cole liked the aura of power.

There were practical things to be considered... Car payments and the two-story house on three acres that made him remember all the best things about the ranch where he had grown up. His house was far enough away from Denver's lights that he could see more constellations than the Pleiades.

Cole had hoped his house would be filled with children by now. When he bought the land five years ago, the dream of family had been foremost. And he had met Susan Stranahan. Tall, cultured, well educated and highly intelligent, she had a fine mind and a body that he loved loving.

She had career aspirations of her own that eventually took her to a Fortune 500 company in Chicago. Reluctantly, he had put his house up for sale, had spent time with her in Chicago. They had found a great apartment in the Near North Side. Trendy, upscale and very urban. Susan had loved it.

Cole had wanted the lifestyle, because living there would prove to his family that he had made it. He had interviewed with a couple of good Chicago law firms and knew he would be offered a position. The final piece fell into place when his house was sold. The house where he had imagined the new trees growing into tall, shady ones. The house where he had imagined raising his children.

And he hadn't been able to sign the sales agreement. A breach of contract that cost him thousands of dollars. Susan told him he had never stopped being a farm boy. In the end, she had moved to Chicago alone.

Cole began scribbling notes on the pad, rehearsing how to ease himself away from Roger's workload without causing a breach. He filled one page, then another, his chaotic thoughts becoming more orderly under his forced discipline.

"Cole, we've got to talk," said Roger Markham from the doorway.

Cole looked up and motioned the older attorney into his office. "I was just on my way to see you." He would have liked another few minutes to rehearse what he wanted to say, but also welcomed the chance to get his concerns on the table. "Have a seat."

Roger walked across the office and wrapped his hands over the back of one of the navy blue leather chairs in front of Cole's desk. "Thank you. No."

"Bates came to see you."

"Yes. He tells me that Miss James left without signing the agreement. That you advised her not to sign it."

"She didn't understand that she was confessing to a felony."

"That isn't your problem. Mr. Bates is our client. *My* client. And I put him in your trust." Roger picked up a brass sailboat off Cole's desk. "It's his feeling you betrayed that trust."

"I drew up the agreement he wanted." Cole set down his pen.

"And then you recommended that Ms. James not sign it, didn't you?"

"In actual fact, no!" Cole responded with heat.

"Isn't it up to her attorney to—"

"Her attorney hadn't done one damn thing to protect her!" Cole watched fingerprints appear on the shiny sails of the boat. The boat normally reminded him of the exhilarating sense of freedom he felt sailing. Today, he was reminded of sudden storms, of hidden rock formations beneath the surface of the water.

"That also isn't your problem."

"What about justice? What about ethics?"

"The court dispenses justice, Cole. Not you. Not me. As officers of the court, our place is to present information." Roger's arguments were as hard and clear as lacquer over brass. "Justice is not ours to hand out. As for ethics, yours are seriously lacking. I need some assurance this incident will not be repeated."

"That's something I can't promise," Cole said. "I don't have any regrets about this."

Roger ran a finger down one of the sails of the brass boat. "That's unfortunate. You failed to give our client your best representation...as required by your oath as an officer of the court. The same things you accuse John Miller of. Mr. Bates believes you have compromised any chance he has of collecting the money due him.''

Cole folded his arms across his chest, and tried to assume a calm exterior. Somehow there was a way to make Roger understand.

"She doesn't have any money. She doesn't have any assets that I can find. She doesn't own anything that can be attached. No property. No car. She doesn't have a dime in savings. All she had going for her was her business—which is so deep in the hole, she'll be years clearing it up if she doesn't declare bankruptcy."

Roger smiled. "Then at last you understand."

"What?"

"If this debt is recorded as resulting from fraud—"

"I know, I know. It's immune to bankruptcy," Cole interrupted. "She has to pay. She gets labeled as a felon, and she could go to jail."

"Exactly."

"Never mind that it wasn't."

"Fraud? How do you know?" Roger countered. "She may be a very touch cookie behind a vulnerable and pretty face. In any event, that fact is irrelevant."

"It isn't enough to have me off the case." Cole unfolded his arms and pushed his chair away from the desk. "He wants you to fire me, doesn't he?"

"Naturally."

"And?"

"Given what you've told me, I think that may be the only logical course of action."

"But?"

Roger set the sailboat down. "There are no 'buts.' I don't think you understand the obligation an attorney has to his clients."

"Unfortunately, I do. I'll have my resignation on your desk within the hour, Roger."

An expression that was more regret than relief passed over Roger's face. "I'm sorry it ended this way, Cole."

Chapter 3

"Hey, Brenna," one of the sports bar patrons called. "Who won the World Series in 1955?"

"Brooklyn," she responded cheerfully, setting another beer in front of him. "Played against the Yankees in seven." It was the sort of question George and his assorted buddies had been asking her since she began working in the sports theme bar two months ago, and they'd discovered she had an uncanny memory for all sorts of baseball trivia. It was the sole arena in her life where she had outshone her brother, Michael.

"Told ya!" George grinned, poking one of the other men at the table. "Pay up."

Brenna tapped her sneaker-clad foot on the floor and put out her own hand. "That's right, George. Pay up."

He laughed and set a bill in her hand. "Bet you don't know who the Iron Horse is," he said.

Brenna counted out the correct change. "That's a bet you'd lose, George. And, since he's dead, it's *was,* not is." She paused for effect. "Lou Gehrig."

He raised his mug in a salute. "Not only does she know everything about baseball we can throw at her, she never forgets an order. Tell the boss to give you a raise.''

"I'll do that." She winked at him, took the orders for another round of beers, and left the table.

The good-natured banter made the nights go pretty fast, but Brenna still would have preferred to be somewhere else. It wasn't that she disliked the job or the people she worked with or the patrons who came to the bar. It wasn't even dressing up like a cheerleader, complete with ponytail and bobby socks, though she wasn't fond of that at all. What she missed, what she longed for, was challenge.

The litany that she needed challenge like she needed another lawsuit was automatic. Her cleaning service had provided more than enough challenge—finding new customers, hiring good people who needed a chance. Good people—seventeen of them—she reminded herself, lost their jobs when she got into trouble with *challenging*.

Give it a rest, she silently reprimanded herself.

She gathered up the last empty glasses off a vacant table, wiped it down, and returned the glasses to the bar. Theo, the bartender, gave her an absent smile as he took the glasses from her. His attention, like everyone else's in the bar, focused on the big-screen TV where a Rockies player was up to bat against the Cardinals in the bottom of the sixth inning.

When the door to the bar opened and a tall man in a business suit entered, Brenna watched to see where he sat so she could promptly serve him. She didn't expect to recognize him. When she did, her palms instantly became clammy.

Cole Cassidy. This was the last place she imagined seeing him. If she had imagined him at all, which she hadn't. He gave the bar a thorough once-over, his gaze lingering on Theo a moment, then made his way toward a deserted table at the back of the bar.

Anger surged through her. Its intensity surprised and upset her. The lawsuit was long over. She would be living with the consequences for years, but she could deal with that. She would do what she had always done. Survive.

She couldn't remake the past. But she learned its lessons well. Trust wasn't a bond unless written on a piece of paper. Honor wasn't your word unless spoken in front of a witness.

"Customer, Brenna," Theo said, snapping his fingers.

"Yeah, I see him." Picking up her tray, she closed her volatile emotions behind a mask of calm. She had learned from her mother, a military wife first and always, you never let the world see your emotions—happy or sad or angry or scared. Brenna learned early and well just how right her mother was.

She would deal with Cole Cassidy by imagining he was just one more man stopping by for a couple of beers on the way home from work. That's all. And he did look as though he had just come from work, though the hour was late for the come-from-work crowd.

He looked comfortable in his charcoal dress slacks and a pale gray sports coat. The top button of his crisp white shirt was open behind a conservative tie. He was taller and more broad-shouldered than she remembered. Gone was the razor haircut in favor of a more casual, slightly disheveled style. His face was tanned, the top layers of his brown hair sun-streaked. Much as she hated admitting she liked anything about the man, she thought the new look suited him better.

She reminded herself that a man wasn't necessarily worth knowing simply because he looked good.

Cole Cassidy wasn't a man she wanted to know, and if she was lucky he wouldn't recognize her.

He sat down, his face expressionless as he focused on the TV.

Another wave of anger washed over Brenna as she approached his table. She hadn't thought anyone would ever again be able to stir her this deeply. Beneath the anger, she was filled with that same sense of panic she felt only in her father's presence. Nothing about Cole Cassidy, though, reminded her of her father, the Colonel. She licked her dry lips and resisted the urge to run.

Brenna set a napkin in front of Cole Cassidy, then asked, "What can I get for you?"

Instead of the direct, unblinking predatory stare she remembered so well, recognition was followed by surprise and pleasure.

"Brenna James?" He smiled. It lit his face, crinkling his eyes, revealing a dimple in one cheek. "It's great to see you. I've wondered every day what happened to you."

His warmth almost undid her, contradicting all the reasons she had to dislike him.

"Now you know. What can I get for you?" Her voice was too curt, too defensive, her control less than she thought, far less than she wanted. *So he has a good memory. So what? Why does he look at me like he gives a damn?*

His smile faltered as though her biting reply bothered him. "What do you have on draft?"

She gave him three choices, shifting her glance away from his eyes. After taking his order, she checked with her other customers and took their orders for refills. She returned to Cole's table a few minutes later with his beer, aware he had been watching her the whole time. He was silent as she set the drink on a napkin, picked up the five-dollar bill, and made change.

"You're looking well," he said, giving her another smile, this one more tentative.

Her gaze caught his and held. It took all her self-control to keep from returning his smile.

"Thanks." Her reply was automatic, but her throat felt dry, her palms clammy—a reaction to a man's subtle opening gambit that he was interested. She didn't like her reaction, and she didn't want to like him or his smile. With this man, nothing could be so simple— if he appeared to be interested in her, there had to be a reason.

"Can I talk to you a minute after you've delivered those?" he asked, motioning to the other drinks on her tray.

"I can't think of a single thing we have to say to each other." At least her hunch about that had been right.

He sighed. "We have a lot to say to each other."

"I don't think so," she replied, her tone even, and walked away from his table.

She would never let him know that he had stripped her of all her defenses, leaving her with only her deepest held secret all but laid bare for him to discover.

Or maybe he knew, maybe John Miller had told him. Never had she felt so powerless as she had during the long months of the lawsuit. Losing her business had been bad enough, but the lawsuit had been worse. To this day she didn't understand Mr. Bates's animosity toward her or his greedy assumption that her father was responsible for her debts. As if she would have asked her father for the money.

Two things she did know. First, she never wanted to be that powerless again. Second, she wanted that chapter of her life closed. She wasn't about to agree to discussing anything—not even the weather—with Cole Cassidy.

She turned to look at him and found him watching her with an expression that was eons away from the way she felt. He looked pleased, genuinely pleased. Not a cat-playing-with-a-mouse pleased. More like a cat that had licked up a bowl of cream. His smile, from anyone else, would have been impossible not to return.

Okay. So he's attractive. So what? He's also aggressive, hardheaded and too masculine. And trouble.

His beer disappeared too quickly as he divided his attention between the ball game and her. Brenna would have preferred walking over hot coals to waiting on him again.

"Another beer?" she asked him after cleaning empty glasses off the table that had been vacated next to him.

"Please."

She brought him the beer, hoping the sooner she gave it to him, the sooner he would be gone. He smiled again when she set it down and handed her another five-dollar bill.

"Are you getting along okay, Brenna?" he asked, his index finger sliding down the condensed moisture on the outside surface of the mug.

"Define okay." She set the correct change down on the table, watching his big hand close around the glass. It looked more like a laborer's hand than an attorney's, callused with a scrape across one of the knuckles. The contrast between his hands and his clothes unwillingly intrigued her.

A workman's hands. And expensive clothes.

She would bet the shirt was custom-made. The jacket stretched perfectly across his shoulders without so much as a wrinkle. Remembering the attorney's fees and court costs that had been attached to her judgment, Brenna figured he could probably afford a very upscale lifestyle.

A BMW. A fancy townhome in Cherry Creek. A wife who bought her clothes in one of the trendy boutiques along Second Avenue. Kids with a silver spoon in their mouths and no worries about whether their daddy could afford health insurance.

She understood her anger, but the bitterness of her thoughts came as a surprise. Blinking, she brought Cole's hands back into focus.

Where he lived or what kind of car he drove or whether he was married or how he spent his time—none of those things mattered.

His eyes had taken on their familiar gold-flecked glint that made her want to drop her gaze. Defiantly, she held it. As always, he left her with the unsettled feeling that she was as transparent as a mist dissipating beneath a hot sun, that she had nothing that could be hidden from him.

"I wasn't trying to make polite conversation. I asked because I wanted to know," he said at last.

Did he really want to know that in addition to losing her business, she sold her condo and its furnishings. Instead of having money to start over, she had paid her attorney, paid the taxes she owed the IRS, and made a small dent in Harvey Bates's judgment. Did he want to know that she would have been homeless without her brother's charity?

Did Cole really want to know that her take-home pay after Harvey Bates's garnishment left her too little to cover her basic living expenses? Did he really want to know that she wondered whether she would ever be independent again?

Of course not.

"I'm all right," she finally responded. "And how are things at Jones, Markham and Simmons?" There was a trio of names she wouldn't soon forget.

"I don't know. I left there some time ago."

Nothing in his voice indicated how he felt about that. Secretly, his admission pleased her.

He pulled a photograph out of his pocket and laid it face up on the table. "I'm looking for information. Recognize him?"

Brenna glanced at the picture. The man in the photograph had nice features and just a hint of a smile. Zach MacKenzie.

"What kind of information?" she asked cooly. If Zach was on the receiving end of Cole Cassidy's brand of justice, he had her sympathy.

Zach was a frequent patron of the bar. Or he had been until he had been involved in a car accident a month ago. At the time, he had been on his way home from Score. Zach was charged with vehicular homicide and drunk driving, which had come as a shock. Theo swore Zach had been drinking only ginger ale that night.

Brenna wished she could remember. When the police came a couple of days later to question her, she hadn't been able to confirm Theo's assertion, much as she wanted to. She was positive she would have remembered, though, if he had left the bar drunk. And she had no such memory.

"I want to know as much as I can about the last time Zach MacKenzie was here. May 26. How long he was here. What he drank. How much he drank."

"I suppose this is what you did to me." Her conversational tone did little to hide irritation that swirled just beneath the surface of her control.

Cole frowned. "Did to you?"

"Prying. Asking questions that may not have had anything to do with my case. Digging up dirt—"

"Prying," he repeated. He stared at the table a moment before looking back at Brenna. "I suppose that's how it seemed. When I talked to the people who worked for you, I assumed I'd find corroboration of Bates's accusations. I didn't. In fact, without exception, your employees spoke very highly of you, as did your clients." Cole took a long swallow of beer. He set the glass down. "You think I went looking for dirt?"

"That's what you were paid to do."

"I'm paid to uncover the truth."

"Spare me," she said, wrapping her hand around the towel, twisting it. "I think you'd do whatever it takes to win. I think—"

"I represent Zach MacKenzie," he said, reaching out to touch the back of her hand with a finger. "And, yes, I like winning." The glint she knew too well returned to his eyes. "And, I took no pleasure at all in winning Bates's case."

"Is that supposed to make me feel better?" She rubbed the back of her hand where Cole had touched her.

He smoothed a hand over his hair, then laid his palm face up in a gesture of supplication. "No."

Brenna's gaze was drawn from his expression of closed confusion to the silent entreaty of his callused palm. She hadn't expected him to have hands that were so large, so hard. A man didn't get calluses like that from writing notes on a legal pad. His palm reminded her of her grandfather's—equally deft at coaxing open a stuck valve on an irrigation ditch or cleansing a scrape on his small granddaughter's knee. She glanced back at Cole's face and found him watching her, his eyes again warm.

This time she really looked at him, trying to see the man, not just the adversary. His cheekbones were high and fell away into blunt hollows above the rigid line of his square jaw. Not a single thing about his face was soft, but she saw none of the cruelty, either, that she was used to seeing in men with the hard ruthlessness Cole Cassidy had subjected her to.

"You're really Zach's lawyer?" she asked.

He nodded and wrapped his open hand around the glass of beer. "If he was obviously drunk when he left here, I need to know that. If he wasn't—"

"He wasn't," she interrupted.

"What was he drinking?"

"I can't remember. A beer, maybe. Most likely, ginger ale."

Cole raised an eyebrow.

Brenna shrugged. "He sometimes had a beer. Never more than two that I can remember. Then he usually switched to ginger ale. He mostly just hangs out when he comes."

"He's a regular?"

"More than some. Less than others. He and Theo are friends."

"I know." Cole glanced at the bartender. "Theo told me if I'd stop by about eight-thirty, he'd have time to talk to me."

Brenna frowned. "Why didn't you say so when you came in?"

"I wanted to see what the place was like."

She left Cole and told Theo that Zach's lawyer was here to see him. She watched as the two men shook hands. While they talked, she kept an eye on the customers, refilling drinks and pretzel dishes as needed. Theo and Cole's conversation ended just before the ball game.

Brenna expected Cole to leave. When he didn't, she had no choice but to wait on him again. "Another beer?"

He shook his head. "Coffee." When she returned to his table with a steaming cup, he asked, "Do you like working here?"

"It's okay."

"I never pictured you as a barmaid."

Given Harvey Bates's opinion of her, she didn't want to know how Cole thought she earned a living. "It's honest work. It pays the bills." *Almost.*

Cole grinned and brushed his finger across the back of her hand. Warmth lingered on the trail from his finger.

"I did it again, didn't I?" he said.

"What?" His smile was stunning. Her resolve to continue disliking him slipped another notch.

"Put my foot in my mouth." He stuck out one of his feet, covered in a size-twelve black wingtip. "It sure tastes awful. I wasn't casting aspersions about your job. Maybe we can start over."

"Start over?" She shook her head, lost in the direction his conversation had taken.

"Hi," he said, extending his hand toward her, a smile creasing the corners around his eyes. "I'm Cole Cassidy."

She stared at him.

He took her hand in his and in a stage whisper, said, "You're supposed to tell me your name. This is the first time we've met."

She was unable to say a word, aware of his hand on her arm, his eyes on her face. Somehow, in the last five minutes, reality had shifted subtly. The attorney who had been Harvey Bates's tool in her destruction became a man she found alluring.

Never in her life had she felt so off balance. She had spent years trusting her instincts. Which did she believe now? Instincts that were drawn to the caress of his hands and eyes, promising compassion and understanding? Or instincts that warned her of danger and urged her to run?

"Brenna James," he said as though she had just told him her name. "I like your name. Brenna is Irish, isn't it?"

"You're nuts. Certifiable."

He laughed and released her hand.

"That's the nicest thing you've ever said to me."

She resisted smiling. "I thought we had just met."

"Then it's true, because it's also the first thing you've said to me."

The corner of her mouth lifted. "Okay."

He took a sip of his coffee. "Nice outfit," he said, indicating her uniform. "Makes you look about fifteen."

His tone echoed her sentiments exactly. She glanced down at the green and white uniform, bobby socks and tennis shoes. "Makes me feel about fifteen."

"That can't be all bad." His voice became light and teasing.

"The worst year of my life was when I was fifteen." The confession fell from her lips without conscious thought and was followed by an instant of disbelief that she had spoken aloud. Blindly, she picked up glasses and debris from the adjoining table. "I've got to get back to work."

She never slipped. Not ever. Her defenses were bone-deep and governed by a simple rule. She never talked about herself. She couldn't afford to. This time, her anger was directed at herself.

By rote, she moved through the bar, doing her job. Unwanted memories interrupted her concentration.

Two deaths and Brenna's entrance into adulthood had marked her fifteenth year. First her mother, then Nonna.

Her mother had been powerless to defuse the growing resentment between father and daughter. When Brenna had decided to leave home, her mother did the one thing she could—let go. At the time, Brenna hadn't understood or appreciated how difficult that choice had been for her mother.

And her grandmother. Nonna had been the one person who cared enough to reach out to an angry adolescent and love her unconditionally. Even now, when Brenna felt herself slipping into an abyss of hopelessness, all she had to do was close her eyes and think of her grandmother. Within moments, Brenna would feel better.

She didn't think anything would ever be as devastating as being fifteen and discovering she had just one person she could depend on—herself. Eleven years should have been long enough for the shattering desolation to be gone. It might as well have been yesterday.

Chewing the inside of her lip and lost in her thoughts, she waited on her customers without responding to their banter, straightened chairs and wiped down tables. Other customers left the bar, but Cole remained, nursing coffee that Theo refilled several times.

Brenna wanted to run from his attention, and she wanted to rant at him for stirring long-dead, painful memories. She wanted to sit with him to find out how he got calluses and scraped knuckles, and she wanted time alone to absorb his subtle flirting.

Months ago, that first day in his office giving the deposition, she had been intensely aware of him. He dominated her memories of that day, and he dominated her awareness now. What was it about the man?

The night dragged by at a snail's pace, and she knew exactly when Cole left. Fifteen minutes before the bar closed. The tip he left her was average, but a note left for her on a napkin was not. She stared at the words, unable to make sense of the bold strokes of his handwriting. She set it on the tray with his empty coffee cup.

Behind the bar, she set the tray next to the sink. "Theo, can you decipher this?"

Theo glanced at the napkin. "See you soon."

"See you soon," she repeated, staring at the three words, then putting the napkin in her pocket.

"You knew him before tonight, didn't you?" Theo asked.

"Yes."

"Are you two good friends?"

"No. Not friends. We met last year, but I haven't seen him in a while," she said. Two months and three weeks exactly, she thought, remembering that last day at his office.

"Might as well pack it in," Theo said, glancing at his watch. "When is your bus due?"

"It comes by at five of."

"Get going then. I don't want you to have to wait another half hour for the next one."

After changing into jeans and a loose T-shirt, Brenna pulled her hair out of the rubber band and brushed it out.

She found it impossible not to think about Cole and gave up trying. She had seen him as an extension of Harvey Bates—a man intending to do her harm. But that wasn't the man she had seen tonight. The Cole Cassidy she met tonight was charming. Nice. A man she could like, a man she found...alluring.

"Grow up, Brenna," she told her reflection. "You and Mr. Cole-Justice-Cassidy? Not in your wildest dreams."

What's so wild about wanting him to see you as an interesting woman, came the persistent voice inside her head that had once made her think almost anything was possible. What if you had met him some other way?

But I didn't.

But, what if you had? What if he liked the person you are?

Fat chance of that.

She threw her hairbrush in the bottom of the canvas tote bag that had once been beige, but that was now held together with patches in a variety of faded colors and shapes. In her mind, the tote bag symbolized their differences perfectly. Cole was cordovan leather, and she was patched canvas.

Even if they had met some other way, it was just that simple.

Hoisting the tote bag over her shoulder, she held that thought firmly in mind as she walked out of the bar and into an empty night.

The traffic was a little less than usual, even for the middle of the night. The homeless man who had slept on the bus-stop bench the last two nights was nowhere to be seen. The only pedestrian on her side of the street was a drunk sprawled against the building, his legs bent, a hat pulled over his eyes. A couple of other men stood in front of a bar at the other end of the block, their arms wrapped over the top of a parking meter, their laughter carrying to Brenna.

This neighborhood wasn't as rough as some where she had worked, a fact she had pointed out to her brother Michael when he told her no sister of his was going to sit at a bus stop in the middle of the night. The conversation seemed stupid to her, since she had been following similar patterns for years. She wasn't about to impose on her brother by having him pick her up from work at one o'clock in the morning. Michael hadn't agreed willingly, but he eventually had agreed.

Giving the block one last perusal, Brenna left the shelter of the entry and walked the block and a half to the bus stop. If she was lucky, the bus would be early tonight, instead of ten to fifteen minutes late it sometimes was.

She was halfway to the bus stop when she saw movement next to the shadowed building out of the corner of her eye. Automatically, she reached for the cylinder of pepper gas in her tote bag that she should have been carrying in her hand.

A man materialized out of the shadow, his voice and his eyes dark as the night. "Hey, baby, wanna party?"

Chapter 4

Brenna had never seen this man before. Avoiding a direct challenge, her own gaze skittered away from his sharp eyes, her assessment quick. Baggy jeans, black T-shirt, a narrow face and the wiry muscularity of a jackal.

Dirty. Drunk. Dangerous.

A predator to whom she could show no weakness. Making sure she didn't turn her back to the man, she edged away from him.

Did she want to party? Not hardly. She didn't trust her voice to be as stern as she wanted, so she shook her head and kept walking toward the bus stop. With every step, a lurch in her stomach kept pace. She fought the urge to run. It was too far back to the bar, and she doubted she'd find any good Samaritans driving down Colfax at this time of night.

The man lengthened his stride to catch up with her. "Hurrying home to your boyfriend?" He reached for Brenna, and she sidestepped to avoid his grasp. "Hey, I'm just trying to be a nice guy," he protested. "Ain't safe around here for a pretty thing like you. Betcha your boyfriend don't know where you've been." He nodded toward a strip joint across the street. "You a stripper?"

Brenna looked down the street, hoping she would see the bus, hoping the man didn't have the money or the inclination to board the bus when she did.

"Whatchername?" he asked.

Brenna didn't answer. Instead, she walked toward the bus stop. Purposeful. Calm. Her fingers closed around the pepper spray in the bottom of her bag. Again, she looked down the street. For the moment, it was deserted as a country road.

Where was the bus?

His glance followed hers down the street. "Expecting someone?" he asked.

Brenna met his gaze. "Yes," she said, her voice crisp with the conviction of truth.

Bus or no bus, at the moment she'd be happy to see anyone. Otherwise, she might have to spray the guy.

And hope her reflexes were faster than his.

He was too close, enough so she could smell his sweat and the beer on his breath. She edged toward the curb, trying to put some distance between them. He followed, his swagger more confident.

A single car drove past, its driver staring straight ahead. No help there. Where was the bus? A cop? The cavalry?

Ahead of her, a black Jeep came toward them. Brenna recognized the driver.

Cole Cassidy.... An unlikely answer to her prayer.

She waved.

Cole stared hard at her, then made an illegal U-turn in the middle of the block. He pulled to a stop next to the sidewalk.

"Brenna?" His eyes swept over her then went to the man on the sidewalk next to her.

He set the emergency brake and got out, his movements as controlled as a lion stalking its prey. He had taken off his coat, revealing muscular shoulders that had been only hinted at beneath his jacket. Brenna was struck with the raw power of his presence. He had rolled up the cuffs of his dress shirt, and the muscles of his forearms bunched when he curled his hands into loose fists. He looked altogether...dangerous.

Next to her, Brenna felt the man shrink back a little.

"Hi," she said, her voice breathless.

"Are you all right?"

Brenna nodded and glanced from Cole to the other man, who moved closer to Brenna, his chin high, his chest out.

She touched Cole's arm. "You're late," she said, urging him back toward his Jeep.

One of his eyebrows rose and his gaze again fastened on Brenna's uninvited companion.

"Sorry," Cole said, taking her arm in a possessive gesture that she normally wouldn't have allowed.

"Your boyfriend?" the man asked. When neither Brenna or Cole responded, he added, "Hey, man, that's a fine set of wheels."

"Back off," Cole said, pushing his hand into the man's chest.

"Hey, man, I ain't doing nothing." He shook his shoulders. "In fact, I've been doing you a favor. This neighborhood is downright dangerous for a pretty filly like your woman."

"Get lost," Cole snarled.

Cole's complete lack of civility stunned Brenna. She stole another glance at him. He looked ready to kill. Quite literally.

Cole opened the Jeep door for Brenna and held his hand out to her. He wasn't looking at her, though, she noted as she took it and climbed into the vehicle. He watched the man with unblinking intensity.

The man shrugged his shoulders and walked away, grumbling under his breath. Cole skirted around the vehicle and climbed in behind the steering wheel. Without a word, he put the car into gear and drove down the street.

A breeze swept over her as the vehicle gained speed. Brenna shivered, nerves stretched taut. As much from Cole's close proximity as their brush with the drunk.

"Thanks," she said. "You don't know how glad I was to see you."

"Where's your car?" he asked.

"I don't have a car. I was headed for the bus stop." She motioned toward the end of the block. "This bus stop is a little too close to that guy back there. If you'll just let me out at the next stop—"

"You ride the bus?" Disbelief filled his voice.

"It's the usual way of getting to and from work if you don't have a car." She brushed away strands of hair that blew across her face.

He jerked his head in the direction they had driven from. "And how often does that happen?"

"The guy?"

"The guy," Cole confirmed impatiently. "The one you're so eager to get away from that you'll put up with my company."

Brenna glanced at him. His anger tonight was far different from his courtroom persona. This man was...earthier. No suave sophistication here.

"How often?" he repeated. "Weekly? Nightly?" He pinned her with a hard glance. "What would you have done if I hadn't come along?"

"I'd handle it," she said. "Just like I'm used to doing."

"I could see how you were handling it," he said. He shook his head. "You shouldn't be out here at this time of night."

"What I should or shouldn't be doing is none of your damn business," Brenna said, her temper slipping. Never mind she agreed with him. She pointed toward the end of the next block. "You can let me out down there."

"And then what?"

"And then I'll wait for the bus," she replied. "Just like I do every night when I get off work."

"Great," he muttered. "And I get to go on my merry way, worried about the next scumbag who makes a grab for you."

She pulled the pepper spray out of her tote bag. "Next time I'll be ready." Again, she gestured toward the bus stop ahead. "You can let me out there."

"Not bloody damn likely," he muttered.

"What's that supposed to mean?"

"What kind of man do you take me for?"

He glanced at her when she opened her mouth.

"On second thought, don't answer that," he said. "I don't want to know. But, for damn sure, I'm not letting you off to wait for the bus." He jerked a thumb toward the canister. "What if the nozzle jammed? What if he took it away from you? What if—" Abruptly, he closed his mouth and wrapped his fingers around the steering wheel. "I'm taking you home."

"That's not necessary," Brenna said tightly.

"You might as well tell me where you live, fair lady. You've got two choices here. I'm taking you home."

"That sounds like one choice," Brenna said.

"Your home." He looked at her. "Or mine. Lady's choice."

Clearly, he had called her bluff. She didn't know him at all, but she had no doubt. The man was serious.

His attention returned to his driving, which gave her a chance to study him. She had simply hoped for an easy way to get away from the drunk, and if anyone had a right to be angry about the encounter, she did. Cole's unexpected anger puzzled her, intrigued her. As did his confession that he would worry about her.

I took no pleasure at all in winning Bates's case. Cole's statement floated across her mind, and with it, his expression that last day in his office. "Handle it," he had said to her attorney. "Tell her she's confessing to a felony." Brenna frowned. Cole's intervention had made even less sense to her than John Miller's actions had. She'd assumed he had some complicated legal reason for his actions. Now, nine months later, she wondered if he'd tried to protect her.

Protect her. Just as he had tonight. Was it that simple?

He glanced at her. "What's it going to be, Brenna?" His voice had thawed some, as had his expression.

"Why are you doing this?"

"My good deed for the day," he said shortly.

Pointedly, she looked at her watch. "One per day, and a mere few minutes past midnight. It's a good thing I caught you early, isn't it?"

"Brenna."

There was no mistaking the warning in his voice. She gave him the address for her brother's apartment that was within walking distance of the University of Colorado Medical School where he worked. Telling the man where she lived shouldn't have been a big deal. Except it felt like one.

At rare moments in her life, she recognized the forks in the road where a simple decision led in a whole new direction. This was one of those moments.

The high road, or the low? She didn't know. Would her life include Cole Cassidy, at least for a while? If it did, she was sure things would never be quite the same again.

When she looked back at him, she found him watching her. He smiled. "Was that really so hard?"

"You've no idea," she grumbled. Darn the man for smiling, for being nice...for having a protective streak that made her feel cared for, for showing up when she really did need help. Her well-guarded dislike of him slipped another notch.

"You always this stubborn? Or is it just me?" That smile invited her to respond in kind.

"Stubborn is my middle name." Brenna slid down in her seat a little, wrapping her arms more firmly around her tote bag. What did he want? Really?

"That's what I figured."

"Why were you still here?" she asked. She never had this kind of luck. There had to be another reason why he conveniently showed up in the nick of time. "You left the bar quite a while ago."

Surprisingly, a stain of color appeared on his face and he ducked his chin. "I...wanted to see which car was yours."

"Were you thinking I might have an asset I hadn't told the court or Harvey Bates about?"

"Hell, no." He glanced at her as though genuinely shocked by the train of her thoughts. Meeting her gaze, he repeated, "No."

"Then why?" she persisted.

The flush returned to his cheeks. "I was curious," he said finally. The traffic light turned red, and Cole braked. His gaze direct, open, he added, "You know—find out where the lady works, what kind of car she drives. Find a way to be around her a bit until you figure out if she'll say yes or no when you ask her out."

It was Brenna's turn to be shocked. Sure, she had sensed his interest—except deep down, she had been convinced she was mistaken, sure that he must have some other motive. She hadn't expected an open declaration that felt like the truth.

A long moment passed while Brenna mulled that over, her impressions again altered. A couple of hours ago, she had been sure what kind of man Cole Cassidy was—and he wasn't one she wanted to know.

How could she continue to nurse her dislike of him?

Easy. Look at everything you lost because of him.

Not him. Harvey Bates.

He cleared his throat. "You have every reason to think the worst." He glanced at her, the smile gone. "I wasn't stalking you. I was just...interested."

She met his gaze. "I believe you."

The light turned green, and he pressed on the accelerator.

She closed her eyes and inhaled deeply. For an instant, she allowed her imagination to take flight, wondering where Cole lived. A Jeep, not a BMW. She stole a glance at his hands, noting the lack of a wedding ring.

What else was she wrong about?

A man with a Jeep might like the country the way she did. Where the sounds filling the night would be from crickets instead of traffic. Where the aroma of freshly cut alfalfa would fill the air instead of exhaust fumes. She opened her eyes. Where stars would light the night instead of neon.

She stole a glance at Cole and gave herself a firm reality check. The man was an attorney, for Pete's sake, in a big city. If he wanted the country life, that's where he'd be. A Jeep didn't mean a thing. It was probably no more than a yuppie, macho symbol to match his image of himself. Her visions of his house shifted to one of those expensive lofts in Lodo.

"What do you dream of, fair lady?" he asked, turning to look at her, letting her know he was aware of her study of him.

The simple question nearly brought tears to her eyes. She ought to know better than to dream, but dream she did. Her parents' voices echoed down the cluttered corridors of her mind. *Daydreaming again, Brenna James? Get your head out of the clouds.* And beneath her father's scorn, the gentler, more soothing tones of her mother that had lately come more often to the surface. *Dream, Brenna, for in dreams are the seeds of possibility.* And her grandmother's words that simultaneously gave her hope and made her feel like a failure. *Dream it. Then be it.*

She cleared her throat and said the words out loud—words that had been alive only within her mind. "I dream of...going back to school."

Cole nodded as though he understood. "That is sometimes a big step. Hard to fit in with a job."

"Yes."

Cole grinned at her. "Hell of a thing, school. Can't wait to get out while you're there. Can't wait to go back when you're out."

She nodded, remembering the way she had hated school, always feeling like the outsider she was, forever the new kid on the block.

"What else do you dream of, Brenna?"

She shrugged, pretending nonchalance she didn't feel. "The usual things, I guess."

"Like what?"

"A nice place to live. Having interesting work."

"Working in a bar isn't interesting?" he teased.

"Hardly. It's okay, and most of the people are nice, but..."

"What would be? Interesting, that is? If you could do anything?"

She thought a moment, then gave voice to the one wish she had always cherished. "I'd collect stories." She turned in her seat and faced Cole. "You know, we don't talk to one another like they used to. Instead we watch television." She paused. "One of the things I loved about my grandparents were the great stories they told. About their experiences or repeating stories they had been told as children. My grandmother had the best stories. About things she did as a girl. About my grandpa courting her."

"An oral history," Cole said.

"That's right," Brenna agreed.

"Sounds nice."

"Yes."

"Thanks for letting me take you home," he said, reaching out and giving her hand a squeeze. "Thanks for sharing your dreams."

Warmth feathered through her as she studied him. She didn't want to like him. Yet, he touched her like he cared. His smile was genuine. Everything about him announced, *You can trust me.*

Could she?

"It's not easy, is it?" he asked.

"What?"

"Seeing me. Just me. Not Harvey Bates's attorney."

His perception surprised her. "No, it's not," she agreed. "Do you see me? Just me?" She was crazy for asking.

"I always have," he responded, holding her gaze a moment longer before starting the Jeep's engine.

Had John Miller told him? she wondered.

"Told me what?" Cole asked.

She cast Cole a startled glance, unaware she had spoken aloud. "Anything about...about me."

"Nothing."

Brenna didn't dare believe he really saw her. He couldn't. If he had, he wouldn't be acting as though he liked her.

"So, you work nights at Score. What keeps you busy during the day?" he asked.

"I take care of my nephew on the days my sister-in-law goes to the university."

"And the rest of the time?"

"I clean houses," she said, flashing him a look that dared him to say anything. Working as a barmaid and housekeeper were her fall-back jobs. Survival jobs. This time she was determined to do more than survive. A few more customers and she would have enough money to get into her own apartment again.

"Sounds like you don't have much time to yourself, then."

"When you've dug a hole for yourself as deep as the one I'm in, there's no other choice."

"No, I suppose not. Tell me about your nephew."

She hesitated only a moment before answering. The topic of Teddy James was almost as safe as the weather. "Teddy's great—the best four-year-old anywhere. Being able to spend time with him has been one of the few good things that's happened to me lately." She paused and watched the passing streets for a moment. "You'll want to make a left at the next light."

"Okay." Cole slowed and made the turn. "If he's like my nieces, he likes swimming and Frisbees."

Brenna smiled. "You forgot baseball."

"My nieces haven't expressed any interest in baseball." His tone was indulgent.

"That's too bad. Baseball is a good game—one girls can play just as well as boys." She worried her lip between her teeth for a moment, then asked one of the questions that had bothered her all night. "Why are you defending Zach MacKenzie?"

Cole's smile faded. "I believe him. I believe *in* him."

"And that's why you represented Harvey Bates?"

"Nope. I represented Bates because he was a case that I was as-

signed by a senior partner in the firm. I did my level best to talk him
into a settlement, but he wouldn't budge.'' Cole slowed the Jeep. ''Is
this the building?''

Brenna nodded as Cole parked the car.

He shut off the ignition and turned to her. ''I'll tell you anything
you want to know. I just don't quite understand what you're really
asking.''

''I've just been thinking about Zach.'' She fiddled with the strap
of her tote bag. ''I mean, he's more like me. A guy who's in a jam.
I didn't think a case like that would be of much interest to you.''

''If I had stayed at Jones, Markham and Simmons, I wouldn't have
had a chance to represent someone like Zach. Or you. You couldn't
have afforded to hire me.'' Cole didn't seem to be bragging, rather
just stating the obvious facts of the situation.

''And now?''

''Now I get to choose who I represent. That's one of the things I
like about being on my own.'' Cole turned more fully toward her and
stretched his arm along the back of the seat, his hand close to
her hair. He touched one of the strands.

She felt the heat from his hand near her face. She longed to rest
her cheek against his open palm, which proved to her just how little
sense she had. Instead, she sat perfectly still to keep from acting on
the urge. He moved his arms away from her and slanted her a grin.

''I always wanted to be the guy in a white hat. The one who made
things better.'' His smile faded. ''Until I went out on my own, it had
been a long time since I'd felt like that.''

''And you think you can help Zach?'' she asked.

''Yes. I know I can.''

''I'm glad. He's going to need someone...'' *Tough. Aggressive.*

A moment later Cole prompted, ''Someone?''

Brenna felt her cheeks heat as she met his gaze. ''You're
rather...um...intimidating, you know.''

Cole laughed. ''I've been told.'' When she looked down, he tipped
her head up with his index finger. ''I can't begin to tell you how
sorry I am that I intimidated you. I believed you.''

She imagined him repeating, *I believed in you.*

''I'd like to see you tomorrow,'' Cole said. ''Dinner. A movie?''

''I don't have time,'' Brenna replied, oddly disappointed that she had to turn down the invitation. "I'm watching Teddy in the morning. The sky would probably fall if we missed story hour at the library. And I have a house to clean tomorrow afternoon, which I'll finish just in time to get to work at Score tomorrow night."

Cole traced the back of his finger down the side of her face. In the wake, her skin tingled. "Another time then?"

Brenna swallowed, enjoying the promise of his invitation, hating the anticipation for things that could never be. "Another time," she agreed, believing no such thing.

Cole got out of the Jeep and walked her to the door of the apartment, taking the key from her and unlocking the door. "See you soon," he said the instant before he bent and brushed a fleeting, gossamer kiss across her lips.

Chapter 5

"Auntie Brennie, I don't want to wear socks," Teddy said the following morning. He dropped his brown leather sandals on the floor next to the kitchen table where Brenna sat, her hands wrapped around a mug of coffee. He looked up at her with beseeching blue eyes.

Privately, Brenna agreed with him. Brenna had been unable to convince her Swiss sister-in-law, Jane, that little boys in Denver, unlike little boys in Zurich, didn't necessarily wear socks with their sneakers and never with sandals.

Deciding whether Teddy should wear socks was easy compared to sorting out her feelings for Cole Cassidy. However determined she had been to put him out of her mind, her thoughts returned to him again and again—like picking at a scab that itched.

His bringing her home was the act of a decent, generous person. Nothing more. She would be a fool to read anything into that. Even if he had wanted to know what kind of car she drove and where she lived.

Yet, she had never remembered a man's touch as vividly. And his scent. It rushed back with a clarity that made her breath shorten in a response that had everything to do with hormones and nothing to do with her head. She had forgotten how warm a man's body was, and Cole's had been as inviting to her as a crackling fire on a winter day.

"Auntie Brennie, you're not listening," Teddy complained, patting her arm. He climbed into her lap and rested his forehead against hers, his expression fierce as he could make it. "Do I have to wear socks?"

Brenna dragged her thoughts away from the enticing, confusing Cole Cassidy and smiled at Teddy, crossing her eyes as she met his. He giggled. She tousled his blond hair. "Yes, you have to wear socks."

"Why?" Satisfied he had her attention, he climbed off her lap and sat down on the floor next to his sandals.

"Your mother says you have to." Brenna slid out of the chair and sat down on the floor in front of her four-year-old nephew. She took the pair of socks out of his hands. "Let me help."

Teddy sat down and stuck his foot out, and Brenna tickled the bottom of it. He laughed and snatched it back.

"See?" Brenna said. "Socks might be good for one thing. They would keep me from tickling your foot."

"Huh-uh." He stuck out his other foot. "I like it when you tickle me."

"Oh, you do, huh?" She grasped his foot and feathered her fingers across his sole, then brought his foot up to her mouth. "Mmm. Yummy foot. Too bad I've already eaten breakfast and I'm not hungry." She offered the foot to the calico cat, Penelope, who sat watching their play with haughty disdain. "Want a bite?"

Penelope blinked her golden eyes and wandered off, her tail in the air.

Brenna blew on the bottom of Teddy's foot before running her fingers over it again. he burst into peals of laughter, wriggling on the floor. She let him go and held out one of the socks.

"Aw, I was hoping you would forget." He smiled. "'Cept, you never forget, huh?"

"Not usually," Brenna agreed, putting a sock on the foot he held up. After putting on the other one, she patiently assisted as he put on his sandals and buckled the straps.

"I still think this is dumb," he said, standing.

"Then talk to your mother."

He plopped down in her lap and tipped his head up to look at her. "How 'bout you talk to her for me?"

"Nope." Brenna kissed his cheek. "This is your battle to fight, Teddy." She stood him up. "You feed Penelope, I'll do the dishes, and then we're off to the library for story hour. Okay?"

"Okay," he agreed.

She and Teddy had fallen easily into a routine since she moved in. Swimming lessons on Monday, Wednesday and Friday afternoons while Jane was in class. Story hour Tuesday morning and playtime in the park on Thursday.

Brenna had just started running the water into the sink when the telephone rang.

"Brenna," came her father's voice across the line when she picked up, "I thought Michael would still be home."

"Hello, sir," she responded, automatically giving him the military address he had always demanded. "He left more than an hour ago."

"You're not at work this morning?"

Familiar defensiveness rose within her. From anyone but her father, the question might have been casual. From him, there was an implied criticism. "It's my morning to watch Teddy while Jane is in class."

"And how is my grandson? Well, I trust."

Brenna's glance fell to Teddy, who was sitting on the floor, feeding Penelope pieces of cat food one by one. "He's fine. He's growing like a weed."

"Have you found some other job yet?" the Colonel asked. The last time they spoke, he had been highly critical of her working in a bar.

"I haven't been looking," she responded.

"And I don't suppose you've been looking for your own place to live, either."

"Not yet." She knew her father thought she was taking advantage of Michael's hospitality. In the three months that had passed since she had moved in with her brother, a single, overriding goal dominated her thoughts—to be independent again.

With more patience than she felt, she asked, "Was there something you needed, Dad?"

"I just wanted to let Michael know that I'll be in Denver the second week in July."

"I'll tell him," Brenna responded.

"I have his work number. I'll call and tell him," came her father's response.

"Fine." Brenna closed her eyes, hating the fact that she cared that her father made her feel small and unimportant. He wanted to let Michael know he was coming, not her. And he didn't trust her to pass along the message.

"Goodbye, Brenna," he said, severing the connection without waiting for her own farewell.

Brenna hung up the phone, staring into space a moment. She was a grown woman, but her father always made her feel about twelve—awkward and unsure.

Twenty minutes later Brenna and Teddy were on their way to the library, which included a ride on the bus, where Teddy said hello to everyone as they made their way to their seats, and a three-block walk to the library. Teddy skipped along beside her, pausing every few feet as something new caught his imagination.

"Why are there cracks in the sidewalk?" he asked.

"It's a seam where the edge of the concrete form meets another block of concrete."

"Oh." Teddy jumped over the crack. "I wonder why they don't make one long strip from there to there?" A squirrel chattered at them from a branch of a tree. "How come squirrels climb trees and rats can't? Daddy says they are both pesky rodents."

Brenna glanced at the tree above them, horrified at the thought of tree-climbing rats.

"Why do flowers smell and leaves don't?" he asked, his quick mind zipping onto a new subject.

"Some leaves smell," Brenna said. "Mint."

"Did you remember to bring *The Little Engine That Could*?" he asked as they climbed the steps leading to the library entrance.

"Sure did." Brenna patted the book she carried under her arm. She opened the door and followed him inside. "I've got it right here."

Teddy ran down the stairs to the children's section with his usual enthusiasm. Three other children were already gathered in the corner.

Teddy sat down next to a little girl and struck up a conversation with the complete confidence of a child who had never met a stranger.

"Brenna, hi!" Nancy Jenkins called from behind the checkout counter.

"Hi," Brenna returned. "How are things down here with your ankle-biters?"

Nancy smiled. "You really should watch that kind of talk, you know. You've entered enemy territory."

Brenna grinned and gazed around the bright room with enjoyment. Nancy's assessment was more accurate than she knew: for Brenna, this was enemy territory. Even so, telling stories to the children wasn't half so scary as she had anticipated when she agreed to be a story-hour volunteer. Even more surprising was that she not only enjoyed telling the children stories, she looked forward to it.

"I found that book of train engines you asked me about," Nancy said, leading the way across the room to the corner where story hour was held.

"Good. Color photos?"

"Of course." Nancy picked up an oversize book from one of the carpet-covered cubes.

Brenna focused on the pictures, ignoring the lines of fine print that would have panicked her. "These are good. If I can just keep the kids from asking me anything more technical than 'Where's the smoke stack.'"

Nancy closed the book and set it back down. "It wouldn't matter if they did. You always know just what to say to them."

"Talking to the kids is easy," Brenna said, ignoring the compliment. She sat down. "Now adults—that's entirely different."

Nancy laughed. "My cue to leave, I think." She took a couple of steps, then turned back around. "Let me know the next time you've got a free Saturday afternoon, and we'll go to the movies."

"No Saturdays any time soon," Brenna said. "I just got a small office to clean." Their mutual love of movies had cemented the friendship after they had discovered that they were both single and both Army brats who had never spent even one full school year in one location. The bond of common experience held them together even as Brenna was sure their differences would eventually drive them apart.

"Sunday then?"

"Okay." Brenna nodded. She picked up the storybook and flipped through the pages, confident that she had thoroughly rehearsed her telling of the story.

"That's my auntie," Brenna heard Teddy say to the little girl next to him. "She's going to tell us our story today."

Brenna lifted her eyes to watch her nephew, then let her gaze wander around the room for the last few minutes she had to wait before it was time to begin. She found the bright colors of the children's library inviting. For a moment, she imagined having a job like Nancy's. Brenna discarded the idea almost the instant it surfaced. She liked kids, and she like coming to the library, but making it her vocation was beyond her imagination. Storytelling. That was something altogether different.

For as long as she could remember, she loved hearing stories. Vividly, she remembered her grandparents' stories about the Great Depression. Her father's memories of his early years in the military were almost as compelling. Brenna's favorite stories, though, came from Nonna, who had told stories of her own grandmother.

Brenna had mostly hated the constant moving that came with her father's military career. The one thing she had liked about moving to new places was the folklore. She had tape-recorded many stories, including those her grandmother had told her. Until last night when Cole had asked her about her dreams, she hadn't ever considered that keeping the oral histories alive could be a job. No, more than a job. A career. A dream, Brenna thought, in this case, most likely a pipe dream.

Dream it. Then be it.

She shook the thought away. No dreams. Not until she had her independence back. Then she'd look beyond the basics.

"Hi, Auntie Brennie," said a little girl who skipped across the room toward her, adopting Teddy's nickname for her.

Brenna smiled. "I'm glad to see you, Lisa. Are you and your sister ready for today's story?" When both girls nodded, Brenna lifted her gaze to include the rest of the children. "Are you ready?"

Vigorous nods and a chorus of "Yes!" answered her.

"Today's story is *The Little Engine That Could,*" she began, her smile automatically including the adult that sat down in a chair behind the children. Absently wondering which child's father the man was, Brenna's gaze rose to his face.

Cole Cassidy smiled back at her.

Her voice trailed into a hoarse whisper.

What was he doing here? Her cheeks grew hot and her hands became instantly cold.

All of Brenna's worst fears pooled into a seething cauldron in her stomach.

Today the deception would end. Today, she would be exposed as a fraud. Today, of all the days of her life, would surely be the worst. The urge to run—run as far and as fast as she could—was nearly overwhelming.

"Brenna?" Cole's gentle question brought his face back into sharp focus. "Do you mind if I stay?"

Of course I mind, she wanted to shout. She wiped her damp palms on her jeans. Instead, she found herself answering calmly, "No. If you like—"

"*The Little Engine That Could* has always been one of my favorites." His brilliant eyes held a message Brenna chose not to interpret, though she couldn't ignore it. Involuntarily, she remembered the caress of his lips across hers, carrying no more weight than a whisper, holding her attention as certainly as a whisper.

Brenna returned her attention to the book she held in a death grip. She closed her eyes for a second, calling for the control and confidence she had spent her life building. The carpet-covered cube where she sat wasn't likely to swallow her any time soon, which meant she had to deal with the problem right now. Brenna opened her eyes, opened the book, and smiled at the children.

"Once upon a time," she began, wishing for the next few minutes to be over with. Most of the children soon became involved with the story. They followed her narrative paced to the illustrations, which she kept in front of the children. A roar in her ears kept her from hearing the words she spoke, and for all she knew she might have been speaking Swahili.

Brenna was glad—really glad—that today was not her first time as the story-hour volunteer. Otherwise, she would have been positive the kids were privy to her secret. One little girl practiced tying her shoes. The pair of twins whispered to each other. Another child ran his palm up and down Brenna's jean-clad leg as though the texture of denim was more interesting than anything, especially the story.

Brenna's mental struggle as she recited the story echoed the little engine's struggles. She had spent years perfecting her defenses. Cole wouldn't suspect, because he wouldn't be looking for anything out of the ordinary. Her mind acknowledged the truth of her logic, but she didn't believe it. Any moment now, he would stand, point his finger, and label her for the fake she was.

Any moment now.

Yet Cole seemed to be enjoying himself, just as the children were. Her pretense was successful. Again.

Yeah, but look at what you got from faking it, came the ever-persistent voice of her conscience. A lawsuit, because you couldn't read the fine print of the lease. Because you couldn't read the back statement. Because—

Go away. This isn't the same.

Isn't it? One more lie built on a foundation of lies.

That was a truth she couldn't deny, much as she wanted.

Up and down the mountain, by himself, the Little Engine That Could overcame all his obstacles, chanting, "I think I can. I think I can! I know I can." The last page of the book came, and the Little Engine That Could sat on top of his mountain, smug and proud.

Smug and proud might have been what the Little Engine That Could felt. Brenna had felt only relief that one more time, the deception had held together.

The children left one by one, most telling her, "Bye, Auntie Brennie," and promising to see her next week. Brenna gathered up the books and stacked them neatly on the cube beside her, aware of Cole's approach.

"You're terrific at this," he said, sitting down on the cube next to her. His suit today was dark, impeccably tailored. A power suit. She couldn't help but compare the suit to her jeans, tangible proof, had she needed any, she and Cole belonged in very separate worlds.

"Thanks," she responded huskily, automatically.

"She's the best volunteer we've got," Nancy added from behind Cole. "It's not often we have one of the dads pay us a visit."

"I'm not a dad," he explained. "I'm a friend of Brenna's." He extended his hand. "Cole Cassidy."

Friend. A single innocent word that echoed through Brenna's mind.

"I'm Nancy Jenkins. It's nice to meet you." She winked at Brenna. "You're holding out on me, girl."

Teddy perched his elbows across Brenna's thigh, and Cole smiled at him. "You must be Teddy."

"Yep," he replied. "Is it lunchtime yet? I'm hungry."

Brenna stood up. "We're almost ready to go, sport."

"Here's the book you asked me about for next time," Nancy said, handing Brenna a large picture book.

"Let me see," Teddy insisted, pulling the book down until he could see the cover. "What's this book?"

"The Bremen Town Musicians," Cole read. "One of the tales from the Grimm Brothers."

"And a very strange story, too," Nancy added, synopsizing the story of four old farm animals who ran away from home and frightened a band of robbers when they sang for their supper. "But, I know you, Brenna. There's some important lesson of life you're getting at here. I mean, you always do. With *The Little Engine That Could,* it was easy to see you wanted the kids to know the importance of trying even when you think you can't. But, this story is too weird for words."

Cole took the book from Brenna and flipped through the pages. Brenna watched him scan the pages, his expression changing slightly as he read. Then he nodded, once, as if confirming something to himself. He looked up, winked at Brenna, and glanced down at Nancy.

"What scared the robbers?" he asked. "The animals themselves? Or what the robbers thought they were?"

"What they thought," Nancy answered. "But I still don't get it."

Cole looked up from the last page of the book. "Appearances are deceiving." He paused and his gaze focused on Brenna. "Right?"

She hadn't expected him to get it, but he had. In spades. Nothing else could have frightened her as much.

"Right," she agreed, forcing the word between dry lips.

"Too bad deception works both ways," he mused.

Brenna was sure she didn't want to know what that meant, but she had to ask, "How's that?"

"In my line of work, things would be easy if breaking through the deception always revealed the truth. But it doesn't work that way. So you never know what is really beneath the deception. The truth or more lies."

Chapter 6

Appearances are deceiving. Never mind that he was right. Brenna felt as though she had been caught in a trap of her own making. Cole would surely see through her deceptions, if he hadn't already. That she cared a flying fig what he thought baffled her. More. Frightened her.

Fighting the urge to run, she blindly reached into her wallet and pulled out a library card, which she handed to Teddy with the book. "Want to check this out?"

"Uh-huh." He smiled and trotted off to the counter, his posture indicating his pride at being given the job.

Brenna looked up and found Nancy watching Cole. Brenna halfway expected Nancy to have that I-think-you're-great, why-don't-you-ask-*me*-out expression. She didn't, and when she glanced back at Brenna she smiled—that secret smile between friends that silently said, *This guy is hot.*

"I still wish you'd tell the kids the story of the *Three Little Pigs* the way you did to Teddy that one time." Nancy grinned at Cole. "You would have loved it. These pigs went off to seek their fortune, all right. But in professional sports. Can you imagine a little pig as a baseball player?'' She put her two fists together as though holding a bat.

Cole's smile returned, and his attention remained fastened on Brenna. ''Baseball, again. Do you like the game?''

''She loves it.'' Nancy echoed. ''And I'm telling you, don't ever challenge her to baseball trivia. She'd whip your derrière.'' She wiggled her fingers. ''Gotta go.''

Cole's attention shifted to Brenna. ''How 'bout a Rockies game?''

''I'm working.''

Cole laughed and made a point of glancing at his watch. ''It's June, and there's only dozens more home games between now and the playoffs. And you're working.''

Brenna felt the heat flood her cheeks. ''I...thought you meant tonight.''

''Ah. And it is true—that you're working. I remember you telling me.'' He leaned a little closer. ''Another time, then?''

Brenna met his gaze, her breath caught painfully in the middle of her chest. Another second chance, when she didn't want it, didn't deserve it...couldn't resist it. She nodded. ''Another time.''

''A woman of many talents,'' Cole said. ''Baseball trivia buff. Entrepreneur. Storyteller. Adored aunt.''

''Ex-entrepreneur,'' Brenna corrected. Nancy had made her sound like something special. What a lie—another deception on top of all the others. She needed some distance and time to think. That conclusion didn't keep her from asking, ''Why aren't you at work?''

He grinned. ''And direct, too.''

''Well?'' She wanted to give in to his grin. He looked great—what woman wouldn't be charmed by him? She couldn't allow herself to be.

''Who says I'm not working?''

''Unless you're suing the library, I can't imagine what you're doing in a children's room at ten o'clock in the morning.''

His smile widened, and she sensed he would deliberately ignore her baiting him.

''It's not ten o'clock, Brenna. Would you and Teddy like to go to lunch?''

''Lunch?'' she echoed.

"Yes," Teddy responded from her side, handing her the book and library card. "McDonald's. Okay?"

Brenna shook her head and stood up. "Not okay. I've got to go to work."

"All work and no play isn't good for you," Cole murmured, following her through the library.

"All play and no work doesn't pay the bills."

"Now there's a news flash." Cole had appreciation for her point of view, one he hadn't had until he struck out on his own. No more frills, if you could call a paralegal and an investigator frills. Things could be worse, he reminded himself. David Simmons had sent him several referrals, which Cole appreciated. When he had called to thank the senior partner from his old firm, the conversation had been surprisingly amiable.

Brenna acted as though she couldn't wait to get away from him, moving toward the door as if it was a lifeline. He followed, reluctant to let her go. Though he admitted he'd earned whatever she thought about him, it rankled that she didn't trust him. That didn't keep him from being attracted in a way he hadn't been...ever.

"Brenna, it's just an invitation for lunch—"

"Thanks," she interrupted, "but I really do have to go to work." She pulled open the door and held it for Teddy. Cole caught up with her in time to keep it from slamming in his face.

"The least I can do, then, is drive you home."

Again she shook her head. "The bus will be along in a couple of minutes. I don't want to put you out of your way."

Her voice had that same calm cadence she used in court, but he sensed that beneath the surface, she was rattled. Why? he wondered. He caught up with her outside under the shade of a spreading oak. "It's not out of my way. Is that really the problem? Or something else?"

She glanced at him in that almost defiant way she had, challenging him, wary as a barn cat.

"I guess I was hoping for too much," he said. "God knows you don't have any reason to trust me, much less like me." When she didn't contradict him at all, he decided the time had come to retreat and regroup. His gaze left Brenna, and he dropped to his haunches in front of Teddy, offering him a hand. "Take good care of your aunt, okay, Teddy?"

In grown-up fashion, the child took Cole's hand. "Maybe we can go to McDonald's some other time?"

Cole chuckled. "We can." He stood up, and unable to resist, tucked a strand of Brenna's hair behind her ear. "Okay, Auntie Brennie?" She didn't answer, and he cocked his head to the side. "I'll see you soon, then."

She swallowed and nodded, holding her hand out to Teddy. Cole watched them walk away, wondering if she believed him. If she didn't, she'd know soon enough. Tonight. He didn't have a clue about how to breach her defenses. But, he promised himself, by the time she got off work from the bar tonight, he would have a plan.

You should have told him to butt off, Brenna told herself as she walked away from Cole.

She had never indulged in casual flings. Cole almost made her wish she was the type. Without a doubt, she knew she couldn't have an easy, fun, casual relationship with this man. And for her, there could be no other kind. The sooner she got that through her head—and his, if he asked her out again—the better. The next time she saw him, she'd tell him in no uncertain terms. She wasn't interested in going out with him. No matter how much she wondered what kissing him would be like.

While they were waiting at the bus stop, Teddy asked, "How come the words aren't the same when you read to me?"

Brenna frowned, aware she had missed something in Teddy's ongoing monologue. "Same as what, Teddy?"

"The same words as Daddy reads," he explained. "Don't you know the words, Auntie Brennie?"

Don't you know the words? Brenna stared at her nephew. If Teddy had figured it out, surely her lack of reading was equally obvious to the entire world. While she was still trying to understand how he had discovered her secret, Teddy jumped up.

"Here comes the bus. Can I put the money in? Please?"

The bus stopped, and Teddy preceded her up the steps, telling the driver hello, and fed the coins into the meter. He skipped to a seat and sat down.

"Look at the funny dog, Auntie," he said as she sat next to him. "What kind is it?"

Brenna followed his pointing finger through the window, marshaling her scattered thoughts with effort. "An Afghan hound, I think."

"I like the way he walks. And his floppy ears."

Brenna sighed, thankful for the curiosity that had made Teddy forget his question. More frightening was Cole's intuition.

Appearances are deceiving.

The three words beat inside her brain, keeping rhythm with the bus. Brenna watched the passing city, remembering every turn, every choice, that had led her here. A choice—a stupid choice, made when she was six—that she wouldn't compete with her brother to earn her father's love. She hadn't understood the consequences of her actions then. And now...now she was an illiterate woman, deceiving everyone.

"Isn't this where we get off the bus, Auntie Brennie?" Teddy asked, startling her out of her melancholy reverie.

She focused her gaze on the pizza parlor and service station that marked their stop. "It sure is, honey. That's very observant."

He beamed. "I'm getting to be a big boy, huh?"

Brenna wanted to scoop him into her arms and encourage him to continue being a little boy. There was plenty of time to be a big boy, plenty of time to face all the challenges of growing up. Instead, she smiled and tousled his hair.

"Yes," she said, giving him the reassurance he needed. "The biggest. The best."

"How do you suppose the bus driver knows where to go?"

"I imagine he looks at the street signs."

Teddy craned his neck and looked up at the sign on the corner. "What does this one say?"

Brenna glanced at the sign, then at the landmarks that identified the intersection to her. "Washington Street."

"I'm going to learn every sign," he said. "Then I'll be able to drive a bus, too."

She had little doubt he meant it. Teddy would make his choices, just as she had made hers. Hopefully the chain that would stretch link by link into Teddy's future would include better choices than she had made.

Brenna moved through the rest of the day like an automaton. As she cleaned Mrs. Johnston's house, doubts returned to plague her, doubts that had been nearly constant since Bates filed his lawsuit. She hadn't been able to make a success of a small, simple business. How did she expect to ever get out of her current pickle?

For more than two years, she had dared think everything would be fine. Her business hadn't required much paperwork, and anyway she'd hired a bookkeeper-secretary to manage those details. Until she had taken maternity leave, things had gone fine. Then, little things Brenna thought she could handle became overwhelming. The remembered helplessness poured through her now. How much longer could she keep deceiving everyone?

At once, dozens of things flitted through her mind. Her brother's casual way of talking aloud to himself when they went shopping—muttering that she paid close attention to so she could identify a baking powder can from a cocoa can. When they were kids, the way he had teased her about important phone numbers—numbers she learned to remember after hearing them once.

At the bar that evening, she waited on customers, responding to the banter out of habit and without conscious thought. Had anyone asked her a few days ago, she would have told them she'd gotten used to her unraveled life. She had been wrong. She wanted to be in control again, but she didn't have a clue where to even begin, not to mention she no longer trusted her own judgment.

"Has everything been okay, Brenna?" Theo asked toward the end of the evening. "You seem a little down tonight."

"Everything's fine." Except that it wasn't.

She made countless trips through the bar, doing her job, but unable to push away the feeling that a great void had opened beneath her feet. Two months ago she thought she could handle knowing it would be years before she'd be free of the debt from the lawsuit. Those years loomed before her now in an endless stretch where little more than survival would be possible. By then, she'd be closer to forty than thirty.

Somehow, she thought, I've got to figure out a way.

You know the way, came the ever-taunting voice from inside.

Leave me alone. I don't want to deal with you right now.

Closing time arrived, and Brenna went into the rest room to change out of her uniform. She emerged and paused in the doorway studying the street. *If I could read, I'd have a driver's license and I wouldn't have to worry about catching a bus in the middle of the night.*

Like last night, Colfax Avenue was nearly deserted. The homeless man was back tonight, asleep on the bus-stop bench. Two couples left another bar at the end of block and disappeared behind the building at the corner. The only car parked on the street was a black Jeep in front of Score. A tall, broad-shouldered man wearing a huge white sombrero leaned against the vehicle, his arms folded across his chest.

Brenna studied him from the shadows of the entry, knowing immediately that Cole Cassidy was, for whatever reasons, waiting for her. The hat, which looked like something he had picked up as a booby prize at a carnival, made her smile. She couldn't think of a single reason he'd be wearing a monstrous white sombrero edged in red and green braid. No reason—except, perhaps, to make her laugh.

Such a simple thing. She couldn't believe he was here. Not after the way she'd practically run away from him this morning.

She couldn't deny the pull he had for her. *He's the kind of man I'd choose if...*

If what?

She swallowed.

If you could read, prodded her little voice, gently this time. If you could read, even this would be possible.

Brenna ignored the quake of fear that thought filled her with and pushed open the door.

Cole looked up, levered himself away from vehicle, and moved toward her. The hat fell over one eye. His sheepish grin dissolved what remained of her apprehension. Deliberately, she pushed her promise that she'd send the man packing to the back of her mind. Tonight, she would enjoy what he offered and face the consequences later.

"Hi, Brenna." Two ordinary words that primed her awareness of him.

"Hi, yourself." She tipped her head, studying the hat. "I see you've added something to your wardrobe since this morning."

"Good guys wear white hats." He hooked his thumbs in the belt loops at the front of his slacks and sauntered forward.

"They do, huh?" She remembered him telling her that he had wanted to be one of the good guys in a white hat. Not only that, he looked great. Long tapered legs. Flat stomach. His eyes met hers. She felt the jolt of awareness to her toes.

"They do," he confirmed, nodding. The ridiculous hat slipped further over his eye. He pushed it back into place. "I wanted to make sure you'd recognize me."

"I knew you were one of the good guys." She had spent a lot of time thinking about that. Too much. "Why are you here?"

Even to herself her voice sounded husky.

"Thought you might need a lift home."

"A lift is what you'll get if you drive with that thing on."

He grinned. "Like it?"

"I've honestly never seen anything quite like it," she said, unable to keep from smirking.

"Me, neither." He slid the bright red bead down the chin strap and took it off. He held out his hand. "I'd love a cup of coffee and a piece of pie. Join me?"

She moved out of the doorway. More than anything she wanted to be able simply to say yes. In spite of her resolve to live tonight as though it existed without connection to all her days before, nothing was as simple as she wanted.

"Why are you here? Really?"

He placed his hand at the small of her back and guided her toward the Jeep. "Because I wanted to be. Really."

"And this morning?"

"I wanted to see you."

"Why?"

"Does it matter?"

Brenna nodded.

Cole smoothed the frown lines between his eyebrows with his thumb. "I was curious about you." He met her gaze. "I'm attracted to you. And...when I saw you last night...I hoped I'd...we'd have another chance."

"We're an unlikely combination."

"Plaintiff's attorney and defendant?"

"Cocktail waitress and attorney." Among other things, she silently added.

"We can work through that."

He tempted her to believe him. Her gaze moved over his face, his expression as open as his declaration had been. He kept pushing at the limits she had imposed on herself. She wanted to stretch them, wanted to believe in the possibilities he offered. She wasn't frightened of him. But she was scared to death she wouldn't live up to her own expectations of herself.

He clapped the sombrero over his heart, his expression imploring. "I'm inviting you for pie. Not proposing marriage."

His leap from pie to marriage struck Brenna's sense of the absurd, and she laughed. It surprised her as much as it did him. He stared at her, the lines around his mouth relaxing as he at last smiled.

"You're not?" Brenna teased, taking the hat from his hand and tossing it into the back seat of the Jeep. She understood that Cole had worn the hat to put her at ease, to soften her image of him, to replace the stern lawyer with someone full of boyish appeal. That he'd gone to such lengths for her made keeping him at a distance impossible.

"No," he said. "I mean, yes. And I take it all back. You're beautiful when you laugh. I love the way it sounds. Will you marry me?"

Another jolt of awareness sizzled through Brenna's stomach. She climbed into the Jeep and kept her voice deliberately light. "Maybe. Let me think about it while we have pie."

Chapter 7

"What a nice surprise to see you, Cole. Come in," came Jane's voice through the open window as Cole came up the walk toward Brenna's apartment. Opening the door, he stepped inside.

He admitted to himself that knowing he'd receive a warm welcome from Brenna's family was one of the inducements to stopping by unannounced. He had met them all a couple of days ago, and he liked them. There was no doubt Michael and Brenna were brother and sister, sharing the same dark hair and athletic build.

Michael was the sort of man Cole liked, not as bookish or as serious as his Ph.D. degree suggested—at least, not on the surface. Michael had invited him for a game of handball. Thus far, neither of their schedules had allowed it.

Jane was equally warm, including Cole for no other reason than the fact that he liked Brenna. It was the sort of acceptance his grandmother gave people.

Meeting Brenna's brother and his wife did little to shed any light on how or why Brenna had landed herself in so much trouble. They had professions in academia, and Brenna's life, both with her defunct business and her working now as a barmaid, was at the other end of the spectrum. No closer now than he ever was to understanding her choices, Cole knew only one thing. He wanted to know Brenna better—much better.

His plans to pursue her had been frustrated at every turn. He'd taken on two new cases this week: one, a woman being stalked by her ex-husband; the other, a man who wanted sole custody of his son. Both had added hours to his already heavy workload.

Brenna's schedule was just as hectic, and Cole suspected she was as determined to keep him at arm's length as he was to get closer. Whether because of his part in Harvey Bates's case against her or something more, Cole wasn't sure. Spend enough time with her, he reasoned, and sooner or later she'd believe him when he told her he hadn't been happy with his part in it.

"We're just fixing root beer floats," Jane said as Cole came into the spotless kitchen. "If you'll get another glass off the top shelf of the cupboard, you can have one, too." She opened the door and pointed to the glasses.

"Root beer floats, huh?" Cole said, smiling easily. He hadn't had one of those in years and was reminded of Fourth of July celebrations as a kid. He set the glass on the counter next to the others. Jane handed him an ice-cream scoop and a carton of ice cream, and he grinned. Another aspect of her personality that reminded him of his grandmother—no one was guest.

"Brenna," Jane called down the hallway. "Cole is here." Stepping back into the kitchen, she said, "She forgot to mention you have a date tonight."

"No date," Cole said. Brenna had been okay with his dropping by the bar or the apartment. As for a date, a real bona fide date—she wouldn't have anything to do with one. He smiled at Jane and dropped his voice. "I keep hoping, though."

She smiled back. "Nothing good ever comes to the faint-hearted."

Brenna's wariness had made Cole reevaluate his approach to dating, a routine that, on reflection, made him cringe. Dinner at a nice restaurant, and if that went well, a play or concert. Then dinner at one of his favorite restaurants, followed the next day by flowers. Often as not, the lady would invite him over, then an invitation to spend the night. Then the chase would be over, the allure gone. And, he realized, he had never given enough of himself for any of those relationships to have a chance to blossom.

Seconds later Teddy skipped into the room followed by Brenna. "Ymm. Floats," he said. "My favorite."

"Hi," Brenna said from the doorway. "I see you've been put to work."

"When you mentioned you had the night off," he responded, looking up at her, "I thought you might like to go to a movie or something." She was dressed in a pair of running shorts and a T-shirt, her dark hair pulled away from her face in a loose ponytail.

Her glance skipped away from his, and she reached for a glass in the cupboard, which she filled with water. He watched her drink and knew she was going to turn him down again.

"Or we can just hang out," he said, retreating. He picked up the ice-cream scoop and put some ice cream into the first of the glasses lined up on the counter. "It's been a hectic day, and I'd probably fall asleep in the middle of the movie."

"That's what happens to me," Teddy said, solemnly. "I think it's 'cause it's dark."

Cole chuckled. "Could be." He glanced back at Brenna. "Okay if I stay?"

"Of course it's okay," Jane interjected.

Cole appreciated her vote of confidence, but he watched Brenna, who nodded as if she didn't trust her voice.

Brenna's brother, Michael, came into the kitchen from the back of the house and grinned when he caught sight of Cole.

"Look who keeps turning up, like an old penny," Michael said. "Third or fourth time this week, isn't it, Brenna?"

"Yeah," she countered, "but who's counting?"

He laughed, then pointed toward Cole's tie. "You're a little overdressed for hanging-out-and-root-beer-float kind of night."

Cole glanced down at the silk tie, remembering that he had intended to take it off when he took off his jacket.

"We wouldn't want you getting ice cream all over it, would we?" Brenna asked.

To his surprise, she stepped close, expertly loosened the knot and pulled it from under his collar. Cole stood perfectly still, the carton of ice cream cold against his hand, acutely aware this was as close as he had been to her since that first night when he kissed her.

The clean fragrance of her hair assailed him as she unbuttoned the top button of his shirt. the featherlight brush of her fingers against his Adam's apple made him swallow. She looked up at him and smiled. The rim at the edge of her gray irises was dark, something he hadn't noticed before. As he watched her, her eyes became smoky, and he would have bet all he had to know whether she was as bothered as he was. Lord, but he hoped so.

He fought the urge to lower his head and kiss the freckle at the corner of her eye.

"Better?" she asked.

"Yeah." He swallowed the dry lump that lodged in his throat. "Thanks."

"No problem." Stepping away from him, she folded up the tie and set it on the end of the counter near the door.

He returned his attention to filling the rest of the glasses with ice cream, all the while completely aware of Brenna. He wanted to believe he'd destroyed her concentration as much as she'd destroyed his. When his attention wasn't directly focused on a case, he thought about her. All the time.

Sleeping was a damn nuisance, interspersed with languid, hot dreams of her wrapped in his arms. He ached to share the intimacy of sleep with her, which surprised him. He liked having a woman in bed with him, but going to sleep with one wasn't anything he'd wanted, not even with his former fiancée. He wanted Brenna in his bed, wanted to fall asleep with her, wanted to awaken with her in his arms.

Teddy pulled a chair across the kitchen floor to the counter and clambered up on it. "That's too much ice cream," he said with authority. "You've gotta leave room for the root beer."

With more instructions from Teddy and Jane, the floats were finally all made, and they settled around the kitchen table. It was strewn with snapshots, an assortment of papers, and a couple of bank passbooks.

"What's all this?" Cole asked, picking up an old photograph, recognizing Brenna as the child in the photo.

"All these things, their father sent," Jane replied. "He's moving again, and he doesn't want them. Can you imagine such a thing? You'd think he'd want the memories of their childhood."

Cole studied the picture of Brenna in a stiff pose with her brother and a man in military dress whites.

"This is my daddy and Auntie Brennie when they were little," Teddy said, pointing to a picture of a pair of toddlers playing in the sand on a beach.

Michael provided additional explanation for the other photographs, which, Cole gathered, had arrived in the mail today. He learned they had lived in England, Germany, Japan, and more places in the United States than either of them could remember. Michael's history of the family stopped about the time he went away to boarding school, and Brenna had little to add.

All the photographs were of people, except one of an old frame house. It was badly in need of paint, protected by huge trees, nestled at the base of a gentle hill and surrounded by fields that had been misted with a recent rain.

"Our grandparents' farm," Michael explained when he met Cole's glance. Michael picked up the picture and studied critically. "I could never figure out what you liked so much about it, Brenna."

She took the photograph from her brother. "I don't remember it like this." Her voice was soft, laced with memories. "It couldn't have been this shabby."

Between the pages of one of the passbooks peeked one last picture. Cole pulled the photo from between the pages and gazed down at another picture of Brenna, this time in her early teens standing with a woman. They were smiling at each other. "Your mother?" he asked.

The last of any smile left Brenna's face, and she slowly took the photograph and passbook from him. "Yes." After a moment, she passed them both to her brother.

"I don't think I've ever seen this one," he said.

Cole watched as Brenna stood up, carried a couple of the glasses to the sink and methodically rinsed them.

"Brenna?" Michael prompted.

Shutting off the water, she glanced at her brother, then looked back through the window above the sink. "That was taken on her birthday." She cleared her throat. "Her last birthday."

Brenna hadn't enjoyed going through the pictures the way her brother had. In a way Cole could not have explained if he'd been asked, she made him ache for her. He had watched her disappear behind a wall of reserve again, and he was positive she hurt. Regretting that he had asked anything that brought her painful memories, he stood up.

"Let's go for a walk." He set his glass in the sink, then guided her toward the door, giving her no chance to refuse.

"See you later," Michael said as they stepped outside where the setting sun had painted the sky in brilliant crimson.

Cole bet not many of Brenna's memories as a child were good ones. The little girl in the photographs looked desperately unhappy. He'd pegged Brenna to be fourteen or fifteen in that last one. The worst year of her life, she had said. What she'd been through since had been no picnic, either.

He wanted to know why she had shadows in her eyes, why she had looked so panicked when he first arrived at the library the other morning. Most of all, he wanted to know why she worked at menial jobs when she was so bright. How had she ended up in this position when her brother was working as a post-doc researcher at the University Medical Center?

The direct approach wouldn't give him the answers he wanted, he thought, gazing down at the top of her head. Her own gaze seemed focused on the concrete beneath her feet. He lifted his head and looked around, hearing the chirp of birds in the trees above them, inhaling the aroma of someone's freshly cut lawn.

"I like this," he murmured, hoping to draw Brenna from her private, painful melancholy. "Sharing a sunset with you." He clasped her hand and pulled her close, matching his stride to her shorter one. Subtly, slowly, she began to relax.

"At home," he said, "Mom and Dad and Grandmom are probably all sitting on the porch."

"Where is home?"

He grinned, pleased that she allowed herself to be led away from her thoughts. "A ranch in western Nebraska."

She gave him a surprised glance. "A ranch?"

His grin widened. "Is that so hard to believe?"

"I thought..."

A moment later, he prompted, "What?"

She glanced at him again. "I just thought you'd probably grown up in Cherry Creek Village or somewhere similar."

"A silver spoon in my mouth?" He waited for her to look at him again. "Not even close."

She easily imagined him outside surrounded by wide-open spaces. He'd be as confident and as at home there, she thought, as he was in a courtroom. She did have trouble imagining him lounging indolently against the steps of a porch while he watched a sunset. He seemed to have too much energy, too much drive. It was easier to imagine him running or finishing up that last chore of the day before the daylight was gone. The thought made her smile.

Cole touched the corner of her mouth. "What's this about?"

"You. Being lazy enough to watch a sunset."

"I can be lazy with the best." He took an affronted tone that broadened her smile.

"That's what we did at my grandmother's farm, too," she said. "We'd sit on the porch at sunset. Nonna always had something to do. Beans to snap or corn to shuck."

"What about when you were with your parents?"

Cole instantly felt the change in her. Where there had been softness, she became rigid.

"I don't remember." Her voice was carefully neutral. "The Colonel—he's not the kind of man to notice a sunset."

"Once I thought the same thing about my dad," Cole said.

Her glance encouraged him to continue.

"I was supposed to inherit the farm. Dad had it all mapped out. I'd go to college. I was supposed to major in horticulture or agricultural economics." Cole smiled. "Actually, I almost did that one. Those ag economists are sharp. I just knew I didn't want to be a rancher."

"I loved my grandparents' farm," Brenna said. "When it had to be sold, it was awful."

Cole nodded. "Since I won't be around to take care of my parents' farm, I suppose we're looking at that someday, too."

"Don't you care?"

Cole met her gaze. "I care. But ranching is damn hard work. Unpredictable, with one certainty—if the weather can do you in, it will." He paused and looked at her. "And I couldn't ever quite figure out how to have what I wanted and please my dad, too. We had some terrible fights.'' Cole tucked Brenna more firmly against him as they strolled through the park while the evening dusk gave way to night. "Once I even walked out on him. Told him I wouldn't be back.''

Brenna's hand tightened around his.

"You fought with your dad?'' Cole asked, sensing he had struck a nerve.

"All the time,'' she admitted, glancing up at him. "I left, too.''

Cole didn't have to ask when. He knew. *The worst year of my life was when I was fifteen.*

"Damn all those pictures,'' she said softly. "Damn him for bringing it all back now.''

"What, Brenna?''

"I don't want to remember,'' she whispered.

"Maybe it's the only way you can forget. Just get it up and out and gone,'' he returned, his voice as soft as hers.

She glanced at him, and the torment in her eyes made him gather her close. Within his arms, she felt small, feminine, and fragile as a newborn lamb. Within his arms, she felt...perfect. "You can talk to me, fair lady.''

Surprisingly, she did. "I never measured up to his standards. The night I left home, it all started because I stayed out too late at a girlfriend's house.''

"Brenna, get in here.'' Her father's imperative command had come from the living room.

She sighed and adopted a relaxed don't-give-a-hoot posture. She'd rather die than let him know she bled a little inside each time he spoke her name in that particular tone. She sauntered into the living room and leaned casually against the doorjamb.

"Hi, Dad. Where's Mom?''

"She's gone to bed.'' He folded the newspaper and set it aside. "Stand up straight and come here, young lady.''

Brenna moved away from the doorway and stood in front of him, but she kept her posture deliberately slouched.

"Where have you been this time? You're an hour and twenty-seven minutes late.''

"I've been at Sally Peterson's." She met his gaze, then added, "Studying."

"Studying?" He picked up an envelope from the table and withdrew her report card. "Here are the results of your studying, Brenna James. English F, history F, phys ed, A, algebra D, science F, home ec C. I shudder to think what your grades would be if you *didn't* study."

Brenna folded her arms across her chest and waited for him to finish. These "talks" followed a pattern that had varied little since she was in the first grade. Her gaze fixed on the wall behind him, and she let his angry words wash over her without hearing anything, simply knowing Michael was valued and she was worthless.

Once Brenna had overheard an argument between her parents as her mother tried to explain the constant comparisons did neither child any good.

"Brenna's a normal child—not gifted like Michael. Just a child," her mother had said.

"Neither of my children are *just* children," her father had answered. "Brenna is capable of doing anything, *anything,* that Michael is. She's *just* lazy."

That hurt. Brenna pushed aside the memory and waited for the next part of the Colonel's talk—the part where he told her excellence counted. Lives depended on excellence. It wasn't enough to do your best if your best didn't keep other people from dying.

He surged to his feet and slapped her. "You'll show a little respect when I'm talking to you." He grasped her arms and forced them down her sides. "You *will* pay attention. You *will* stand up straight," he commanded, one of his hands at the small of her back and the other on her shoulders. "Now, do I have your attention?"

"Yes."

"Yes, what?"

Rather than give him the "yes, sir" she knew he wanted, she remained stubbornly silent.

"I've had it with you, young lady," he said, giving her a shake. "You're disobedient." He grasped her arms with one hand, unbuckled his belt with the other.

"What's all the shouting in here?" her mother asked from the doorway.

"Tell her," the Colonel commanded Brenna. "Go ahead, tell her."

"I'm lazy," Brenna said dully, watching her father. "And disobedient. May I be excused now?"

"No, you may not be excused!" He pushed her toward the kitchen, where he expected her to obediently bend over the table.

For years it had ended like this. Brenna closed her eyes as she stumbled forward.

In a little while, it would be over. Just a little longer.

Years of tension snapped.

She whirled around. "No! Not this time."

"No? You tell me no?" His face twisted with fury.

"John, stop!" Brenna's mother cried.

He struck with the belt. Brenna lifted her arms. Too late! With a snap, the tip stung against her cheek.

She ripped the belt from his hand and threw it across the kitchen. He grabbed her. She slipped past him and ran toward her room.

His voice followed her. "I never wanted you."

"John!" her mother cried.

"It's the truth. Not from the day you told me you were pregnant."

"You don't mean that. You can't."

"We'd be better off without her. My God, Michael doesn't give us a bit of trouble and she gives us nothing but."

Better off without her. The words echoed through Brenna's head as she slammed her bedroom door. *Never wanted you.* Without conscious thought, she pulled a suitcase from under the bed. *Better off without her.* Tears blurred her vision as she opened the suitcase and began throwing clothes and belongings inside.

The door opened, and Brenna flinched. Escaping the Colonel in the small room would be harder. But, she would not submit to another beating. Not now. Not ever. Instead of her father, her mother stood in the doorway.

"Oh, Brenna. Oh, baby, no."

Brenna wiped away the tears with the back of her hand. "I'm not staying, Mom."

"You can't just leave. Where would you go?"

"Nonna's," Brenna replied with sudden decision. The farm had always been her favorite place.

Brenna's mother stared into space, then nodded. "Okay. Maybe that is best." She left the room.

Her reaction puzzled Brenna. She assumed she'd have to fight both of her parents. She stared at the contents of the suitcase a moment longer, then began organizing more neatly. A quarter-hour later her mother returned.

"Nonna is expecting you," she said. "I called Greyhound, and a bus leaves for Philadelphia in an hour. You can get a connecting bus in the morning." She touched Brenna's cheek. "Are you sure this is what you want, baby?"

Brenna nodded.

Her mother helped her finish packing while they both cried, then drove her to the bus station. During the last moments before the bus came, her mother tried to give her a passbook for a savings account.

"This was for your—for college. But you need it now."

Brenna looked with blurred eyes at the insignia on the outside of the book. College? Right. She had as much chance of going to college as Michael did of flunking out of school. Another reminder that she had failed. She hadn't come close to the excellence the Colonel demanded. Hadn't even tried. For the first time in a long while, she wished she had.

Tears filled her eyes as she shook her head. "I can't, Mom. Dad would…"

Her mother's eyes welled with tears. "I wish I could do more for you." She shook the passbook for emphasis. "This is yours. Any time you want it, you call me." She gave Brenna a fierce hug. "I've made so many mistakes. I can't take away what I let happen. I wish…"

Brenna returned her mother's hug. "Me, too, Mom."

"It was the last time I saw her," Brenna finished, her eyes feeling gritty from unshed tears. "Two months after I went to Nonna's, Mom was killed in a car accident." She swallowed and gripped Cole's hands. "Six months after that I came home from school one day. Nonna always took a nap in the afternoon. That day, she never woke up."

Dusk had given way to darkness, and sometime during Brenna's story, Cole had directed her to a bench beneath a huge silver maple tree. He had wrapped his arm around her and kept her close while she talked. She'd never felt more vulnerable—or safer.

She risked looking at him. His gaze was focused unseeingly on the night, his expression pensive. She held her breath, waiting. For what, she could not have said.

He finally looked down at her, and a sad smile touched his lips. "You make me feel like my dad was a saint," he said. "I think you'd like him."

Relief whispered through her. She wasn't sure what she wanted from Cole, but she knew she couldn't have borne his pity.

"Thank you," she whispered, pressing her cheek against his.

"For what?"

"Being here."

"You're welcome." He made sure his voice was calm. More than his next breath, he needed her to know she could trust him, wanted to prove to her that he'd never use his strength or his anger against her. Carefully, he held her, making sure none of the rage he felt toward her father was transferred to her.

He brushed his cheek with hers, and in passing, she gave him a quick kiss. Her lips were inviting. Soft. Unable to resist, his lips returned to hers, not deepening the kiss, teaching both of them how sweet the mere touching of lip to lip could be. He sensed she wanted more. Hell, he wanted more. But for now...for now, this was more important.

Take it slow, he cautioned himself. He'd be gentle, and he'd cherish her the way she deserved.

Two hours later, Brenna lay in bed without sleeping. Either Michael or Jane had put the photographs and papers from her mother on the dresser. Brenna's gaze drifted to them, unable to make out more than the rectangular shapes in the dark. She hated the feelings all this looking into the past had evoked.

The dark teardrop of a crystal hanging in the window was her only memento of those months she had lived with Nonna. Brenna remembered that her grandmother had hung it in the window of her room the night she had arrived at the farm.

"Something pretty to look at," Nonna had said. "Sometimes to find the good things in life, you just have to be standing in the right spot to see them. And sometimes, you're already standing in the right spot. You just have to pay attention.''

Brenna was standing in the right spot to know just how special a man Cole Cassidy was. She felt an undeniable flicker of hope in her heart. He was perfect for her.

She was not perfect for him.

When he called the following morning to invite her to go sailing on Sunday, the truth that would push him out of her life remained stuck in her throat.

She knew she should turn him down, but she didn't.

Chapter 8

"There are better places to sail," Cole said after they climbed into his Jeep, his sailboat in tow. "Next time we'll get started sooner, and we'll go to the mountains." He flashed her a smile, then squeezed her hand. "At Lake Dillon there are a dozen secluded coves to explore."

Brenna smiled at him. "That sounds nice."

Next time. However alluring that promise was, she didn't dare hope for a next time. If she had a lick of sense, she would make sure the man never asked her to go sailing or anywhere else after today. When she was with him, their worlds didn't seem so different, nor did the differences seem that important. She liked him, darn it, and she hadn't expected to. She certainly hadn't wanted to.

Who was she kidding? She loved being with him. Loved the way he looked at her—as though she was the only woman he had ever seen. Loved the way he listened to her—as though what she had to say was important. Not only had he listened to her, he had held her as though her pain hurt him, too. How could she resist that?

Lame excuse though she knew it was, she fell back on her sister-in-law's take on the situation. "Let it happen, Brenna," Jane had advised. "Don't be looking for trouble where there might be none."

During their short ride to the marina, his manner was more relaxed than she had ever seen it. He obviously loved sailing, revealing an endearingly boyish aspect to his personality.

When the boat was in the water, Cole pulled the cover off the sail, readying the boat. He moved with easy confidence, his smile telling her all she needed to know about how he felt.

Then he extended a hand to her, and murmured, "Welcome aboard," as she stepped in. She took the narrow seat in the bow, and they moved away from the shore, Cole maneuvering the craft with the smooth coordination of having done so hundreds of times.

Brenna trailed her hands in the water. Cool. Too cool for swimming, but not by much, she thought, enjoying the rush of exhilaration that came from the water's contrast to the warm sun.

Cole let out the sail, which instantly filled with wind. As soon as they had moved into less crowded water, he raised the sail further still, and they picked up speed at a rate that surprised Brenna. Fresh air, beautiful colors, penetrating sunshine. Life didn't get much better than this. She smiled and lifted her arms into the wind.

Cole grinned at her enjoyment and found himself making comparisons he'd promised he wouldn't. Susan had tolerated sailing, but she usually found a dozen other things to do when he asked her.

"I love this," Brenna said, lifting her face into the wind. "Does your boat have a name?"

"It doesn't meet the minimum size requirements to have a name," Cole said, his tone and expression deadpan.

"That's stupid. You mean some rule says you can't name—"

He laughed, and she looked at him.

"That wasn't nice, Cole." She flicked water at him. "So why doesn't it have a name?"

"I never thought of one that seemed quite right."

"No lost loves?"

"None that mattered."

"No favorite celebrities?"

"I can't see naming my spinnaker the *Mickey Mouse*. And *His Honorable Justice John Marshall* seems…ah…a little pretentious."

"Ah," she agreed. "I can see how that could be a problem. Who is John Marshall?"

"He was the Chief Justice of the Supreme Court during the early 1800s."

"One of your contemporaries, huh?"

Cole aimed a casual swipe at her head, at the last moment smoothing his hand over her hair.

"So what else, Counselor?"

"John Marshall was the author of *The Life of George Washington*—all five volumes. And he established the right of the Supreme Court to have the final say about the constitutionality of any law." Cole met her gaze. "Enough?"

"More than. Is there a quiz later?"

"Nah," he returned. "You'd ace any test I could think up.

Little did he know, Brenna thought, a sliver of fear pricking her, reminding her of the promise she'd made to herself. Tell him the truth or back off before you get hurt.

"Ready to hear what I know about Mickey Mouse?" Cole asked.

This time, Brenna laughed, as much from a release of her tension as from his earnest expression. "Yeah. I am."

Cole's face lit up, like a little boy trying to think of just the right thing to impress a teacher. "His dog's name is Pluto."

"I didn't know that."

"Honest."

"I'm surprised you have any room up there for any fun stuff," she said, gesturing toward his head, "after hearing about John Marshall."

"My grandmom used to tell me, 'It's a funny thing about brains. They never seem to get full.'"

Brenna chuckled. "Mine is stuffed with all sorts of useless stuff."

"Baseball trivia."

"I'll have you know there's nothing trivial about baseball."

"Not compared to the junk in the tabloids—you know, the aliens having lunch with the First Lady and the aunt's grandmother's daughter who bore her sister's twin sons."

Brenna laughed. "That's possible?"

He joined her laughter, then cupped her cheek with his palm, his own laughter fading.

"What?" she asked.

"It's the first time I've heard you laugh. Really laugh." He rubbed his thumb against her cheek. "I love it."

Brenna's throat grew dry. Her breath caught when his fingers caressed her skin as he pulled his hand away. One moment stretched into two, and never had she been more aware of another person.

"What other kind of trivia do you like?" he asked, his husky voice at odds with the let's-lighten-the-moment question.

"Baseball's about my favorite, but I like all natural history, too."

"A woman of many interests," Cole said. "My kind of lady."

She only wished she were.

Several strong gusts of wind pulled hard on the sails, and the craft lurched to one side. Cole's attention shifted to the boat, where he made a couple of quick adjustments, again bringing it under control. Brenna watched him, enjoying his confidence in himself and his ability to keep the boat on the course he wanted.

"I better pay attention to what I'm doing, or we could end up in the drink," he said.

Brenna smiled. "That's one way to impress a woman with your sailing prowess."

He chuckled. "Never mind that the woman in question is too damn distracting."

"Yeah?"

"Yeah."

As if by tacit agreement, they let the silence stretch between them—a comfortable, easy silence. Gradually her attention focused beyond Cole. Farther away she heard the call of other voices, the endless traffic moving across the dam, the distant roar of an airplane as it made its approach to Denver International Airport. She imagined being with Cole when the only sounds were those of the vessel gliding through the water, punctuated occasionally by the calls of birds soaring overhead.

She closed her eyes and lifted her face into the breeze, giving herself to the wind and the flying mist with an abandon she usually did not allow.

She loved the feeling of racing across the water. "Maybe you could teach me how to sail."

"Any time you want," he answered. "Ready about."

"Aye, aye, Captain," she said with a smile, ducking under the boom as Cole skillfully turned the sailboat back in the direction they had come. Bright sails from other boats dotted the lake, and the high-rise office buildings to the northwest stood in sharp relief. Cole never tired of the view, but just now he had something better to watch. Brenna.

Mahogany highlights glinted in her loose hair. Fine strands blew across her face in a continuing caress that made Cole wish he could touch her. Her legs seemed longer than they had in the cheerleader's uniform she wore at work. Her faded cutoffs, nearly white from countless washings, faithfully clung to every curve between her waist and thighs. An oversize pale blue cotton shirt was knotted at her waist over a darker blue tank top. The wind billowed through the fabric, hiding a lush body that he had undressed only in his dreams.

"Want to eat lunch yet?" he asked.

"I'll probably be starved later, but right now I don't want you to stop. This feels too good."

"Yeah," he agreed, his gaze again sliding over her. He imagined her coming to him as she was now—her face lit with a smile of pure sensual enjoyment.

Brenna let her mind drift. She felt as though the wind had caught all her worries and blown them away. Through half-closed eyes, she watched Cole tack the craft across the lake with the complete ease of a man who had spent hundreds of hours sailing. He grinned when he caught her watching him.

She decided the way he looked today was her favorite. No unap-proachable, stern lawyer. He wore tan cotton shorts and a loose red T-shirt. Even as she watched, he stripped away the shirt, revealing an expanse of tanned chest rippling with a hard washboard of muscle that made her breath catch. She looked away, licked her lips, then looked back. The swirls of hair that covered his chest were the same golden brown shade as his head, and every bit as inviting to touch. Then, she imagined him without even the shorts. Heat chased through her, and she tore her gaze away.

"Hungry yet?" he asked, steering the craft toward a secluded ex-panse of shoreline.

"God, yes," she murmured.

"Like Italian subs?"

"Love them," she replied.

"Gee, too bad I only brought one. I figured you were more the liverwurst type." His eyes lit with teasing.

"Fat chance," she answered.

Cole lowered the sail, and the boat slid soundlessly toward the shore. He threw a rope tied to the bow into the water, and eased himself out of the boat. Picking up the rope, he waded to shore, anchored it under a rock, and came back.

Brenna started to stand, then immediately sat back down when the boat rocked.

"You make that look so easy," Brenna said, eyeing the shallow water, convinced she was about to take a dunking.

"Piece of cake," he said. He caught her under her knees and across her back, and effortlessly lifted her out of the craft.

"I—" *Can walk,* she whispered in the deep recesses of her mind. Except, she didn't want to.

Caught against Cole's chest, she was assailed with his warm scent—soap, deodorant and him all blended together in an aroma that made her stomach tighten. So much skin touched her, burned her, drew her irresistibly closer. She looped her arms around his neck, acutely aware of his hand searing her bare leg, his other hand scorching through the cotton of her shirt.

She turned slightly in his arms, enjoying the sensation of being fully pressed against him.

He stopped walking, the water lapping around his legs, his gaze caught with hers. Her breath hitched painfully in her chest, and she looked at his mouth, then back at his eyes. On a groan, he closed them and lowered his head.

The instant his mouth touched Brenna's, she opened hers wide, inviting—demanding—his possession. Heat and the nubby touch of tongue gliding over tongue consumed her. She pressed her hands against his neck, which felt nearly as hot as his mouth.

Sharp need flowed through her and pooled low in her belly. Her focus narrowed to the sensation of their mated mouths. The other night he'd taught her yearning and wanting. Now he taught her combustion, paling all her previous experiences.

The roar of a speedboat and catcalls from a group of teenagers as they sped by shocked Brenna out of the consuming kiss. Cole's gaze roamed over her mouth and face before he looked away. He took a deep breath.

"We left lunch in the boat," he said finally.

She wiggled her toes. "Probably because you had your...um, hands full."

He grinned, squeezed her, and waded out of the water. He set her down, steadying her as though he knew her legs wouldn't hold her upright. She glanced around the small cove. For the moment no one else was close by, but the shore had about as much real privacy as a department-store window.

"Damn," Cole said on a ragged sigh, his thoughts apparently echoing her own.

"Damn?"

He smiled and tilted her chin back with his finger, then gave her another thorough kiss. "Yeah. Damn. I want you, and I wouldn't have brought you here if I'd known you'd have this kind of effect on me. I would have taken you home to the privacy and comfort of my bed."

Another surge of heat lanced through her. Simple words that painted a vivid picture. He raked his hand through his hair, bent and brushed her nose with his, then kissed the corner of her mouth.

"Be right back." He waded to the sailboat. He wanted to take Brenna in his arms, and hold her until they were so close nothing separated them. Only then would he find relief from the aching need that had consumed him for the past week. Which was fine, he admitted, if a quickie was what he wanted.

It wasn't.

"Cool off," he muttered to himself. "You've got plenty of time." Easier said than done. At least she wasn't so wary of him. And she wasn't running. He glanced around the cove. A fisherman with a couple of kids was a hundred yards in one direction and a family having a picnic on the beach was a bit further away in the other. She didn't have to run. They had chaperons to spare.

Brenna watched the play of muscles on Cole's back and legs as he waded to the boat. For a moment, his profile was to her, and she had no doubt he was as aroused as she. He gripped the edge of the boat, and bowed his head as if in deep thought. A moment later, he reached inside for his T-shirt, which he pulled over his head. Lifting the cooler out of the boat, he headed back toward her.

By the time he returned, the evidence of his arousal was mostly gone. She didn't have that much control, she silently admitted, wanting to be in his arms again.

Her promise to herself slammed into her. End it or tell him the truth before things went too far. She didn't want to end it. And telling him the truth would surely do that. What she wanted, quite simply, was to be the kind of woman he would be interested in. His intellectual equal, someone who would understand him the way he seemed to understand her.

He stopped a scant foot in front of her, squatted, and waved a hand in front of her eyes. Her gaze snapped to his. He smiled, and she smiled back.

"I didn't think you saw me, you were staring into space so hard. Sunstroke?" he asked, then answered himself. "Nope. Not hot enough."

"I'm plenty hot," she murmured.

He laughed and sat down beside her. "You're an unmerciful tease, Brenna James."

"I'm just trying to figure out how to convince you the Italian sub is mine, if you really brought a liverwurst sandwich."

"Hunger pangs are the problem, then?"

She cast him a dark glance at his double entendre.

"If you can do it, so can I," he said with a wicked grin.

"Trade you my tennies for the sub," she said.

He glanced at her size-six feet. "Tempting offer." He reached past her and pulled out two white-paper-wrapped sandwiches, handing one to her.

She unwrapped it and inhaled the aroma before taking a bite. The sandwich tasted just as good as it smelled.

"Heaven," she murmured.

Cole sat down next to her and took a bite of his own sandwich. "I could almost live on these."

"You said the same thing about apple pie."

"How does that saying go? If you can't have the food you love, love the food you have."

"Girls, too?"

"Nope," he replied without looking at her. "I'm much more particular than that."

Brenna savored another bite from the sandwich, pleased at his admission. He'd deliberately lightened the mood, and she decided to follow his lead.

"So what made you interested in John Marshall?" she asked. The technique was one she'd learned from her mother. Fill any social situation with small talk, and if you're with a man, get him to talk about himself.

"He was assigned. Literally," Cole said. "I was taking an American history class taught by an old guy who was Ebenezer Scrooge incarnate. He assigned a term paper. We were to research eighteenth- or nineteenth-century people whose influence is still felt today. I couldn't think of anyone, so he assigned me John Marshall."

Cole's eyes lit as he stared across the water, his sandwich temporarily forgotten.

"It was wonderful, Brenna. Here was a person who was just a name from history—not even a well-known name. But his ideas reached across more than a century. He was one of the first to see the constitution as a dynamic instrument that could help government act effectively, in 1820 or now. For a while I thought about going into politics. Then I got interested in law." He glanced at her. "I guess that was the first time I figured out what college was all about."

"How so?" Brenna asked. Her need for small talk was gone. She really wanted to know what made Cole tick.

"I thought I was supposed to be in school to get a skill so I could make a living. That's secondary. Ideas. Thousands of ideas. Things I've never thought about or heard of," he said, "that's the important part. To be able to open up a book and find out what someone else thought about the world, what they did about it." He glanced at her. "You know?"

She swallowed. "I know. I feel the same way when I hear a grandparent pass on a story to a child." She looked away from him. "You're very lucky to have such a clear vision, Cole. To know what you want."

"Is that why you're working at Score?" he asked. "To give yourself time to think about what you want to do next?"

"With my job skills..." Her throat closed. She was used to lying, but she found she couldn't lie to Cole.

"You'll figure it out, Brenna," he said, reaching for her. He pulled her against his side and draped a companionable arm around her shoulder. "God, if I'd been through what you've been through the last year, I'd be working at the most mindless thing I could think of."

His explanation provided an easy out, and she grasped it like a drowning woman reaching for a lifeline.

Chapter 9

"And so the Bremen Town musicians decided to stay at the house. The robbers ran away and were never seen again," Brenna said to the children gathered around her in the reading corner of the library. She closed the colorful picture-book. "And?" She smiled in response to their expectant grins.

"And they lived happily ever after," chorused several of the children.

"Yeah," Brenna agreed.

"That's a good story, Auntie Brennie," Teddy said.

Another little girl leaned against Brenna's leg the way Teddy often did. "I think story hour should be longer."

Brenna chuckled. This was the same child who often started yawning the minute she opened the first page.

"You did great," Nancy said, sitting down next to Brenna on the carpeted cube. "As usual."

"Thanks."

"I sure wished you were here the other day."

"Why?" Brenna asked, watching the last of the children wander away from the reading area.

"We have a new volunteer. She was so nervous I wasn't sure she was going to be able to finish. She botched things up so much that I was sure she had never read a book in her life.''

Nancy's tone painted the woman as an imbecile.

''She was probably just nervous because of the kids,'' Brenna responded.

''Maybe,'' Nancy agreed reluctantly. ''Except this woman couldn't tell which side of a book was up.''

''Sounds like she was scared.'' Brenna had been there often enough herself to know too well all the variations of being scared. ''In that situation, there's only one thing to do.''

''Which is?''

''Fake it,'' Brenna said with a smile. ''No matter what.''

Nancy laughed. ''Right. Just like you do.''

''Exactly.'' Brenna knew Nancy would never suspect the truth even though she'd just been told.

''Want to go see a movie this weekend?'' Nancy asked, changing the subject to one of their shared interests.

''I can't.'' Brenna shook her head. ''I'm working all day Sunday. My latest cleaning job is a small office complex. After I get into the routine, it should only take me a half day. But, I'm giving myself the whole day the first couple of times.''

''You're a glutton for punishment,'' Nancy said. ''There's a new Tom Cruise flick.''

''Sounds tempting,'' Brenna said. The long days were a means to an end—an end that was in sight. She touched Nancy's arm, unable to keep her anticipation to herself. ''If this works out like it should, I'll be able to move into my own apartment again within the next two months.''

''That's great,'' Nancy responded with a grin.

Teddy skipped across the reading area toward them and pulled on Brenna's hand. ''Come help me,'' he commanded. ''I'm looking for a book about ducks that I found the other day. Now I can't find it.''

''What did it look like?'' Brenna asked as he led her to the bookstack. She knelt beside him.

''It was red.'' He gave one red-covered book a glance, then put it back. ''I'll never find it.''

''Sure you will.'' She peered more closely at the titles. He might. She surely never would. Gnawing at her lip, she pulled a red book off the shelf. She flipped open the book, and elephants figured prominently in the illustrations. She returned the book to the shelf and pulled out another one.

Her annoyance with herself increased as she peered at the words of the title. Duck began with the letter *d,* she thought, mentally sounding out the word as she had been taught a lifetime ago. Identifying one letter from one word surely wasn't that hard. The words of the title were blocks of indecipherable symbols, and she wanted to scream her frustration. She ought to be able to read enough to find the title of a book for a four-year-old. She was just ready to return the book to the shelf when Teddy pulled it from her grasp and opened it up with a quiet sigh of delight.

"This is it!" He set the open book on her lap. "See. *Baby Mallard Takes a Trip.*" He turned one page, then the next, his smile growing wider. "I'm going to get Dad to read it to me."

I'm going to get Dad to read it to me. Just once she'd love Teddy to say that to her. *Auntie Brennie, please read to me.* Except that he'd already figured out her stories weren't read. They were told. For reading, he needed someone else.

"Do you have the library card, Auntie Brennie?"

She stood up and handed Teddy the card, who skipped off to check out his book on ducks.

Unexpectedly, Cole's words rang through her head. *Ideas I'd never thought of.* Teddy, like Cole and her brother, was discovering he could explore almost any world he wanted through books. New things. Worlds that she'd miss entirely if she didn't learn how to read. Soon.

The last time she had tried had been a humiliating disaster. She didn't want to face stories geared for a five-year-old, and she wouldn't face another teacher who treated her like a five-year-old.

"Dream it, then be it," she whispered.

This time, somehow, she would find a way.

Cole gave his notes on the Zach MacKenzie case one last thorough scan before asking Myra to show him in. Dozens of details about the case bothered Cole and simultaneously challenged him. This was exactly the kind of case he'd wanted to represent when he left Jones,

Markham and Simmons. Had he stayed there, he would never have had the chance.

That Zach MacKenzie was so perfect a suspect for the drunk-driving charges against him had been one of the things that drew Cole to take the case. Zach was athletically good-looking, single, drove a sports car, liked to have a good time, had a history of drinking and driving. One night last May, he had been at the wrong intersection at the wrong time.

Cole trusted his instincts. Zach MacKenzie was telling the truth. And they already had been through Cole's standard talk. "You can lie to your mother. You can lie to the world. But you sure as hell better not lie to me. I guarantee you, we'll both look stupid if you do, and if there's one thing I won't tolerate, it's a client making me look stupid."

Cole buzzed Myra on the intercom. "Show Zach in, please."

"Sure thing, boss," came her prompt response.

He grinned. He'd asked her a dozen times since she'd followed him from Jones, Markham and Simmons to please call him by his first name. She did so only when she was worried. So long as she referred to him as "boss," everything was fine.

He got up from his desk and opened the door to admit Zach, clasping his hand as he came through the door. Cole motioned Zach to sit down, noting that his eyes were filled with worry. And to be honest, the man had cause.

"I finally got discovery from the D.A.'s office," Cole said.

"It took long enough," Zach responded, sitting down. "Maybe it's a sign they don't have much of a case."

"Don't bet on it." Cole leaned against the edge of the desk next to Zach.

Zach glanced down at his hands a moment, then asked, "What do they have?"

"Some good points, and some not so good." Cole picked up the folder and opened it. "In our favor, they didn't administer the breath analysis test until more than an hour after the accident. The D.A. will probably try to disallow their own evidence since they didn't handle it well."

"And that's good, right?"

Cole nodded. "That's good. Not in our favor, the arresting officer swears he smelled liquor on you at the scene."

"He's lying," Zach said.

"Or maybe he's confused. There was an open bottle in the other car, which may have made the crime scene reek." Cole searched through the papers in the folder, and handed one to Zach.

"What's this?"

"The statement from the accident reconstruction team. According to the report, you both entered the intersection within a split second of each another." Cole paused, waiting for Zach to look at him before he continued. "You both were speeding. If there's anything in our favor here, it's that you hit your brakes sooner."

Cole took another sheet out of the folder and handed it to Zach, who read the top line of the report, then said, "They can use this?"

Cole nodded. "Your prior arrest record is the strongest evidence the D.A. has in the case."

"I thought a trial had to focus on only the facts directly involved with the case." Zach glanced at Cole. "You hear about that all the time."

"Maybe, but your drunk driving record is public, and the D.A. will use it," Cole said. "Right off the bat, it gives us a credibility problem."

"But I went through rehab last year," Zach said. "Doesn't that count?"

"It all depends," Cole answered. "If we go into court asserting that you haven't had a drink since then, we'd be lying."

"I haven't been drunk," Zach insisted.

"But you have a record of driving drunk prior to that," Cole said, holding up a finger, then adding a second. "And your buddy Theo at Score admitted that you have a couple of beers pretty regularly—"

"Never more than two. And I switch to ginger ale before I drive, and I always give myself at least an hour."

Cole nodded. "I know that, too. I don't want any surprises. No storekeepers saying that you buy a case of vodka a month. No acquaintances who've seen you drive under the influence. No family members with tales of public...or private...drunkenness."

"No one will say any of those things, because none of it is true,"

Zach said. "I've made mistakes. Plenty of them. But this accident wasn't one of them."

"But you did have a couple of beers in the bar earlier." Cole folded his arms across his chest.

Zach stood up, his gaze unwavering. "I did. Why the hell are we covering this ground again?"

"I'm just making sure."

That night, when Cole went to pick up Brenna after she got off work, he went inside to wait for her. She smiled at him from across the room, and he ordered a beer from one of the other waitresses.

Cole looked critically around the bar, thinking of the damaging points the prosecution could make about the place. His biggest challenge would be convincing a jury that Zach MacKenzie was more than the prosecution would make him out to be.

"Are you worried about something?" Brenna asked a few minutes later as they left the bar.

"Just thinking about the MacKenzie case." Cole took her hand and pulled her close to him as they strolled toward his car.

"Are there problems?"

"No more than the usual," he said. "I'm just trying to figure out what surprises the prosecution will have for us."

"I thought they had to share all their evidence with you ahead of time."

"They do," he agreed. "That doesn't mean there won't be a surprise or two, though."

"You don't like surprises?" she teased.

"Only nice ones. By definition, that excludes anything that comes up in court."

"Would you like to come to dinner on Sunday?" she asked.

Cole laughed at the sudden change of subject. "A surprise?"

"I hope not. My cooking isn't *that* bad," she said. "It's Michael and Jane's anniversary. I'm watching Teddy while they go out."

"A date with you and Teddy," he said.

"Not a date," she hedged. "I'm baby-sitting."

"And this—us right now, going to have pie—"

"That's not a date, either."

"Dating isn't such an awful thing, Brenna."

"It implies a whole bunch of stuff I'm not ready to get into," she responded. "Boyfriend, commitment, plans for the future—"

"Whoa." He held up his hands. "I don't want to be your boyfriend."

She stopped walking and faced him. "No?"

"No. I'd rather be your friend."

"That sounds nice." A smile lurked at the corner of her mouth, and she resumed walking, slower this time.

"I don't want any commitments from you. I'm not asking for anything from you."

"That would be a first," she murmured.

This time Cole stopped walking, pulling on her hand. "Maybe, but get this straight, fair lady. You don't want the pressure of commitment, and hell, I couldn't give you one if I wanted to. My life is a mess."

"So, I'm safe."

He gave her a quick kiss. "You sure are," he drawled. "As long as friends can kiss friends." He squeezed her hand. "As long as they can bring wine for a dinner that's not a date."

Brenna ought to have been reassured that she could be friends with Cole without getting hurt. The man had just given her everything she had asked for. No commitment. But friendship. And kissing. No dating. But time spent together. Contradictions, every one. Just like the man.

Charm that hid steely determination. An easygoing manner that masked his intensity. Gentleness that almost hid his protective streak.

Having him for dinner wasn't that big a deal, but she worried off and on about it over the next several days.

She took Teddy shopping with her the morning of their no-date dinner for the groceries they needed. She had taken shopping for granted for years, but she had a sudden anxiety attack. What if she confused baking soda with corn starch—never mind she didn't intend to purchase either one. She wished she could afford scallops and hated the idea of serving anything as mundane as chicken.

"Jeez, Auntie Brennie," Teddy complained after they had been in the grocery store for half an hour. "It's only dinner. How 'bout pizza?"

"No pizza," she said, his statement echoing her own internal scolding. *It's only dinner.*

In deference to keeping the apartment cool, she decided on cold boiled shrimp with an assortment of vegetables. Her choice pleased her even more when she slid the platter into the refrigerator.

"What's an anniversary?" Teddy asked, following Brenna into her bedroom where she went to change her clothes.

"Like a birthday," she told him, sitting down at the dressing table. "Except it counts the number of years since your wedding."

"When will Mommy and Daddy be back?"

"Later tonight. Probably not until after you've gone to bed."

She opened a jar of face cream and smoothed it over her cheeks and forehead while Teddy leaned against the table and watched her.

"Are you gonna get married?"

"I hope so. Someday, anyway." She replaced the lid on the jar of cream and reached for the eye shadow.

The doorbell rang and Teddy scampered down the hall. "I bet that's Cole!"

"Ask who it is before you open the door."

"I will," he promised, then loudly called, "Who is it?"

Brenna didn't hear the reply, but a second later she heard the door open. She brushed the eye shadow on and picked up the mascara.

"Cole. I knew it was you. Hi!" Teddy's voice carried toward Brenna. "Did you know that Auntie Brennie says she's getting married? Are you?"

Cole's laughter floated to Brenna. "She is, huh? Well, I guess I could, too, then. Where is your Aunt Brenna?"

Brenna paused with the mascara wand halfway to her eye. She stared unseeingly at the mirror as a flash of images swirled from her imagination. In the back of her mind she heard her own voice telling the man she wanted only to be friends. Except the pictures in her mind were more than friendship.

Herself. Cole. A two-story house with a big wide porch and a swing. Starched priscillas hanging at the dining-room window. Wide-open spaces with enough room for a big dog and little kittens. Children with golden brown hair and blue eyes.

Her fingers clenched around the wand. Dare she hope for a future she saw so clearly? She had friendship for a while. But a future with a man like Cole? How could she dare hope for that?

"She's putting stuff on her face," Teddy said. "We're having shrimp for dinner. I helped."

Brenna quickly finished getting ready, then gave herself a last check in the mirror. Smoothing her hands down her skirt, she left the bedroom.

"Hi," she said a moment later from the living-room doorway.

"Hi." He stood up and held out a paper sack, which was wrapped around a bottle of wine. He gave her a thorough glance, then grinned. "You look great."

She took the sack from him and pulled out the bottle. "White wine. Thanks. It's just right for dinner."

"Where do you keep the corkscrew?" he asked, following her into the kitchen.

Brenna rummaged through a drawer and handed him the corkscrew.

"Can I have some wine, too?" Teddy asked as she took down three goblets from the cupboard.

"No. But I'll put your Kool-Aid in a goblet if you want. If you promise to be careful."

Teddy smiled. "I promise. Can we make a toast, too?"

Brenna filled his glass from the pitcher in the refrigerator.

"Sure you can." Cole pulled the cork out of the bottle and poured the wine into the two glasses Brenna had set on the counter next to him. He handed one of the glasses to Brenna, took the other one, and knelt on the floor, at eye level with Teddy. "Who do you want to toast?"

Teddy's face screwed up as he thought about it.

"How about to your aunt?" Cole suggested.

Teddy nodded in agreement.

"What do you want to say?"

Brenna handed Teddy his goblet of Kool-Aid and knelt next to him. He lifted his glass, sloshing a few drops over the rim. "I wish Auntie Brennie had her own house again. And...I wish...she had a daddy."

"I have a daddy. Grandfather James."

"Oh. I mean a daddy. You know, Auntie Brennie, like Mommy and Daddy."

"You mean a husband?" Cole asked.

Teddy's face brightened. "That's it."

Brenna suspected her own face was beet-red when she glanced back at Cole.

Seeming not to notice at all, Cole clicked his glass with Brenna's. "To Brenna. May you have all the things that make you happy."

Chapter 10

"Thank you. Both of you." Brenna took a sip of the wine, her eyes never leaving Cole's as he also sipped the wine. Cole took her hand and stood up, pulling her with him. She recognized the longing in his eyes, feeling his hunger as though it were her own.

His eyes still intent on hers, Cole lifted Brenna's fingers to his lips, pressing a warm kiss on each of them. Each separate caress pooled in her stomach, which tightened into knots just shy of painful. Then he turned her hand over and pressed a lingering kiss into her palm, the most sensual caress she had ever received.

"Is this part of the toast, too?" asked Teddy.

"Sometimes." Cole kept Brenna's hand within his own when she would have pulled it away. He took another sip of his wine and offered his goblet to Brenna. "Just like sharing glasses is part of the toast, sometimes."

Teddy lifted his glass, now only half full of Kool-Aid. "I'll share mine."

Brenna glanced down at Teddy, whose upper lip was covered in a red Kool-Aid mustache.

"You should never mix your drinks," Cole said with a chuckle.

Teddy proved to be a diversion during the rest of dinner. Cole couldn't decide if that was a blessing or a curse. He had never wanted to kiss anyone as much as he wanted to kiss Brenna. Throughout the evening, he was caught within the visceral memory of that instant when her breath had caught and her wide luminous eyes had reflected a need as great as his own. Little boys were a diversion he didn't want—not for the kind of grown-up games he had in mind with Brenna.

That thought was uppermost in his mind as he helped Brenna get Teddy ready for bed. Cole recognized stalling tactics when he saw them. Teddy proved his mastery beyond any doubt when he asked Cole for one more bedtime story. Nothing could have topped the two stories Brenna told Teddy. Cole was relieved when she gently insisted lights-out time had come.

"I'd forgotten how exhausting kids can be," Cole said after they left his room. He went into the kitchen, poured the last of the wine into a single goblet and brought it into the living room.

"Kid," Brenna corrected. "Although, I admit Teddy sometimes makes me feel like he's more than one child."

"My sister has two little girls. At least they have each other to play with."

"Do you get to see them often?" Brenna turned on the stereo, and the soft sounds of a Vivaldi concerto filled the room. She sat down at the opposite end of the couch Cole had claimed and curled her bare feet under her.

"Not often enough. Three or four times a year. They live in Cheyenne. Dinner was delicious." He took a sip of the wine, then offered the glass to her.

"I bet you say that whenever you're invited to dinner," she teased. She took a sip of the wine. "And this is lovely wine."

He took the goblet back and set it on the coffee table. "Now that we have all this polite stuff out of the way, do you want to know what I really think?"

She glanced at him.

"I think you're a special lady. You're wonderful company. I like being here with you."

Her eyes dropped, the color in her cheeks high and her expression full of a discomfort that bordered on...pain, he decided with surprise.

He wanted to ask her what she was thinking, which would have been fine if he had thought she'd tell him. He doubted she would.

"That embarrasses you?" he asked, wishing he understood what had made her so uncomfortable.

She shook her head. "No."

"But?"

Her eyes met his. "The gracious thing to say is 'thank you.' Right?"

He grinned. "Right." For the moment he'd content himself with returning to the more neutral topics she seemed comfortable with. "Dinner was delicious. Shrimp is my favorite. I ate too much, and I'm stuffed."

"That's good," she said.

Staying away from her was impossible. Gently Cole pulled on her arm. When she didn't come closer to him, he slid across the couch, eliminating the distance between them. "I'm glad cooking is one of your talents."

"I always thought being domestic was overrated, myself." She tipped her head back, and the corners of her eyes crinkled when she smiled up at him. "Besides, maybe this is the only thing I know how to make."

"Suits me," he said. "I make a great steak. Between your cooking and mine, we'd eat real well."

She chuckled. "Expensive, too."

"Then I'll just have to round up a few more clients, preferably ones that pay a fat monthly retainer."

"I thought getting away from that very thing was one of the reasons you left the old law firm."

"Nope. I just wanted to get away from having to accept cases I didn't want." He picked up the goblet and offered to it Brenna again, watched as her lips left a faint mark against the glass. He traced the side of her face with one long finger, then wrapped a strand of her hair around it.

"You're so beautiful," he whispered.

Her eyes grew wider, and she gave her head a tiny shake.

"You are to me," he insisted. "From the very first time I saw you, I wanted this."

His hand slid behind her head, his fingers raking through her dark hair, drawing her closer. He brushed his lips lightly over hers, feeling as though she left a mark on him just as she had on the glass.

His warm lips barely touched hers before drawing a hairsbreadth away, then touched again, each separate surface of her lips brought to life under his touch.

Torture. Wanting to feel his mouth completely. Wanting more to extend the moment, to let the anticipation stretch until she thought she'd die from it.

She opened her eyes and found Cole watching her, the gold flecks in his blue eyes hot, molten.

"My beautiful Brenna," he whispered against her mouth. His eyes closed and his tongue traced the inside line of her lips. Brenna sighed and leaned against him, her lips parting under his unspoken request. Cole increased the pressure of his mouth against hers, but withheld what she wanted. He wrapped his arms around her, drawing her across his lap.

Brenna put her arms around his neck and slid her hands through his hair, feeling each strand against her fingertips, giving herself to the moment. If he wanted to tease, two could play that game. She touched his lips with the tip of her tongue, feeling his warmth to her core. He imitated exactly her gossamer caress, then deepened the caress ever so slightly, which she answered in kind. Kissing—mere kissing—had never been like this. At once satisfying and making her hunger for more.

At last long last his tongue touched hers.

She moaned, moving her mouth over his, taking as much from him as he took from her. A spark ignited and blazed into flowing heat that erased all thought. Nothing was more important than being in his arms, than feeding the fire with the slow bond of tongue caressing tongue.

Cole shuddered, passion flaring into timeless need. He loved kissing Brenna. That he already knew. What he hadn't expected was this yearning—so deep he wanted to nurture as well as possess. The feeling was new, unlike the aroused pulsing of his body. Other women had desired him, but not one had trembled within his arms or whimpered softly with her own need.

He knew what it was to enjoy a woman, but he wanted to cherish Brenna. He was accustomed to wanting the unique softness of a woman, but he needed Brenna with an intensity that bordered on pain. He understood desire, but what he felt for Brenna made desire seem superficial and one-dimensional.

He lifted his head and looked at her. Her breath was as shallow as his own.

She sighed and trailed a line of feathery kisses along his jaw. She pressed her nose against his skin, and inhaled deeply, her pleasure in him heightening his own need to painful intensity. She sighed again, then smiled contentedly.

Her smile hit him in the gut. No touch, not even her kiss, had ever been as erotic to him as her drinking in his scent, then smiling as though nothing could be better.

Cole pressed his mouth against her cheek, caressing each plane of her face before claiming her mouth again. He wanted to feel the hot satin of her skin, wanted to see her lying beneath him with the gold chain around her neck and his body the only things touching her.

He didn't want to remember Teddy, who might interrupt at any moment. He didn't want to remember Michael and Jane, who might return at any time. He didn't want to face the long drive home and yet another restless night as he considered all the ways to fit Brenna's supple body against his.

None of those intrusive thoughts kept him from seeking her mouth in one last deep kiss before gently...slowly...pulling her arms from around his neck. "No more. You're killing me."

She smiled, her glance sultry, her eyes sparkling with sudden devilment. He loved that look on her.

"What a sweet way to die." The tip of her tongue touched her own lips, swollen from kisses—the ones he had taken and the ones she had given.

He laughed. "You'd tempt a saint." He brushed his lips across hers, keeping the kiss chaste in spite of his need and her invitation. "And I'm no saint."

He stood up, pulling her with him. He glanced around the room in search of a diversion. Any diversion. Even that last bedtime story Teddy had wanted. Several board games on the bookcase next to the stereo, including his favorite, caught his eyes.

"How about a game of Scrabble?" he asked.

The question shattered Brenna's euphoria.

Why not chess? she wondered. Or backgammon? Or even Monopoly, whose cards she had memorized long ago. Of all the games sitting on the shelf, why Scrabble?

The sudden acceleration of her heart had nothing to do with passion and everything to do with panic. She might be able to set fire to his body, and her own, but she couldn't share anything else—not really. Not like she wanted to.

"How about backgammon?" she asking, hearing the tone of desperation in her voice.

"I'm better at Scrabble."

God, no. Not tonight.

When then? After this has gone on long enough to hurt him? Hurt you?

She was already long past that point, she realized, her heart sinking at the thought. Managing a smile had never been more difficult. "All the more reason to play backgammon."

"You don't want to play Scrabble," he said, his eyes full of devilment as he dropped a kiss on her mouth, "because you're scared of me. And you have reason to be."

Scared of him? She sure was. She folded her clammy hands and waited for the other shoe to drop.

"Know why?" he asked.

Mutely, she shook her head, hating the idea the moment had come. He'd use the Scrabble game to tell her, gently of course, because that was the kind of man he was, that he had been privy to her inability to read from the beginning.

"I'm the champion triple-word scorer," he announced with a grin. "My sister won't play with me anymore. Or my mom. So, it's time to pick on somebody new."

"Me?"

He winked. "You."

"Count me out," she said. Relief flowed through her. "If we're going to play games where one person has a decided advantage, it ought to be me." She lifted her chin and gave him what she hoped was a teasing smile. "After all, it is my house, and—"

"Your marbles, so to speak?" He took the backgammon game off the shelf. "You'll have to teach me." He set the case on the coffee table and opened it. "It's been years since I played."

"It's easy as falling off a log," she said, sinking to the floor and sitting down Indian style. Easy, she thought. Unlike lots of other things—teaching myself to read, for instance. "Do you want the dark stones or the light ones?"

Cole chose the dark ones, and Brenna showed him how to line them up and explained the strategy for moving around the board. He caught on quickly, liking, as she did, the combination of luck, skill and aggressive playing the game required. She won the first game, barely. He won the next two, and by the time they reached a fourth game, Brenna was determined she wasn't going to lose another one to him.

The luck of the dice wasn't with her, though, and after Cole tossed his third set of doubles, sixes no less, she threw her hands into the air with a sound of disgust.

"I like this game," he said, leaning across the table to give her a searching kiss, then casually put three of her stones on the bar. As he was ready to begin bearing off his stones, she had no doubt that's where she'd remain for the rest of the game.

"This really isn't fair," she complained, resting her chin on her hand. "I teach you my favorite game and you take unfair advantage of me."

Cole slanted her a wicked grin and followed it with yet another kiss. "Do I?" He returned to cherish her mouth once more. "Is this your favorite?" He tossed the dice again as entitled by his last doubles. The numbers that fell gave him more than enough to finish the game. "Or this?" This time when he returned to her, he brushed her nose first, then claimed her mouth with sensual abandon that made her tremble.

"You're driving me crazy, woman," he whispered against her mouth. "I keep thinking I can stop, and I keep being wrong."

"That's the way it is for me, too," she admitted with a husky sigh.

"One more game?" he asked.

She grinned. "But of course. I'm not going to let you whip me again. I may be down, but I'm not out. Not by a long shot."

"I never meant to whip you in the first place," Cole replied, referring not to the game of backgammon, but to the lawsuit. He hoped she'd hear what he was really saying. Not once since the first night had they discussed the lawsuit.

"Ha," she responded, aligning the stones on the playing board. "You took after me with greed in your heart and malice in your soul."

Her tone was light, but their implied truth twisted through Cole. He knew she was still talking about the game that lay on the table between them. Inexplicably, for him the outcome of the lawsuit was there, as well.

"I never meant for you to be hurt."

At first Brenna thought he was uttering a little-boy apology in the vein she was teasing him. Something in his voice, though, made her raise her head. He watched her with such intensity that she touched his cheek with her finger tips.

"I'm sorry, what did you say?"

He placed his hand over hers, pressing it against his cheek. Then, he turned his head and kissed her palm. "The lawsuit cost you so much—not just in terms of money. I'd change the outcome if I could."

Brenna couldn't take her eyes away from him. She had already figured out that he carried almost as many regrets about the lawsuit as she did.

"You don't have anything to feel guilty about," she assured him. "I got exactly what I had coming."

He shook his head.

"My stup—"

Abruptly she closed her mouth. *Don't rush this,* she told herself. *He's given you the perfect opportunity to explain why the lawsuit happened. All of it.* "My actions got me into the mess." She went on. "I don't have anyone to blame but myself. If you hadn't represented Harvey, someone else would have. I know you did what you could that last day when I came to your office." She bent her head, then looked at him. "Cole, when did you leave the law firm?"

"Several months ago."

"When?" she insisted. "It was right after the lawsuit, wasn't it?"

"Yes." He didn't have one regret about the way that had turned out, and he didn't want her to, either. "By the time I was finished representing Harvey Bates, the handwriting was on the wall. If I hadn't left then, it would have been soon. It just happened to be then."

She gripped his hand. "I'd hate knowing your standing up to Harvey had anything to do with—"

"Harvey Bates," he interrupted, "got way more from you than he deserved, way more than was reasonable under any circumstance. And John Miller could have done a lot to minimize the damage." Cole's anger with both men was nearly as great now, months later, has it had been at the time.

She smiled sadly. "John Miller proved that old saying. You get what you pay for."

"That's a damn poor excuse—"

"I wasn't about to complicate my life even further by having a huge debt to him when I knew I'd owe Harvey money no matter what happened."

Cole shook his head. "He did the worst job of defending your case I've ever seen. You have grounds to sue, Brenna."

"With what? In case you hadn't noticed, I'm flat broke. Suing someone takes money I don't have." And besides, she thought, in the end I'd have what I have now. Nothing.

"I know." Cole brushed a strand of hair away from her cheek. "Bates was always convinced you had money. My investigation never indicated you had a cent, but he kept telling me you could get it."

Brenna's face lost all animation, a return of the mask she'd worn when he first met her.

"Brenna?"

"It's funny," she said finally, "how things come back to haunt you. I always wondered why Harvey wouldn't accept payments."

"He thinks your father is wealthy."

"He is. I don't know how Harvey knows that. But it does explain a lot."

"Would your dad loan you—"

"I won't ask him. Not now, not ever," she said, her voice low, fierce. "Not in this life!"

"Brenna—" He gripped her hand, remembering her history with her father too late. In her shoes, he would have felt the same way. "I didn't mean to upset you."

"You didn't." She swallowed, dropping her head a moment.

"I'm sorry." Cole was sorry that she didn't have the kind of relationship with her father he had with his. Sorry that her father hadn't been able to accept her for what she was rather than what he wanted her to be. Sorry that after all this time, she still hurt. Sorry most of all that he, too, had hurt her.

"I don't blame you. I don't." She squeezed his hand.

"You should."

"And how would that change anything?"

He gazed at her, more drawn to her now than he'd ever been. A hundred different images of her flooded his mind. Brenna at work, doing a job that fulfilled a fraction of her potential. Without complaint. Brenna with Teddy, sharing her humor and affection. Without reservation. Brenna with him, trusting in spite of all the reasons she had to be wary of him. Without condition.

"I'd give my right arm to make things easier for you," he said. "You're a unique woman, Brenna James. You don't blame others, even when you have cause. And you don't shirk from anything. I admire that."

"I'm not like that," she whispered. "If you knew—"

"I've never see seen anyone work harder. A couple of weeks ago you told me how many customers you needed to get your own apartment again. Now, you're nearly there. And I'm happy for you."

He cupped the side of her face and leaned closer. "I love watching you explain things like playing backgammon to me. You're so clear, every step built one onto another. And I love watching you read to the kids at the library. Your face is so expressive, so alive." He paused, swallowed, and when he began talking again, his voice was barely audible. "I'm half in love with you."

Tears appeared in her eyes.

"Shh," he said. "We'll take it as slow as you need, Brenna. But, someday, fair lady, I'm going to understand what's really going on with you." His lips touched hers softly. "Someday," he whispered again, before taking her mouth in a deep hungry kiss.

Someday...she'd have the courage to tell him.

Chapter 11

The following morning, Cole let himself into the office, automatically flipping on lights and heading for the back room where Myra kept a coffee maker. He had just poured in the water when he heard the front door open and close.

He went back to the front of the office. Zach MacKenzie stood leaning against the doorway, his head thrown back, and his eyes closed. His shirt and sports coat were disheveled. His tie hung out of a pocket, and his slacks appeared slept in. Zach looked as though he hadn't shaved in a couple of days.

Ten feet away from Zach, the reek of old alcohol hit Cold. His concern vanished under a wave of awful disbelief. "Zach?"

He opened his eyes. "We've gotta talk."

"You've been drinking," Cole said, unable to keep his irritation out of his voice. Zach wasn't the first of his clients to lie to him, and he likely wouldn't be the last. But damn, Cole had been so sure Zach had been straight with him about his drinking.

Zach lifted a hand toward Cole. "If I want a lecture, I can go see my mother."

"With everything that is at stake, how could—"

"Don't start on me, Counselor." Zach pushed himself away from the wall and headed toward Cole's office. "What I could really use is a friend."

"You came to the wrong place, pal. I'm your lawyer." This was not the time for Cole to admit it, but the truth was he would have liked being friends with Zach. "You told me you were on the wagon."

"And now I'm off. If you're determined to lecture me, you could at least offer me a cup of coffee first."

"Coffee?"

Zach turned around and gave him a bleary smile, full of regret and apology. "Yeah. Black and strong as a fickle woman's heart."

"With or without a bourbon chaser?" Cole retorted.

Zach raised an eyebrow. "I probably deserve that. But don't tempt me. You wouldn't like the answer."

Cole stared at his client who sat down and dropped his head into his hands as though he didn't have the energy to continue holding it up.

"Aspirin to go with that coffee," Zach added. "I've got a bitch of a headache."

Cole headed for the back room, feeling the onset of his own headache. His client—who swore he hadn't gotten drunk since before admitting himself to rehab last year—was sitting in his office. Hungover.

The coffee maker stopped dripping, and Cole poured two cups of coffee. Black and strong, as ordered.

In frustration, Cole slammed his hand down on the counter. "Stupid, stupid son of a bitch," he muttered under his breath.

"Made so by the alcohol, Cole," said Myra, suddenly appearing at the doorway.

Cole jumped and whirled around to face his secretary.

She offered him a faint smile of apology. "Sorry. I thought you heard me come in. You look about ready to strangle someone," she murmured, picking up cups from the counter.

"Damn straight."

"Losing your temper won't do either one of you any good. Why don't you take five minutes. Walk around the block or something until you're—"

"Calmer?"

She nodded.

Cole stared at her a moment, remembering that he'd asked her to help him keep his temper in check when she came to work for him. He valued her astute assessment of people, but just now he wasn't all that pleased that she had so accurately read him. Cole nodded, and leaned against the counter folding his arms across his chest. A moment later, he heard Myra talking to Zach.

Pouring another cup of coffee, Cole drank it slowly. After his watch ticked away another four minutes, he returned to his office, carrying the half-empty pot.

Myra sat in the chair next to Zach, and Cole had no doubt that she had been successful in her favorite-aunt routine to temporarily defuse the situation. When Cole appeared in the doorway, she patted Zach's hand and stood up. Cole briefly met her eyes, saw a warning in them, and refilled Zach's coffee cup. Myra took the pot from him and left the office, softly closing the door behind her.

Rummaging around in his desk drawer, Cole found the bottle of aspirin, which he handed to Zach.

Zach opened the childproof cap with more finesse than Cole expected, and poured a couple of tablets into his palm. He swallowed them with a long drink of the hot coffee.

Cole sat down behind the desk and watched his client, dread sinking into his stomach like the lead weight on a fishing line.

"My dad doesn't believe me."

"Another news flash. So what?" Not believing children seemed to be a common failing of fathers everywhere.

"He told me that I'd made my choices, and that I'd just have to live with them. As if I didn't know that." He took a deep breath. "He told me...that he'd been figuring for years that I'd kill somebody." He met Cole's gaze head-on. "And I did. There's no sugar-coating it."

"That's the kind of talk that could get you convicted. We have to go into court—"

"This isn't about court. This is about..." Zach lifted a hand in frustration. "There's legal. And then, there's right. You know?"

Cole chose to ignore that. "So what drove you to drink last night?"

Zach pulled a ring out of the pocket of his sports coat. He skittered it across the top of the desk, a two-carat diamond flashing. The ring twirled briefly like a top, then fell over.

"Pamela agrees with my father that I'm a no-good worthless bastard." Zach looked up, his eyes old, tired. "I didn't lie about that night."

Cole sensed a "but" coming, and he had a bad feeling about where this was going.

Zach rubbed his hand across the top of his thigh before looking up and meeting Cole's gaze. "That night...the night of the accident...after I left Score, I went over to Pamela's. We had a couple of drinks. Hell, I had more than a couple. I'd planned to spend the night, but we had a fight."

He surged out of the chair. "And I left," Zach continued. "I wasn't drunk. I swear I wasn't. Just upset. Driving mad might be legal, but it's no smarter than driving drunk. I knew I shouldn't be driving. So I went to Denny's, ordered an omelet and pancakes, and drank about two quarts of coffee. I was there over an hour." He turned back around to face Cole. "I swear. I wasn't drunk when I left there."

"Which Denny's?" Cole wanted to know.

Zach named the cross streets.

"I suppose you don't remember the waitress?"

"No."

Cole pulled a pad toward him. "No matter," he said, jotting down a note. "We can find out who worked that night. Show your picture around. Something will show up." Cole glanced up. "How'd you pay for the meal? Cash? Credit card? Check?"

"Hell, I don't know."

"It's important. A credit card leaves a paper trail."

Zach surged to his feet, thrusting his hands into his pockets. "I don't remember, okay? The bill couldn't have been more than ten dollars, so I probably paid cash. What's the big deal?"

"The big deal is that this could go a long way toward proving you weren't drunk at the time of the accident. How long from the time you left Denny's until you—"

"Killed someone?" Zach interrupted.

Cole looked up from his notes and set down his pencil. "If that's how you want to put it."

Zach shrugged. "Ten or fifteen minutes, I think. No more than a half hour."

"Why didn't you tell me this before?" Cole asked.

"I didn't think you'd believe me."

"You'd be amazed at what I believe." A trace of anger edged Cole's voice.

Zach met his glance squarely. "I haven't lied to you."

"You didn't tell me the whole truth, either." Abruptly Cole pushed himself away from the desk. His temper seared through the edges of his control. Recognizing just how close he was to losing his temper, he grabbed both empty coffee mugs and went to get them another cup of coffee. He stood in front of the coffee maker a moment, irritated with Zach, furious with himself. His belief in a man's guilt or innocence didn't have anything to do with the case. Ensuring the prosecution played by the rules, finding every scrap he could to cast doubt on the evidence—those counted. Somehow, though, Zach's innocence had come to matter. Plain and simple, Cole resented the sense of betrayal that came with this morning's revelations. He swore.

When he returned to his office, Zach was sitting down again, straighter this time, though his attention was still focused on the noisy traffic just beyond the window.

Cole set one of the mugs in front of Zach and went himself to stand in front of the window. The convenience store across the street and the steady stream of rush-hour traffic were a far cry from the view of Cherry Creek Reservoir he'd had at his old office. He turned around and looked at Zach. So were his clients. Bad as things were with Zach, this was still an improvement over Harvey Bates and his ilk.

Zach cleared his throat. "She's testifying for the prosecution."

"Pamela?" So that was what had pushed Zach over the edge, Cole thought.

Zach nodded. "It's bad, isn't it?"

"It's not going to help." Cole took a hefty swallow of his coffee, most of his anger fading. He knew what it was like to be ditched by a woman you cared about.

"There's one more thing," Zach said.

Cole didn't want one more thing. This one was enough to make him sweat bullets.

"I'm checking myself into Maizer's when I leave here." The hospital Zach named was one of the best in the area for treating alcohol and drug abuse.

Any other time, Cole would have applauded the move. The trial, however, was a scant six weeks off. The timing stunk. If the prosecution got hold of this, they'd use it as another piece to build a solid, if circumstantial, case.

"You're going in for a thirty-day program?" Cole asked.

"Yeah."

"You can't wait until after the trial?"

Zach lifted his head and reached for the coffee cup. "I intended to. But I'm not handling this. I'd promised myself I wouldn't touch a drop until after the trial." He briefly met Cole's glance. "I can't stay away from it."

"This isn't going to look good to a jury. Or the D.A."

Zach gave a short bark of laughter. "Some choice, right? I can pretend like this is all going to be okay, and maybe, just maybe, that's how it'll turn out. That is, if I can get to court without looking like I do this morning. Or, I can dry out and whip this thing." His ironic smile vanished. "Which makes me look guilty."

Cole thought back a moment to all the contacts he had developed at his old firm. A very discreet, albeit expensive, sanitarium was one those. "I know of a place—"

Zach shook his head. "Thanks for the offer, but no."

"What about outpatient?" Cole asked.

"If I'm going to do this, I'm doing it right. Hell, walking out of here and heading for the nearest bar...nothing sounds better. Nothing."

"But?"

"I just don't want to wake up a homeless filthy drunk one day," he said. "The way my dad sees me. The way Pamela sees me." He picked up the ring and put it back in his pocket. "One more thing."

"Another one more thing?"

Zach smiled. "Yeah, Counselor. *One* one more thing."

Cole shook his head. "With your last two bombshells, I don't even want to guess."

"The bar, Score," Zach said. "Theo told me it's being shut down. He said the insurance company raised the owner's insurance to cover their liability."

"You're sure?"

"Theo told me last night. The big boss will be in today to lay off the whole crew. It's not just me I'm hurting anymore. Sure as hell never thought my drinking would cost somebody else their job." Zach pulled out a card and jotted down a phone number. "It'll be a few days before I can talk to you, but if you need to reach me, this is the number." He stood up and extended his hand. "See you in a thirty days, Cole. Clean, sober and clear-eyed as a baby."

After Zach's departure, Cole helped himself to another cup of coffee. The discipline to keep working failed him this morning, and he found himself unable to focus on the other cases that needed his attention.

A part of him was furious with Zach. After Cole thought about it some more, he admitted that another part of him admired and respected the courage Zach's actions required. The man wasn't guilty, but he wasn't innocent, either. In the beginning, Cole had been positive this was a tough case, but one he would win. He was no longer so sure.

Zach's willingness to face problems head-on deserved the best representation Cole could give him. He hoped it was enough.

Zach reminded Cole of Brenna. No blaming someone else for your trouble, no wringing your hands hoping to be rescued. Much as Cole hated the idea of Zach's entering a rehab program so close to his trial date, it was the right thing.

Cole called Brenna, wanting to warn her the bar was closing, but there was no answer. It was late afternoon before he had a chance to call her again. There was still no one home.

Two more appointments with clients kept him at the office until after eight. He headed straight for the apartment Brenna shared with her brother's family.

He needed a break, he decided during the drive. Both he and Brenna did. A few days to be lazy, have a change of scenery. Brenna had loved her grandparents' farm, and he knew she'd love the ranch. He hadn't been there all summer. Long weekends and holidays, his car just naturally pointed in that direction.

A strong pull to go home swept through him.

Home.

The ranch wasn't home anymore. Even so, he needed the sense of renewal and acceptance he always found there. A place he had loved visiting and that had become a bone of contention between him and Susan every holiday. She'd grown up spending holidays in exotic locales. The Christmas he'd spent with her in Hawaii ought to have been fun, but he'd been miserable. Paradise instead of a blizzard. A willing, passionate woman in his bed, but no nieces and nephews to tuck in on Christmas Eve.

He'd invite Brenna to the ranch, Cole decided. Over the Fourth. He knew the connotation his parents and grandmother would put on his bringing her. He had never taken anyone before Susan or since.

He parked the Jeep in front of the apartment, got out, and went to the door.

"She's gone for a run," Michael told him after letting him into the house.

"Did she tell you the bar shut down?"

"Yeah," Michael said. "She surprised us when she walked in while Jane, Teddy, and I were having dinner."

"Is she okay?"

"I thought she was doing fine until our dad called. They talked a couple of minutes, and she left right after that." Michael scratched his jaw. "She usually takes off after talking to him. C'mon in and have a seat."

Cole followed Michael into the apartment. "She still doesn't get along with him, does she?"

"She talked to you about that?" Surprise laced Michael's voice.

"Only that she'd left home when she was fourteen. That your mother and grandmother died shortly after." Deciding there was no point in adding that he knew their father had beat Brenna, Cole asked, "Where does she usually go? Washington Park?"

"Yeah."

"I think I'll head that direction." At the door, Cole turned back to Michael. "If I miss her, tell her I'll be back."

Four blocks from the house he saw her, walking toward him her head down and her shoulders slumped. He recognized the feeling. It was the same one he'd had the day Roger Markham gave him a choice between resigning or being fired. As if sensing she was being watched, Brenna lifted her head, and looked straight at him. He quickened his pace.

"Hi," he said, draping both his arms over the top of her shoulders and pressing his lips against her forehead. "I'm sure glad to see you."

Brenna didn't want to be, but Lord, she was glad to see him, too. Without speaking, she wrapped her arms around his waist, shaken at how relieved she was that he'd come. She wanted—needed—him with an intensity she didn't understand and hadn't realized until he held her within the circle of his arms.

"The bar closed," she said.

He rested his chin on top of her head. "I know. Sometimes, it's just one damn thing after another, isn't it?"

"How'd you find out?"

"Zach MacKenzie told me." Cole stopped under the spreading branches of a giant silver maple tree and pulled Brenna into his arms. "I'm here for you, fair lady. I'll help you in any way that I can."

"Will you?" she asked, almost absently, staring into his eyes.

"Sure." He smoothed her hair away from her face. "What are friends for if they can't be around when you need them?"

"Are you my friend, Cole?" she whispered.

"If you'll let me close enough to be."

"I'm trying," she said, as much to herself as to him.

He gathered her closer and nuzzled the hair away from her ear.

She leaned into his caress. Shivers spread through her. She felt his lips on her jaw, and she turned her face, needy for the kiss she knew was coming. He didn't immediately give it to her, though. He watched her through half-closed eyes, his lips near, but not near enough. She wrapped her arms around his neck, pulled him toward her, and stood on tiptoe until her mouth touched his. His lips parted, and she drank hungrily from him as though the sheer merging of their mouths could make her feel whole.

He groaned and shifted his hold on her, bringing her in more complete contact with his body. Another surge of heat rushed toward her center. She pressed herself closer. His hands slid under her shirt. She was sure she had never felt anything half so wonderful as his hard palms on her back.

Cole trembled as his body clamored for more. He had never wanted a woman so much as he wanted Brenna in this instant. He had to back off. He knew it. This was too public a place, and he was no longer a teenager willing to bear this hungry teasing. Yet, he barely had control enough to lift his mouth from hers.

"No more," he said, his voice hoarse with need. Ignoring his own command, he pressed kisses all over her face before claiming her mouth again. She came to him in kind. Knowing her need was great as his own made him shudder and again threatened his resolve.

His hands traced the contour of her buttocks, then followed a path from her waist to her soft breasts pressed against him. He tore his mouth from hers. "I could almost lay you down right here on the sidewalk, and to hell with the consequences."

"Take me home with you," she whispered against his neck, inhaling the aroma of his skin.

He dragged in a big breath and framed her face with his hands. "You're sure?"

"Yes."

He ran the pad of his thumb across her lower lip. "Now?"

She nodded.

He took her hand and they walked silently, swiftly toward the apartment. She tried to calm her emotions, to think. All she wanted to do was climb back into his arms. Her legs were shaking so badly, she trembled as she walked. Never had she wanted anyone like this.

She channeled her thoughts into mundane matters. Like an explanation to her brother.

"I have to go in and let Michael know where I'm going. I don't want him to worry when I'm not here in the morning.

Cole chuckled. "You make me feel like I'm stealing my high-school sweetheart off for the night."

"No chance of that," she said. "I was never in high school."

"Michael's not—" Cole stopped talking suddenly, then stopped walking, as well. He faced Brenna. "What did you say?"

"When?" But she knew when, and silently cursed herself. She had slipped again. How could she? How?

Chapter 12

"You never finished high school?" A puzzled frown drew Cole's brows together.

"I never *went* to high school." She lifted her chin and faced him squarely, familiar defensiveness surfacing. "I'm a dropout, Cole."

A look of complete bafflement passed over his features, followed by a frown. "You're so bright, so—"

Acting out of years of protecting herself, a habit so old she scarcely recognized it as such, she attacked before he could attack her.

"Going to school wasn't exactly a priority, Cole. Survival was." She thumped herself on the chest. "Take a good look. I've been on my own since I was fifteen years old. This is who I am. A barmaid. A housekeeper."

He stood in the middle of the sidewalk, his arms loosely at his sides.

"It's not exactly what you had in mind, is it?"

He shook his head, and she died a little inside.

"Who were we fooling, Cole? This was never going to work."

She held her hands out as though weighing a ball in each, one much heavier than the other. "Your world is here. And mine...is here. They don't match worth a damn, do they? Chemistry between us or not.''

He extended a hand toward her. "I thought it was more—"

"Goodbye, Cole."

Without waiting for his reaction—his rejection—she stomped away from him, nearly ran up the walk, wrenched the door open and slammed it behind her.

Cole watched her go, feeling as though the knots in his gut might strangle him. He supposed he ought to have figured it out. He'd just never taken the things she'd told him to the logical next step. She'd left home at fourteen. Her mother and grandmother had died. She wouldn't have gone back to live with her father. And Michael would have been sixteen or seventeen at the time, too young to help her even if their father had permitted.

A dropout, though. Dropouts were stupid. Content to slide through life letting someone else shoulder the burdens. Working at subsistence jobs that took minimal skills and had no future. Like housekeepers. Like barmaids.

Like...Brenna.

Cole hung his head, shocked at the turn of his thoughts. That wasn't how he thought of Brenna. It wasn't. When he was with her, her jobs didn't matter to him. Quite simply, he liked being with her. She was bright, funny, easy to be with. She had dreams that she had shared with him. But...a dropout.

Much as he wanted to believe she had finished school some other way—with a GED or something, he instinctively knew she hadn't. If there was one thing he could count on with her, it was her truthfulness. It was as she said—she had never finished, had never begun, high school.

He wished he didn't hate the idea quite so much.

Unexpectedly, one of Susan's last taunts came to him. *Farm boy.* She'd said it with the same derision his thoughts had about dropout. His roots were a piece of what made him who he was. And Brenna...was who she was because of those same roots.

He took a couple of steps toward the apartment, then stopped again. She acted as though she had expected him to look down on her, demean her, hurt her. Hell, he already had.

With a mutter of disgust, he headed for his Jeep wondering how to approach this latest facet of the ever-more-complex woman he was half in love with.

Brenna jabbed the pillow and tucked it under her chest, no closer to sleep now than she was hours ago. She rested her chin on her arms and silently counted all the ways she was a fool.

One of the problems with sexual attraction, she decided, was that it rendered her brain a useless quivering mass completely at the mercy of her hormones. Twice now she had slipped, and twice now she had hurtled herself into a bottomless well full of her worst fears.

If only she had kept her mouth shut, she'd have her arms full of a warm, vibrant man instead of a lumpy pillow. A wave of complete wretchedness washed over her. If only...

If only... The phrase that measured all the lost possibilities of her life.

What if you didn't have anything to hide?

But I do.

But what if you had told him? Everything.

He'd be gone in a flash.

But he didn't leave you tonight. You ran.

I didn't run.

Didn't you?

She dropped her head onto her pillow and let the tears come. Starkly, she pictured Cole's face as she had walked away from him. Bewilderment—not censure. Concern—not judgment. Expecting the worst from him, she ran. Ran, just as she always had.

She fell into a restless sleep to the relentless beat of her own ever running footsteps.

She awoke five hours later with a pounding headache and all the events of the previous day clamoring for her attention. She didn't want to think about being unemployed. She didn't want to think about looking for another job. She didn't want to think about her almost-come-to-fruition plans. But she did.

Most of all, she thought about how she had driven Cole away, how she had judged him more severely than she had anticipated him to judge her.

She owed him an apology, and she knew it. *I'm sorry,* she mentally rehearsed. *I shouldn't have...what? Quit school when I was fifteen?*

Shouldn't have told you about leaving home? Shouldn't have run? Shouldn't have lied to you.

A word she hated almost as much as *if only*. *Should*.

She got out of bed, slipped into a robe, and hoped a cup of coffee would help clear the fuzz out of her brain. In the kitchen she found her brother.

"Good morning, Brenna," he said to her over his newspaper.

"What's good about it?" she muttered under her breath, reaching for a bottle of aspirin.

"Pardon?"

"I said 'good morning.'" She filled a glass with water from the tap and swallowed two tablets. She poured herself a cup of coffee and checked Michael's cup, which was full.

He met her eyes when she sat down across from him. He folded his newspaper.

"Headache?"

"Mmm." She took a long swallow of coffee, ignoring that it was too hot.

"Want to talk?"

"No." She stood up. "I'm going for a run. Maybe that will help."

"Maybe," Michael agreed, watching her with narrowed eyes.

Five minutes later Brenna went through her warm-up and stretching exercises before she took off toward the park at a pace she kept deliberately slow. She intended to run until her body was as numb as her mind. That would take some time. She intended to run until all she felt was the throbbing muscles in her legs and until she could think about nothing at all.

By the time she had circled Washington Park once, she had worked into a comfortable, loose rhythm. Her mind was still keeping pace, tormenting her with all the *what-ifs* and *should-have-beens* in her life. By the time she started her fourth lap, she doubted her conscience would ever leave her alone.

"Brenna, wait!" came a call from a feminine voice behind her.

Brenna turned around and jogged lightly in place, watching as Nancy Jenkins ran toward her. A few inches shorter and twenty or thirty pounds overweight, she ran toward Brenna as though each step was torture.

"I thought that looked like you," Nancy said, panting, beads of perspiration running down the sides of her face, and trying to smile. "I didn't know you jogged this early."

"I usually don't. And it's running, you know, not jogging," Brenna said.

Nancy grasped her side. "What it really is…is agony."

"I used to think so, too," Brenna replied, slowing her pace to match Nancy's. "You're not working at the library today, huh?"

"Nope. We're on a new schedule. Just have to work every other night now," she said. "You haven't even worked up a good sweat. Did you just get here?"

"No. I'm about half way through my fourth lap."

"Four? God, there has to be an easier way to get into shape."

"You shouldn't be in this much pain," Brenna said.

"I thought 'no pain, no gain.'"

"That's for weight lifting," Brenna said, slowing her pace some more.

Nancy patted her side. "I decided if I couldn't stay away from the peanut-butter cups, I could run the calories off."

"When did you start?"

"Yesterday," was Nancy's breathy reply.

"Did you warm up first?"

"Warm up?"

"Yeah. Stretch your muscles out? Walk a couple of blocks first?" Nancy shook her head.

Brenna stopped running. "Let's walk for a while."

"Good idea," Nancy said with relief. "Warm up, huh?"

Brenna nodded. "Yes. You should be walking for a couple of blocks to get the blood flowing before you run. And you should be stretching your muscles out before you run at all."

"Okay, coach." Nancy grinned. "I always wondered what the secret of your great body was." She sank down on a park bench. "How I'd love it if somebody discovered that a dozen chocolate chip cookies a day was the key to perfect health."

Brenna smiled and used the bench for a series of stretches that would keep her muscles from kinking up later.

"So how are things going?" Nancy asked. "I haven't seen you much lately. What have you been doing?"

"Working," Brenna said, sitting down next to Nancy. "Until yesterday, anyway.'' She related the circumstances surrounding the closing of the bar.

"I bet Cole will be glad about that," Nancy said. "There's a guy who strikes me as the type who wants to spend more time with you."

Brenna had successfully avoided thinking about Cole for five whole minutes.

"C'mon, girl," Nancy encouraged. "You're still seeing him, aren't you?"

"Yes."

"Why do I get the feeling there's more to this than a simple 'yes'?"

"Cole's terrific," Brenna admitted. That was the core of the truth she couldn't deny. She didn't want him just sexually. She wanted all of him. She closed her eyes and sighed.

Nancy touched her arm. "Are you okay?"

Brenna opened her eyes and started to respond with an automatic, "Sure." Instead, she shook her head.

"What can I do for you?"

Brenna looked at Nancy, surprised at the concern in her voice.

"C'mon. 'Fess up, girl. What are friends for?"

Indeed, Brenna thought, feeling her composure crack a little beneath the weight of all her deceptions.

"Oh, Nancy, things are such a mess." The dam broke open, and the words poured out. "I've just lost my job—a job I really needed. The roof over my head isn't even my own. And I'm falling in love with an attorney. An attorney, for God's sake. You'd think I'd know better."

"What's the matter with attorneys?"

"I can't read." The words just slipped out. Brenna met Nancy's shocked gaze and repeated, more softly this time, "I can't read."

"Of course you can. You do story hour every week."

Brenna shook her head. "I tell stories I already know."

"But—"

"It's not that hard," Brenna said. "My grandfather told me great stories when I was little, and my mom read me bedtime stories. I really don't read to the kids. Honest."

"Why?"

"Because I don't know any other way."

"That's not what I meant," Nancy said.

"Oh. Why. The big why. As in, *why* didn't I ever learn to read?"

Nancy nodded.

Brenna stared at her feet. "At first..." Her voice trailed away. How did she explain, she wondered. "I don't know."

"Books were my refuge," Nancy said. "You know what it's like being at a different school every single year. And I was lousy at making new friends."

"I didn't do that so well, either."

"I still don't understand, Brenna. You're the most determined person I know. When you told me about the nonsense with the lawsuit, I thought, Boy, I'm glad this wasn't me. I'd never survive it. But you did. You're bright, one of the brightest—"

"I'm not."

Nancy smiled. "You are." Her smile grew into a laugh. "You're so great with the kids—a natural teacher. I was hoping to recruit you to be a tutor for the library's literacy program."

Brenna's eyebrows rose.

"Yeah. Instead, we need to get you matched with a tutor. And I know just the person, if you agree."

"Who?"

"Me."

Brenna stared at her friend as ideas began to bubble to the surface. "I'm ready to start. What do we do first?"

"I'm not completely sure. This is a first for me, too. I do know that you need to be tested so we know—"

"Tests?" Brenna interrupted, initial elation giving way to wariness. She hated tests.

"Just to see what level you read at."

"But I already told you. I don't—can't—read."

"You probably read more than you know. I mean, how do you know which is the ladies' rest room and which is the men's?"

"I'm careful."

Nancy grinned. "Me too. Listen, I'll talk to the director of the program this morning and find out what we need to do. Then I'll call you, okay?"

Brenna gave Nancy a spontaneous hug. "Okay."

They alternately walked and jogged the rest of the way around the

PLAY "LUCKY 7" AND GET
THREE FREE GIFTS!

HOW TO PLAY:

1. With a coin, carefully scratch off the silver box at the right. Then check the claim chart to see what we have for you — **FREE BOOKS** and a gift — **ALL YOURS! ALL FREE!**

2. Send back this card and you'll receive brand-new Silhouette Intimate Moments® novels These books have a cover price of $4.25 each, but they are yours to keep absolutely free

3. There's no catch. You're under no obligation to buy anything. We charge nothing — ZERO — for your first shipmen And you don't have to make any minimum number of purchases — not even one!

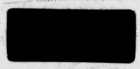

4. The fact is thousands of readers enjoy receiving books by mail from the Silhouette Reader Service™ months before they're available in stores. They like the convenience of home delivery and they love our discount prices!

5. We hope that after receiving your free books you'll want to remain a subscriber. But the choice is yours — to continue or cancel, any time at all! So why not take us up on ou invitation, with no risk of any kind. You'll be glad you did!

YOURS FREE!

PLAY LUCKY 7 FOR THIS EXCITING FREE GIFT!

*THIS SURPRISE
MYSTERY GIFT
COULD BE
YOURS FREE WHEN
YOU PLAY*

LUCKY 7!

PLAY THE

LUCKY 7 SLOT MACHINE GAME!

Just scratch off the silver box with a coin. Then check below to see the gifts you get!

YES!

I have scratched off the silver box. Please send me all the gifts for which I qualify. I understand I am under no obligation to purchase any books, as explained on the back and on the opposite page.

245 SDL CH5M
(U-SIL-IM-07/98)

Name

PLEASE PRINT CLEARLY

Address   Apt.#

City   State   Zip

7	7	7	WORTH TWO FREE BOOKS PLUS A BONUS MYSTERY GIFT!
🍒	🍒	🍒	WORTH TWO FREE BOOKS!
♣	♣	♣	WORTH ONE FREE BOOK!
🔔	🔔	🍒	TRY AGAIN!

DETACH AND MAIL CARD TODAY!

The Silhouette Reader Service™ — Here's how it works

Accepting free books places you under no obligation to buy anything. You may keep the books and gift and return the shipping statement marked "cancel." If you do not cancel, about a month later we'll send you 6 additional novels, and bill you just $3.57 each, plus 25¢ delivery per book and applicable sales tax, if any.* That's the complete price — and compared to cover prices of $4.25 each — quite a bargain! You may cancel at any time, but if you choose to continue, every month we'll send you 6 more books, which you may either purchase at the discount price...or return to us and cancel your subscription.

*Terms and prices subject to change without notice. Sales tax applicable in N.Y.

BUSINESS REPLY MAIL
FIRST-CLASS MAIL   PERMIT NO. 717   BUFFALO, NY

POSTAGE WILL BE PAID BY ADDRESSEE

SILHOUETTE READER SERVICE
3010 WALDEN AVE
PO BOX 1867
BUFFALO NY 14240-9952

NO POSTAGE
NECESSARY
IF MAILED
IN THE
UNITED STATES

park. After they took their separate routes home, Brenna felt as though she was running on air. She was going to learn to read.

She was going to learn to read!

She'd get her driver's license. And she'd learn how to type. She'd buy recipe books. She'd read stories to Teddy. She'd read a menu instead of asking for the daily special. She'd play Scrabble with Cole. She'd read the text in the *National Geographic,* instead of simply looking at the pictures.

Michael and Teddy were playing catch in front of the apartment when she arrived.

"Auntie Brennie," Teddy called. "Catch!" he threw the large softball at her, which she deftly caught and tossed back to him. He made a perfect catch.

"I take it you're feeling better," Michael said.

"Much." She smiled. "Sorry I was such a grump earlier."

"Cole called while you were gone." Michael sat down on the step and Teddy came to sit beside him. "He sounded a lot like you felt this morning. Crabby."

"Thanks for the message," she said. She owed Cole an apology. A knot tightened in her stomach as she recalled that he had held out his hand to her just before she'd run away from him. Inside the apartment, she took a deep breath, then dialed his number with trembling fingers.

"Hi, Cole," she said when he answered.

"Are you okay this morning?" he asked.

"Better." She wrapped the cord around her finger. "I'm sorry about last night."

"It's okay. I—"

"I don't know what happens to me, Cole. I wasn't being fair. And—"

"Brenna, it's okay. I'm sorry, too. I didn't mean to bring up things that hurt you."

She swallowed. "I know."

"Someday…" A long silence filled the line before he added, "Someday, you're going to have to decide if you trust me enough to know I won't hurt you."

"I know," she whispered.

"There's a good play on at the Denver Center Theater. Would you like to go tomorrow night? What do you say? We both need a night out on the town."

"Sounds like..."

"A case of the flu," he teased, to fill in the silence. "But that's not right. I'm looking for a word that sounds like sew, flow, toe."

She chuckled. "Go? As in, I'd love to go with you."

"The lady has just won herself an evening of dinner and theater with a dashing—"

"Don't you think you're laying this on a little thick?"

"A lot thick," he agreed, a smile still in his voice. "I'll pick you up about five and we'll have dinner first."

"Okay."

Less than a half hour later, Brenna had just finished showering when Nancy called.

"Good news and good news," Nancy said. "I can be your tutor. And if you have time, you can come in for testing this afternoon. I'll come to the library—sacrificing my day off, I might add—to be with you. If you want me to."

"I want you to," Brenna said. "Is twelve-thirty okay?"

"Make it two and you've got a deal."

"Two it is," Brenna agreed and hung up the phone.

To be able to open a book. Ideas. To find out what someone else thought about the world. Cole's enthusiasm for books revealing worlds she had yet to discover echoed through her mind.

She wandered back into her bedroom. The room was dappled with color from the crystal hanging in the window. She stood transfixed, watching the rainbow of patterns dance across the room. Just as she had so many other times, she'd get another job, and she'd support herself. Of that, she had no doubt.

For the first time in years she had something more.

This time, she dared look beyond simple survival. And she loved the possibilities she saw there.

Brenna surveyed her world with new awareness when Cole picked her up for dinner the following evening. The previous afternoon, the director of the literacy program at the library had told her, "You're reading at almost third-grade level." As she and Cole drove toward downtown Denver, Brenna watched passing stores, traffic signs, and billboards, searching each one for words she knew.

The tests she had taken made her feel inept despite the director's patience and encouragement. Third-grade level sounded like a lot to her. Reading—really reading—was a far cry from recognizing a few words. Recognizing the words *stop* and *exit* without the context of their familiar shapes within a sign didn't seem that big a deal to her.

Even still, she found herself identifying words within billboards that she'd given nothing more than a passing glance to before.

"You look terrific," Cole told her, taking his eyes off the busy traffic of Sixth Avenue long enough to look at her.

The compliment pleased her, especially as she had fussed over her white eyelet skirt and camisole-style blouse, half convinced it was too casual. She'd been equally critical of her hair, and she had finally pulled it into a loose chignon.

"Thanks," she said. "You look pretty spiffy, too."

"Spiffy, huh?"

"I wouldn't want you to get a swollen head by telling you that you're gorgeous," she teased.

Besides, she thought, how did she tell a man she thought he was devastating without sounding like a girl with her first crush. She always appreciated his choice in clothes. Whether dressed in shorts or a pale gray suit like this evening, he always looked good.

"I admit it. I've never been called gorgeous," he said with a laugh.

She grinned in response. "So, Counselor, this is a first?"

"It is."

"Those firsts..." she murmured. "They ought to be memorable."

Cole took her hand and brought it to his lips, his eyes on the traffic. "I intend for this one to be."

Brenna felt as though a line of no-return had been crossed with that simple, sensuous promise. A line she didn't fear half so much as she had yesterday.

"Promises, promises," she murmured, making him smile once again.

Chapter 13

For his part, Cole was relieved that Brenna was teasing him. She had given him a quick hug when he picked her up, but until now he hadn't been sure things would be okay. Another layer of his worry fell away. Though he couldn't quite put his finger on why, she looked happier than she had since he'd known her.

Cole parked in a lot adjoining the Denver Center Theater, and they walked to a Japanese restaurant a few blocks away.

Brenna loved the atmosphere of the restaurant, the decor reminding her of the clean lines of traditional Japanese architecture. Of all the places her father had been stationed, Japan had been her favorite. The natural finished wood and opaque paper walls surrounding them gave her a sense they were the only two people in the restaurant even though she could hear muffled conversation nearby.

A kimono-clad waitress handed each of them a menu, bowed, and discreetly disappeared. Brenna scanned the words, searching for one she might recognize. The script typeface confused her. No matter how hard she stared at it, a maze of symbols as illegible as Japanese ideographs stared back at her. The waitress brought a carafe of wine, an interruption Brenna was grateful for.

"Do you come here often?" she asked after the waitress had poured the wine and left again.

"Not often enough," Cole said. "Japanese food is my very favorite."

"I've finally learned to like it, too," Brenna said, setting the menu aside. "When we lived in Japan, I hated it. I would have traded it any day for a hamburger."

Cole grinned. "I went through a similar stage myself. When did you live there?"

"When I was thirteen. It was the last overseas assignment my dad had before..."

Before I left home. Cole heard the end of the sentence as clearly as if she'd said it. Each time he thought of her leaving home so young, he hurt for her. A flash of memory clouded her eyes, and she looked down. As he had seen her do before, she straightened her shoulders and looked back up, her emotions once again firmly hidden behind a wall of calm.

"Japan was interesting," she said, taking a sip of her wine, then met his gaze. "Strange and exotic. I liked it."

"What did you like best?" Cole asked her, wanting any snippet of her past that might help him understand her better.

"Japanese theater," she answered instantly, surprising him. "Have you ever seen Kabuki plays?"

Cole shook his head. "I've heard of them, but wouldn't know them from Punch and Judy."

Brenna grinned. "Actually, you're closer than you know. Punch and Judy are puppets. Kabuki plays are performed by mimes. Then off to the side of the stage, there's a narrator who tells the audience the story."

"An interpreter instead of subtitles?"

She chuckled. "Something like that."

Her eyes lit, and Cole sat back, smiling as she became more animated.

"It didn't really matter whether you understood the language. The plays are so dramatic, you get the gist of the story just watching the mimes." She went on to tell him a couple of stories, one an ancient historical drama and the other a modern play about a merchant's family.

"I would have thought you'd be more interested in the other kids than Ka...what was it?"

"Kabuki."

"Kabuki," he repeated.

"It was better than the kids," she replied. "I was always the odd man out."

Her statement was said lightly, but the shadows were back in her eyes, the last thing Cole wanted to see. He forced his attention back on the menu, then glanced at her.

"I've always wanted to order yosenabe."

"That sounds good," she agreed, closing the menu.

The makings for the meal arrived a little while later, an assortment of chicken, crab, scallops, shrimp, and vegetables accompanied by sauces with mouth-watering flavors. They cooked the food fondue-style in a clear broth brought to the table.

Brenna's mask of calm gradually gave way, and Cole found her alternately shy and funny, and always articulate. Nothing in her speech hinted that she hadn't finished school.

Equally compelling was his need to know more about her. Over dinner, she told him that her father had been stationed all over the world. Everywhere they had lived, Brenna's overriding interest was in the legends and parables handed down from grandparents to grandchildren. Given her interest in those stories and the lost opportunities that came with her dropping out of school, Cole found her interest poignant. He understood better why she enjoyed volunteering for story hour at the library. In her own way, she seemed to be passing on legends to the next generation.

"You obviously love all those old folk tales," Cole said. "My grandmother had dozens of stories she told me as a kid."

"Like what?" Brenna encouraged.

Cole ducked his head. "At the time, I didn't pay that much attention," he murmured.

"Ah," Brenna said with a chuckle. "There are times when I wish I had paid more attention to my grandmother, too."

"I was too busy telling her what a hotshot I was going to be after I grew up that I didn't listen nearly as much as I should have," Cole confessed. When Brenna cocked her head to the side in silent encouragement, he continued, "About every other week I had a new career I was going to try. And it didn't really matter whether I wanted to be a deep-sea diver or a design engineer, she listened as though she really believed me."

Brenna nodded. "Mine, too."

"She also knew when to knock me down a peg or two, or ten, when I needed it. I was the first in my family to get a college education, and I remember being pretty smug about that. I remember the summer after I graduated, I'd come home to help my dad bring in the hay, and I didn't like the way he was doing anything. Grandmom sat me down and boxed my ears." He smiled. "Literally. Told me a little book learning didn't mean diddly without experience, sweat, and common sense." Cole met Brenna's eyes. "She was right."

Brenna swallowed. "Education is also important."

Cole nodded. "But, my grandmother showed me that other things are equally important. She was the oldest of seven children, and her papa made her quit school after her mama died so she could help take care of the little ones."

"Why are you telling me this?" Brenna asked.

Cole met her glance. "My grandmother would have boxed my ears again," he said, "if she'd heard our conversation the other night. I admire you. I respect you."

Brenna's eyes took on a sudden shimmer and she shook her head. "Don't say things you don't mean."

"I'm not." He wanted to tell her outright that her lack of education didn't matter to him. It's what Grandmom would have expected of him. But it wasn't the truth, and he did wonder why she had never worked for her GED.

He still found it difficult to believe she hadn't finished school. She was eloquent, listened intently when he had something to say, and asked thoughtful questions. Maybe she was one of those people without much education who was widely read, he decided. The apartment was certainly filled with books.

His gut instinct told him there was more to Brenna than met the eye. He didn't know what it was, but he had to find out.

"I'm not judging you," he said, taking her hand.

"I judge me," she returned.

He smiled and touched the side of her face. "Then maybe it's time to stop."

After they finished dinner, Cole and Brenna walked hand in hand the few blocks to the theater, pausing along the way to window-shop. Brenna couldn't have said what they looked at or talked about. Had it been within her power, she would have stretched those moments into hours.

After they were seated in the theater, she found the program nearly as frustrating as the menu. She searched for words she recognized, trying to read as she hadn't tried in years. *The. A. To. Or. His, for, last, and, in, house, wife.* Her recognition of those words came slowly, and she shook her head in frustration. The play, *Paint Your Wagon,* was a lighthearted musical that bore little resemblance to the movie she had seen years before. When intermission came, she and Cole followed the crowd into the lobby. Someone called Cole's name from across the lobby.

"Cole, hello," the woman said, extending her hand.

Dressed in a severe white suit with a sheer navy blue tailored blouse underneath, she was poised as anyone Brenna had seen in a long time. She was reminded of Sunday afternoon teas on broad expanses of manicured lawns, where the officers' wives had tried to outdress one another. Children were to be seen and never heard, and problems were ignored with the same efficiency as dirty plates and glasses that were whisked away by white-coated waiters.

"Hello, Sandra. Frank."

Brenna glanced behind the woman to the man Cole was shaking hands with. He wore a seersucker jacket and tweed slacks that were a definite mismatch. What an odd-looking couple, Brenna thought.

"Are you enjoying the play?" Cole asked. This is it, he thought suddenly. The first time he and Brenna had ever been with any of his colleagues.

"It's a bit much," Sandra replied. "But it is fun, isn't it? I think I would have preferred a good drama."

Cole touched Brenna's arm. "This is my friend, Brenna James. Brenna, Sandra and Frank Wilson."

Sandra tipped her head in a slight nod. "Hello."

Frank clasped both of Brenna's hands in his, and a smile creased his tanned face, deep smile lines making his eyes just about disappear. "We're both glad to meet you. My wife may prefer a good drama, but I like this a lot."

"Me, too," Brenna said with a smile. She glanced back at Sandra. Brenna had the feeling that, despite her pleasant expression, Sandra was a woman who was good at hiding her feelings beneath a chic exterior. Frank, however, seemed as relaxed as Sandra was formal, as warm as she was cool.

"Have you and Brenna been dating long?" Sandra asked Cole.

"Long enough," Cole replied, wrapping a hand round Brenna's and slanting her a warm smile. "Sandra shows the same aggressive style in court. She gets right to the point."

Sandra's mouth curved in a surprisingly friendly smile. "And guess who I took lessons from?"

It was the kind of small talk Brenna knew how to do even if she didn't like it. "If you're referring to Cole, I believe it. I've seen him in action."

"Are you also an attorney?" Frank asked. "Because I'm really going to feel outnumbered here if you are."

Brenna laughed. "Good heavens, no."

"Thank God," he said with real feeling. "I'm safe. You get three lawyers together, and it's a convention." He took a sip of wine from the clear plastic glass he held. "So, Brenna, what do you do when you're not keeping Cole out of mischief?"

The sixty-four dollar question, Brenna thought. Why was it people decided who you were by what you did to earn a living? She squeezed Cole's hand and looked at him with wide eyes, giving her best imitation of a woman completely beguiled by a man. "Who says I'm keeping him out of mischief?"

Frank laughed. "Have you been sailing with him yet?"

Brenna nodded. "Sure have. And, he promised to take me to Lake Dillon the next time we go out." She gave Frank another once-over. "Next thing you know, he'll want to teach me to play golf."

Cole gave her a puzzled glance. Never once had he indicated a liking for golf—in fact, he hated the game.

Frank chuckled. "If you want a good teacher, forget this guy. I'm your man." And he launched into a long dissertation about his favorite "impossible" shots.

Cole's puzzlement gave way to admiration as his understanding dawned. Brenna had accurately gauged Frank's likes and dislikes. In the process, she steered the conversation away from herself.

Cole watched Brenna as the conversation drifted back to sailing and how they each were spending their spare time during the summer. Brenna continued to turn the conversation away from herself, deftly picking up on things Frank or Sandra told her, getting them to expand on their comments.

Cole had to admit to himself that Brenna was far better at the social small talk than he would ever be. She was warm, witty, and Frank and Sandra would walk away knowing nothing about Brenna James. Cole listened, really listened, to her. She sounded as well educated as Sandra, and her diction and grammar were better than Frank's.

The lobby lights flickered, indicating intermission was over. Cole squeezed her hand. "Ready to go sit back down?"

"It was a pleasure meeting you," Frank said. He and Sandra disappeared in the throng of people returning to the theater.

"Are they good friends?" Brenna asked.

Cole shook his head. "Acquaintances. And I never realized before tonight just how nosy Sandra is."

"Unusual couple."

"She's a prosecutor in the district attorney's office, and he's making tons of royalty money off a group of computer programs he developed a few years ago."

Brenna glanced at Cole. "That tells me what they do, but not who they are."

Cole followed Brenna into their aisle where they sat back down. "I don't understand."

"Aren't you more than the sum of your job?" she asked.

"Of course."

"Is what you do for a living the most important part of who you are?"

"It's a big piece," he said.

"I know. But, is it the most important piece?"

He shook his head. "I hope not."

She smiled. "Which is my point. What is Sandra Wilson's most important piece? I bet it's not her job."

Cole grinned. "In her case, I wouldn't bet on it." He took Brenna's hand in his. "But if you're trying to tell me there's a lot more to you than your education or the jobs you've had, I know that, fair lady. And I like all the parts of you."

"Intuitive, too, aren't you?" She slid her arm under his, threading her fingers with his.

He lifted their joined hands to his mouth and kissed the back of hers. "No. But I can add two plus two and get the right answer if I'm pressed."

The curtain rising for the second act kept Brenna from replying. As the play unfolded, she watched Cole from the corner of her eye. Tonight she had been the worst kind of fraud. Pretending she was just like him. Telling him about things she had seen and done while she lived overseas. She loved his approval, and she enjoyed his company. He'd given her the opportunity to tell him she couldn't read when he told her the story about his grandmother. And she couldn't face shattering his attraction to her with the unadorned truth of her life.

When the play ended, Cole held her hand while they walked to his car and stole a kiss when he helped her into the seat.

"It doesn't seem possible Independence Day is this weekend," Cole said.

"Summer always feels like it's half over by then. Even though it's just started."

"What I'd like to do over the Fourth of July, is go to the ranch." Cole took her hand. "You and me."

"You're asking me..."

"To go to Nebraska with me." He smiled at her. "About once a year, I get homesick. And I go to the ranch for a few days, get my perspective back, and things are good again. You know?"

"Yeah."

"So, it's agreed then. You'll come with me."

Brenna sensed the tension radiating from him despite the casual tone of his voice. She wanted to say yes, but she owed it to herself—to him—to think about this a little. Meeting his parents...she wasn't ready for that.

"I'd like you to meet my folks. And you'd love my grandmother," he said, as if reading her thoughts.

Cole didn't know whether he had expected an immediate "Yes, I'd love to come" from her. But he hadn't expected her to watch him with dark eyes as though she was trying to fathom some hidden message.

He pulled into an empty parking space in front of the apartment. "You'd love my grandmother," he repeated. "She's the most amazing person, feisty as ever. She's over eighty now, and she ignores us all when we tell her she ought to slow down a little. Did I tell you that she came to Nebraska on a horse-drawn wagon?"

Brenna shook her head. "She's seen a lot, then."

Accepting Brenna's comment as an invitation for more, Cole told her about his grandmother's trip from Kentucky to Nebraska when she was a girl, then told her how she'd met his grandfather.

Brenna listened with her usual fascination for oral histories passed from one generation to another. Easily, she imagined what it must have been like traveling across the wide prairie to a new and unknown home.

Cole's grandmother came alive to Brenna, and she admitted wanting to meet the woman who had been such an influence on him. Even so, the idea of being important enough to him to meet his family scared her.

"We'll have a great time," he said, finishing his story by repeating his invitation to visit the ranch.

"Do you ask every girl you take to dinner?" she teased. On one hand, she would have a lot less pressure if he took women there all the time. On the other hand, she didn't want to be one of many.

"Only one other," Cole answered seriously. "And that was a long time ago."

Brenna's smile fell away. This was no casual thing for him either. She should tell him no, but instead, she asked, "When would we go?"

"Probably Wednesday. I'd like to spend the weekend there and come back on Sunday night or Monday." Cole's finger touched a tendril that lay against her nape. "It would give us some time together without all the distractions we find around here."

Brenna smiled. "No Teddy."

"If you want a chaperon, my grandmother would do better than Teddy any day."

"She takes longer naps?"

Cole laughed. "Ah, Brenna." He slid closer and touched her temple with his lips. "I know a few places on the ranch where I can have you all to myself."

"What kind of invitation is this?" she whispered.

"Completely honorable." He kissed her cheek, then her hairline below her ear where wisps had escaped the confinement of her chignon. "I want to touch, and look at, and cherish—"

"Oh, Cole," she sighed, putting her arms around him. "Yes."

He hauled her across his lap. "I want you."

"I know."

"I think a change of scenery would do us both good."

"I agree," she whispered against his neck.

"So you'll come?"

She nodded. "I'll have to rearrange the schedule for a couple of my cleaning customers. And I have to make sure I don't leave Jane in the lurch. Maybe one of the neighbors can help watch Teddy for a couple of days."

"Good," Cole whispered a scant second before claiming her mouth as completely as he wanted to claim her body. He wanted to take her back to his house, and conversely, he wanted this tension to increase until she was as consumed by it as he was. Reluctantly, he forced himself to lighten the pressure of his kisses, to tease them both.

When they made love for the first time, he wanted time to play, to enjoy, and to have thoughts of work far behind them. The perfect place would be at the lake, he thought. They would make love beneath the shady cottonwoods, then go skinny-dipping, and play very adult games in the water. He'd never taken a woman there. In fact, he had never made love with a woman out-of-doors.

The idea of making love with Brenna like that tested his resolve to tease them rather than escalate the passion. A few more days, he promised himself. Finally, Cole forced himself to let her go and he walked her to the door of the apartment. "I'll come by tomorrow night," he said. "What would you like to do?"

"I don't know. I can't," she blurted out, her color very high. "I'm...Nancy and I are—"

"Going to the movies, I bet," Cole said. "Who is she dragging you off to see this time? Tom Cruise? The latest Spielberg film?"

"Jealous?" she asked, wrapping her arms around him, a smile lighting her face.

"Only if you think about kissing any one else like this," Cole answered, lowering his mouth to hers.

"Just Tom," Brenna whispered long seconds later, as she hugged Cole more tightly.

"Just Tom," he muttered. "I don't even want to know." He set her firmly away from him. "You two have a good time. I'll call you from work tomorrow."

"Okay."

He playfully swatted at her fanny as she turned to go through the door. "And be good."

She turned and winked at him. "Of course, you won't be around."

Chapter 14

"Hi," Nancy said the following evening when she met Brenna outside the library.

"Hi," Brenna responded. Now that the moment was upon her, she almost wished she hadn't agreed to this. Fear, the flip side of elation, surfaced. She knew just what failure tasted like. She had dined at that plate for years.

Everyone knew kids learned things more easily than adults. The last time she had tried, the experience had been awful. She had felt stupid, and she had hated the teacher. Alarm curled through her stomach and she cast Nancy a quick glance. They were friends. God, what if she ended up hating her friend?

"I just figured out something," Nancy whispered as they crossed the library, headed toward the meeting rooms.

"What's that?"

"I'm scared to death."

Brenna stopped dead in her tracks, her heart pounding, and watched Nancy walk ahead of her. Of all the things she could have said, this was one Brenna had not expected. Nancy opened the door into a small room and turned around to wait for Brenna.

She slowly approached the door. "Why are you afraid?"

Awful things poured through Brenna's head. Maybe she was too stupid to learn, and Nancy knew it. Or maybe she had changed her mind. Or maybe this was going to be just too, too hard.

Nancy closed the door behind Brenna. "Because I've never done this before. When I volunteered, I thought it would be easy. Then, when I went through my training...whew." She rolled her eyes. "They had some exercises to show us what it would be like for someone who doesn't read, and all of the sudden, I figured out this wasn't some lark to feed my ego. This was hard. And important."

"But you volunteered anyway," she interjected. "So why are you scared?"

Nancy looked away from a moment, and when she looked up, her eyes were bright. "I never really thought about who might be my student. And it's you—my friend. And what if I'm not good enough—"

"No 'what-ifs,'" Brenna interrupted, the constriction around her chest easing as she realized Nancy feared her own inadequacies. Brenna understood that. "We can do this. If I can, you certainly can."

She was almost relieved to find that Nancy felt as uncertain as she did. Brenna hadn't imagined this from Nancy's point of view. She knew Nancy would do her best, which was all either one of them could ask for. Brenna would do her best, and that too, was all they could ask for.

"We'll give it our best shot," she added. "If this doesn't work I won't blame you."

"It will work," Nancy responded. "I've seen it work."

"You teach me to read, and I'll coach your running. Okay?"

"Okay." Nancy smiled and sat down in a chair at the table. She opened a folder and pulled out several sheets of paper. "When Brian tested you on Saturday, all he did was determine the level you read at. Our next step is to make sure you have all the basics you need."

Brenna sat down. "What kind of basics?"

"That you know all the letters and their sounds. As we go along, we'll figure out how much you already know. Some of this stuff we may have to spend some time on and some of it we may be able to zip through."

"Okay?" Brenna agreed. "What else?"

Nancy met Brenna's gaze. "Everything we use, we'll gear toward things that interest you. So, I have a bunch of questions to ask you." She read from the top sheet of paper. "Have you read the newspaper in the last six months?"

Brenna shook her head.

"Have you looked through any books in the last six months?"

Again, she shook her head.

"What about the ones you check out with Teddy?" Nancy prompted.

"Oh. That's right. And we have a lot of big coffee table books with wonderful pictures that I like."

"Good," Nancy said, taking notes. "What about magazines?"

"I like *National Geographic*. And Jane gets one of those magazines with recipes in it every month."

Nancy grinned. "You can gain weight just by looking at those pictures, you know."

Brenna smiled back. "Impossible. I heard paper was fat-free."

Nancy laughed, then asked, "Do you read business letters?"

Brenna shook her head.

"Advertising?"

"No."

"Job applications."

Brenna smiled. "As little as possible."

"I don't like them, either," Nancy said. She set aside that sheet of paper. "Okay. The next thing we're going to do is a language experience story—a story about you. Just a paragraph of three or four sentences to start. So, tell me about your day."

"Well, I took care of Teddy, as usual." Brenna paused when she saw Nancy writing. "You're going to write down everything I say?"

Nancy looked up and smiled. "Not everything. We just need a few sentences. Tell me what you and Teddy did."

"We went to the park. Teddy fed the ducks in the lake. He has a new kite, and we flew it. And he likes to swing." Brenna fell silent as she watched Nancy print the words with a black felt tip pen.

She glanced at Brenna. "Tell me if I got this right. 'We went to the park today. Teddy fed the ducks in the lake. We flew his new kite,'" she read, her fingers sliding along each one of the words. "Is this correct?"

Brenna looked at the sheet. "I don't know about correct, but it is basically what I said."

"Do you know any of the words?" Nancy asked.

Brenna studied the sheet for a moment. "Teddy. To. The. Lake. Park. A."

Under Nancy's encouragement, Brenna's confidence increased. All the fear that had plagued her since deciding to do this vanished. Nancy made it seem all so logical. She showed Brenna the name *Ted* in the word *Teddy,* then moved on to *fed* and *bed* and *wed.* Nancy always came back to words and phrases Brenna already knew. They spent the next two hours working through the language-experience story, pulling words from it, using those words to develop other word patterns.

The stack of cards grew as Nancy added new words. They arranged the cards into phrases, and the phrases became short sentences.

The whole thing seemed like a game to Brenna, and she was astounded to discover so much time had passed. Except for a kink in her back that came from sitting so long, she felt energized.

"There's homework," Nancy said.

Brenna stood up and stretched. "That has an ominous ring to it. Do you give out demerits when it's not done?"

Nancy laughed. "Now, there's a thought, but since you're going to coach my running, paybacks could be hell."

"That's right. So, Miss Jenkins," Brenna teased. "What's my homework?"

"I'd like you to read the front page of the newspaper a couple times this week. Circle all the words you know."

"I can do that. It will be a very short list."

"Don't be so sure." Nancy put her papers in a folder and handed Brenna the stack of cards. "These are yours. That way, you have something to practice with."

"Thanks." Brenna put the cards in her tote bag.

"I gather you haven't told your family what we're doing," Nancy said.

"Teddy has already figured it out. If he knows, well..."

"Your brother knows," Nancy said.

Brenna nodded, feeling an odd pang in her chest. She glanced at Nancy. "We'll do this again next Monday?"

"Yes." Nancy fiddled with the strap of her bag an instant, then asked, "Does Cole know about this?"

Brenna shook her head, and her smile faded as she thought about the inevitability of Cole's finding out she was illiterate. On the other hand, if she learned a dozen new words every day, there would some come a time when she could read. Maybe she would get lucky and be able to avoid telling him anything.

"He'll be okay about this," Nancy said.

"I wish I believed that."

"Then you'll just have to choose your moment and tell him when you think he's most receptive."

"I know."

"Brenna?" Nancy hesitated, staring past Brenna at the wall a moment before meeting her eyes. "Learning to read is an up-and-down process, you know. Don't be too disappointed if it doesn't go as well next time as it did tonight."

Brenna smiled and gave her friend a hug. "I understand what you're saying." She drew back. "And thanks for your help. I'm beginning to believe I can do it."

"You've sure been happy the last week," Michael commented, a couple of days after her tutoring session. Brenna and he were putting the finishing touches on dinner in anticipation of Jane's arrival home.

"Yeah," she said, trying to sound offhand.

"The reasons for you being so happy," Michael teased, "wouldn't have anything to do with a certain tall, reasonably good-looking guy that has been hanging around here."

"Mmm," Brenna responded. She couldn't deny that Cole played a part in her good spirits. A big part.

"Don't think I've ever seen you this serious about a guy."

"I'm not serious," she automatically denied.

"He is," Michael stated.

Brenna's hands stilled over the green salad she was making. Without meeting her brother's glance, she shook her head.

"C'mon, Brenna. He's asked you to go home with him."

"Don't go reading anything into this," she said.

"In other words, butt out."

"Smart man." She finished arranging sliced cucumbers on top of the salad. "I knew you'd catch on."

Michael checked on the casserole in the oven, turned it off, and casually added, "Teddy says you've been studying."

Leave it to Teddy to let the cat out of the bag, Brenna thought. She shouldn't have been surprised. Within days of moving in with Michael and Jane, Brenna had discovered you had few secrets around a four-year-old.

"Does this have anything to do with the long conversations you've been having with Nancy the last few days?"

"What is this?" Brenna cast him a you-sure-are-a-pain, big-brother look. "Twenty questions?"

He smiled. "You tell me, sis."

She set the salad on the table. "Just how much has my young nephew told you?"

Michael had the grace to blush. "You mean after I put the thumbscrews to him?" He folded his arms across his chest and faced Brenna. "He told me you have a big stack of words on cards and that you wished you had more. And he's your helper."

"That he is, even if he can't keep a secret."

Michael grinned. "A failing of being four-almost-five. I wish…"

When his voice trailed off, Brenna glanced at her brother. He was studying the pattern on the tiled floor, looking uncharacteristically uncertain.

"Wish what?"

He raised his head. "I knew, even before Teddy told me, that something had changed. I was just waiting until you wanted to tell me. Hoping you'd want to tell me."

"What's to tell? I'm learning to read. No guarantees of success." Deliberately she turned her back on him, fully aware the one thing they had never talked about was now in the open. And she could swear she had heard a thread of hurt in Michael's voice. Not pity, but hurt. Of all his possible reactions, she hadn't anticipated that one. Why would her imperfections make her brother hurt?

She had suspected for a long time that her brother knew of her illiteracy. Of all the people in the world, she knew he'd still love her, but beyond that she hadn't known what to expect. After all, he was a research scientist at a major university hospital, a man who had graduated at the top of his class both in high school and college. A brilliant man who had always, always, made it clear none of that had any importance in their relationship.

Slowly she turned around to face him.

He grinned, and her defensiveness dissolved. She grabbed him by the shoulders, returning his smile with a huge one of her own, a buoyant feeling expanding in her chest. "Oh, Michael. You wouldn't believe it! It's not like being in first grade like the last time I tried. And it's not with some old retired teacher talking down to me like I was stupid. It's..." Her voice trailed away as she searched for the right words.

"Easy?" Michael supplied.

Brenna shook her head. "No. It's not. But this time I think—I know—I can do it."

"I know you can, Brenna." His voice was solemn, a contrast to his smile, which faded.

"But?"

"Does Cole know you can't read?"

Brenna shook her head. "I've wanted to tell him. Oh, Michael, I have. And every time I think I'm close to being able to say the words, something happens."

"I don't want you to get hurt."

If things ended with Cole, not being hurt would be impossible. She knew that. "I keep thinking that maybe—"

"If you ignore the problem, it will go away?"

"Something like that."

"Not a good plan, Brennie," Michael said.

"I know. Cole thinks Nancy and I have been going to the movies."

"I won't lie for you, sis," Michael warned. A smile softened his features. "But I won't give you away either."

Jane arrived home, and the evening routine began, one that Brenna was still adjusting to. Working nights, she had missed the shared companionship over dinner, the relating of the day's activities. Jane expected Teddy to learn something new every day, and she asked him about it every night, a gentle prodding that made her son eagerly share.

As Brenna listened over dinner to his chatter, she wondered if things would have been different if the Colonel had been more encouraging, less demanding. He, too, had expected his children to learn something new each day. She had never measured up. Her inadequacies were pointed out and examined, and her strengths fell too short for praise.

With new clarity, she realized her reluctance to tell anyone—including her brother...and Cole—she couldn't read was rooted as much in her need to protect herself as it was in her shame. A habit that isolated her.

After dinner, she took the front page of the paper to her room, circling the words she knew per Nancy's instructions. Surveying one column of the page, she shook her head in disgust. They were pitifully few.

Taking out the stack of cards Nancy had given her, she reviewed each one, then arranged them into sentences. *Teddy fed the ducks. Teddy led the ducks.* Her attention went back to the paper, and her heart sank. She had so much to learn, and the vast expanses of words on the page she had not circled proved just how much.

Michael tapped on the door, then pushed it open, the cordless phone in his hand. "The Colonel," he said, handing her the phone.

Their father called once a week, precisely at eight, and because Brenna had worked nights, she had been able to avoid those calls. She had preferred it that way.

Brenna stared at it a full second before putting the receiver to her ear. Somehow her father always seemed to catch her at her most uncertain, and tonight was no exception.

"Hello," she said, deliberately omitting the "sir" she knew he expected.

"What's this about your losing your job?" he asked without preamble.

"The bar closed," she said. "It's nice to hear your voice, too, Dad." He hadn't liked her working there, but she knew better than to hope he'd view her job loss as anything positive.

"Don't get sarcastic, young lady," he said. "Do you have another job lined up?"

"Not yet," she said, hating the inevitable, predictable turn in the conversation. "I'm going to be gone a few days—"

"Your number-one priority is making sure you're not a burden to Michael. That you're pulling your own weight."

"I understand that," she murmured with far more civility than she felt.

"If you don't have a job, I don't see how," he said. "Michael understands the need for commitment—"

"The striving for excellence, the goal of perfection." Brenna interrupted, irritated with the comparison he always made.

"That's right." The Colonel paused, as he always did, for effect, to punctuate the importance of what he said next. "You're capable of pursuing excellence, but I'd settle for a little commitment."

Brenna rubbed her temple, rearranging the cards on the bed into a new pattern. *Brenna sin.* She frowned and reached for a new card. *Brenna fled.* Not liking that thought any better than the first, she stacked the cards on top of one another.

"Exactly what is it you expect this time?" she asked. Not that she'd be able to live up to it, but forewarned was forearmed.

"The same as always," he answered, his voice crisp. "But I'll spell it out for you. One. Get a job, Brenna. And this time, be conscientious so you can keep it more than two or three months."

"It wasn't my fault the bar closed," she interrupted.

"Two," he said, ignoring her. "Stop taking advantage of your brother. Do you understand me?"

The do-you-understand-me was his signal he was finished. Thank God. Resorting to the dull obedience that had usually avoided a beating, she repeated, "I understand. Get a job. Pull my own weight."

"Very good."

"You're still coming to Denver?" she asked, hoping he'd say he wasn't.

"I am. I'll be there right after the Independence Day weekend."

"Maybe you should come sooner. Spend the Fourth here," she suggested, fully aware she would be in Nebraska with Cole. Some place where her father wasn't.

The suggestion seemed to catch him by surprise because there was a long pause on the other end of the line. "I'll give it some thought," he said at last. "Goodnight, Brenna."

"Bye," she murmured to the dead telephone line, and hearing a very different conversation in her head.

Hi, Dad, it's so good to hear from you. You wouldn't believe the awful week I've had.

Michael says you lost your job. What can I do to help?

And cows could fly. Her father hadn't offered to help her once, and she couldn't imagine him doing so. She hated that she wanted him to offer. Even more, she hated the realization that she might not turn down his help. After all these years, she still felt as though she could cut herself anytime on the double-edged sword of wanting his approval and wanting to run as far away from him as she could get.

Absently, she rearranged the cards again. *Brenna is a fake.* She didn't like that thought at all. However true, she intended to change. *Brenna make luck.* A better thought.

Chapter 15

"So this is your Brenna." Grandmom's blue eyes were the same shade as Cole's, shot with gold that reflected the bright summer sun, and clear as a young girl's. She released Cole from her welcoming hug and opened her arms to Brenna. "I know I'm going to love you."

Whatever platitude Brenna tried to utter was lost in her awareness of the moment. She took the last step onto the porch of the white frame house and put her arms around Cole's grandmother. Feeling as though she had come home, Brenna swallowed back the lump that rose in her throat.

Grandmom was similar in stature to Nonna, and the indefinable scent of a woman who lived close to the land was the same, too. The crisp aroma of clothes dried in warm sunshine and the faint traces of lotion on her skin assailed Brenna with vivid memories. For a moment, Brenna imagined it was her own grandmother she was hugging. If Grandmom felt her tremble, she was kind enough to ignore it.

"Come in and help me fix each of us a lemonade," she said to Cole. She released Brenna from her embrace and opened the screen door going into the house. "Did you drive straight through from Denver?"

"Left bright and early just so we could enjoy afternoon lemonade with you, Grandmom," Cole said.

"Humph," Grandmom responded. "Tell that to someone who'll believe it." The smile on her face took the sting completely away from her words. She glanced at Brenna and added, "What he really thinks is that he's going to get a piece of apple pie."

"I'd believe that," Brenna said, with a grin. "I've seen how he is about pie."

Following them through the house to the kitchen, she was again overwhelmed with memories. Physically, nothing about the house resembled the one on the farm in Pennsylvania. Yet, she was reminded. Crocheted covers on the arms and backs of chairs, a north-facing window sill full of blooming African violets, and the cheerful tick-tock of a cuckoo clock could have come from Nonna's house.

Cole opened an ancient refrigerator and took an ice-cube tray out of the freezer compartment.

"A long time ago I thought I was getting a deal," he said, breaking the ice cubes apart. "I'd make a bargain with Grandmom to do extra chores, and she'd save me back a piece of pie. Years later, Grandpop told me she always saved the last piece of pie for me."

"Spoiled him rotten, huh?" Brenna said, imagining Cole as a boy, wheedling favors from his grandmother.

Grandmom poured lemonade into each of the glasses. "You bet I spoiled him every chance I got. I still do."

"Are Mom and Dad still in Scottsbluff?" Cole asked.

"They sure are, and you're going to be in a peck of trouble with your mother. She told me they didn't expect you until tomorrow."

"I decided to come early."

Brenna knew first hand just how antsy he'd been. He had become more expansive in his stories about his boyhood as they had gotten closer to the ranch. Brenna had trouble imagining him as a sullen teenager who couldn't wait to leave, his description of himself. The teenager might have wanted to leave. The man couldn't wait to return.

Grandmom led them back to the front porch.

"Cole said you like old stories, folk tales and such."

Brenna nodded. "That's right, I do."

Grandmom watched her steadily for a moment. "Most young folk would rather watch the television."

"She's not most people," Cole interjected. "Did I tell you she volunteers at the library doing story hour for the little kids?"

Brenna glanced at him in surprise. He said it like it was something to be proud of. Compared to the things he did, or those Michael or Jane did, her small contribution at the library was nothing. She found herself wishing, though, it was more.

The conversation turned toward the ranch's activities, the price of cattle, how many head had been sent to a feedlot, and other business. Sipping her lemonade, she let her gaze search to the horizon and back.

The ranch was set in a shallow valley below a bluff. On the way from Denver, Cole told her the original thirteen hundred acres of the ranch came from his grandfather and great-uncle when they filed for adjoining homesteads under the Kincaid Act.

She tried to imagine what the land must have looked like when Cole's grandfather first arrived. The occasional marsh full of ducks and geese and the rolling grass-covered hills were a far cry from the flat landscape Brenna had imagined Nebraska to be. She had a profound sense of homecoming that only deepened as she listened to Grandmom and Cole talk.

Cole swallowed the last of his lemonade and sucked an ice cube into his mouth. He stood up, tucked one hand into the pocket of his jeans, and offered Brenna the other one. "Ready to come see all my favorite hideaways?"

"Sure."

Grandmom waved them off the porch. "You two have a good time. We're going to have a simple supper tonight, so I don't need any help."

"You'll ring the bell when Mom and Dad get back?"

Brenna's gaze followed Cole's vague gesture to a large brass bell that hung from one of the porch posts.

"The minute they get here."

Cole and Brenna strolled hand in hand across the yard and followed a dirt road that led to the barn and several other outbuildings.

"When I was a kid, we had grazing permits that gave us enough range to run five thousand head of cattle," he said. His gaze focused on the horizon for a moment before he glanced back at her. "Those days are gone. Forever, I think."

Brenna sympathized, having listened to enough news and seen enough television to know he was right. "Was that all you raised—cattle?"

"Nope. Everybody had things going. Grandmom always had chickens and she sold the eggs. She still does, but to the neighbors, mostly. There's still one grocery left in Bayard where she sells them sometimes. Nothing like real farm-grown eggs from chickens that actually get to scratch in the dirt."

"And what was your thing?" Brenna asked.

"This." Cole stopped in front of a straw-filled enclosure that had a lean-to at one end. "Come on out, Matilda."

A huge pink pig with almost white hair ambled out, snorting as she came.

"This is Waltzing Matilda," Cole said, "otherwise known as Piglet Factory."

Brenna grinned. "She does kind of waltz, in her own fashion, anyway."

"Matilda, here, is the granddaughter of one of the sows I had when I was in high school. Each little pig was worth over a hundred dollars when we took it to market. After paying for feed and expenses, I got to keep the rest. I paid my way through college with that money."

"No piglets right now." Too well, Brenna remembered the silver spoon she had assumed was Cole's as a child. She knew from her own limited experience with her grandparents' farm just what hard work ranching was.

"She's due again in a couple of weeks," Cole said.

"She gives the phrase 'pig in a poke' a whole new meaning, doesn't she?"

Cole laughed and wrapped his arm around her shoulder. "You're weird, fair lady."

"But you like it," she said, looking up at him.

He dropped a kiss on the tip of her nose. "Yeah," he responded, his voice husky, "I like it."

He was beginning to realize just how much. Every time he'd thought of Susan and Brenna at the same time, he'd deliberately squashed the impulse. Two women could not have been more different. He hadn't wanted to compare, but found himself doing so anyway.

Susan hadn't liked the ranch a bit. She thought the drive from Denver was long and boring and tiring. There was nothing to do after they got here. Cole's parents were boring, and his grandmother was a tiresome old woman. About his parents—sometimes Cole had agreed with that. But his grandmother was a different matter.

Brenna had been interested in the landscape as they traveled Interstate 25 from Denver, and she hadn't seen it as desolate at all. They had talked about the plains Indians, buffalo, sod houses and the dust-bowl years. She'd been curious about the ranch and his family, and he'd told her more than he'd ever told Susan. The rapport that sprang up instantly between Brenna and his grandmother was more than he had hoped for. She was right. He liked her and he liked having her here.

He and Brenna spent the next couple of hours traipsing over the ranch as Cole pointed out buildings and livestock. They walked through fields of waist-high grass, and they laughed over silly things that had no meaning beyond the moment and their enjoyment of each other.

"Of all the places on the ranch," Cole said, "this is my favorite." They followed a narrow path through the tall grass to a clearing, which was dominated by a pond. The rooftop of the house was visible behind a rise on the other side of the water. They sat down on the trunk of a fallen cottonwood. "If we sit here very quietly for a few minutes, we'll see this place come alive," Cole said.

He put his arm around Brenna, more aware of her than of the long afternoon shadows and the muted sounds of lapping water. He pressed a kiss against her temple, his eyes on the pond. A blue heron waded out of the marsh grass and stood stock-still at the edge of the water, its attention intent on something beneath the surface. Cole started to point at the bird, but Brenna had already seen it, her breath held as though even that slight movement would startle the bird into flight.

A mallard, followed by a half-dozen ducklings, swam into view. Cole loved watching them, but that become much less important than watching Brenna's total involvement with them. Her face softened so much Cole realized how tightly in check she usually held herself.

Her expression became wistful, and the sense of longing Cole saw made him want to give her whatever she dreamed of.

He caressed her cheek, softer than the down from ducklings, with the back of his hand. "I'm glad you like my favorite place," he whispered.

She leaned her face into his hand, her eyes still fastened on the serenity of the pond. "I love it."

"What have you been thinking about?"

"My grandparents' farm."

She was silent for so long he almost thought she would say nothing else.

Finally, "It was nothing like this, but it was exactly like this." She glanced at him and made a helpless gesture with her hand. "I don't know how to explain."

"I think I understand," he said, resting his cheek against her hair. "Peace. Serenity. A feeling that the rest of the world is less real than this is."

"Yeah. If this is reality, I'd like to have it all the time."

"And here I thought you were a city kid."

"Not in my heart," she answered. "I spent every summer that I could with my grandparents. And I loved going to the farm more than anything. No matter what else happened, no matter where my dad was stationed, the farm was always there."

"What happened to it?"

"After Nonna died, it was sold."

They fell silent again, and again, Brenna gradually relaxed. She leaned her head against Cole's shoulder. "This is nice."

He brushed his cheek across her hair. "Yeah."

His reply was so soft Brenna felt it rather than heard it. The simple walk around the ranch answered many of her questions about him. She'd bet he still worked hard when he came to the ranch. A gym might help him keep his powerful physique, but it couldn't account for the calluses on his hands. She liked knowing he didn't shirk from hard physical labor even though he had chosen an essentially mental profession.

Cole slipped off the log and sat down next to it, using it as a back rest. He pulled Brenna down next to him, putting his arm around her shoulder and absently caressing the skin on her arm. Brenna closed her eyes and savored the sounds and aromas around her. Still, yes. Serene, too. But hardly quiet. The chirp of birds and the more distant trill of insects filled the air. The aroma of cut alfalfa assailed her, poignantly reminding her of her dream to have a place of her very own.

"How could you leave all this?" Brenna whispered, hardly aware she had spoken aloud.

"I love this place," he answered. "But I'm not a rancher. I don't have the fierce determination to make it work that my dad has."

"Does he mind anymore?"

"What?"

"Your not choosing to be a rancher."

"Nope. We passed that hurdle years ago, thank God."

"You're lucky," Brenna said, thinking of all the times she and her father had disagreed.

"Sure am," he responded, pressing another kiss against her temple. "You know, when I was little, I wanted to be just like him. And every time I'd say so, he'd say, 'Well, what about being an astronaut or doctor or whatever.'"

Brenna gave him a sly look. "You two had no imagination. When I was five I wanted to be one of those guys who guide planes into the gates at the airport. I think I must have thought that was ultimate power, to be so small and yet make something as large as a plane go where you wanted it to go, simply by waving a light."

"I wanted to be a policeman when I was five," Cole responded. "My idea of power was going down the road as fast as I wanted with a siren blaring."

The ringing of a bell in the distance startled the heron into flight with a rush of powerful wings.

Cole stood, pulling Brenna with him, a wide smile on his face. "Mom and Dad are back."

Chapter 16

Cole's parents, introduced to Brenna simply as Norah and Jack, were as charming as his grandmother. Brenna liked them immediately, and she was drawn into the preparation of the evening meal as though she had been a family member of long standing. There were no what-do-you-do and where-did-you-grow-up questions, which made Brenna wonder what Cole had told them about her, if anything.

Rather than being sent to the living room like a guest, her participation was assumed, and she liked it that way. Finding plates and silverware, she set the table. The overflow of conversation between Grandmom and Norah included her, mostly centering on the mundane tasks of meal preparation, but silliness, too, when Cole popped in and out of the kitchen with a boyish attitude Brenna found endearing.

Brenna envied Cole his family. With no difficulty, she could count the number of times her mother had hugged her—that kind of touch had rarely happened within her family. Norah's obvious enjoyment in having her son home manifested itself in the casual touches she gave him. They seemed to be her way of reassuring herself that Cole was in her kitchen.

Jack took pleasure in Cole's achievements without any comparison to his brother or sister and without any apparent judgment over his recent decision to leave a large law firm and strike out on his own. If there had been strong disagreements between father and son, there was no evidence of it now.

After dinner they sat on the porch and watched the moon rise over the bluff. Grandmom sat with a red-and-white enamel colander in her lap and a paper sack full of freshly picked green beans, which she snapped into pieces as they talked. Cole's mother crocheted granny squares for an afghan for her daughter.

Cole and Jack wandered toward the barn to check on minor repairs for a harvester. Brenna watched them talk, and knew the relationship evident between parent and son was the kind she'd like to have with her own children one day. One without the upper hand the Colonel always seemed to hold.

She picked a handful of beans out of the sack, pulled the string off the seam like she had been shown when she was a small girl, and snapped them.

"I haven't done this in years," she confessed. "I guess it's something you never forget. I saw the garden through the kitchen window this afternoon. It was about the only place Cole didn't show me."

Grandmom chuckled. "Cole steers away from there. He might get invited to do a little weeding."

Brenna smiled back. "Never my favorite either, but to be able to eat peas or a carrot fresh out of the garden..." Her voice trailed away as she remembered the times she had spent in her grandmother's garden.

"If you're implying you'll help with weeding," Norah said with a laugh, "you'd better watch yourself. Mom'll take you up on the offer."

"I like peas eaten in the garden," Brenna said, meeting Grandmom's eyes. "Hulled directly from the vine."

"You can have as many as you want," she said.

"Then it sounds like we have a deal."

She and Grandmom finished snapping all the beans before Cole and his father ambled out of the barn. Silhouetted against the evening sky, Brenna saw a resemblance she hadn't noticed before.

Brenna sighed, letting her gaze stray to the sky where the first stars were beginning to light the sky. The old childhood refrain of "I wish I may, I wish I might, on this first star I see tonight" played through her head. She remembered the night she and Cole had talked about sitting on the porch and enjoying an old-fashioned evening with family. Tonight was just as they had spoken, and it was perfect. Crisp evening air, the hum of crickets and the occasional deeper croak of a frog. If she had a wish this very moment it would be for more nights like this one—shared with Cole and with his family.

Her conscience pricked her, reminding her of promises she had made and not kept, of the convenient lies of omission. Some people were lucky enough to skate through life without seeming to pay for their sins. Hers always caught up with her. No matter how much she hoped she could learn to read before confessing her illiteracy to Cole, deep in her heart she knew she wouldn't get away with it.

Wishing on a star wouldn't save her, and it certainly wouldn't guarantee she'd have more nights like this one. No matter how much she wanted it.

From the barn, Cole watched Brenna, pleased that he had brought her here, even more pleased that she fit in with his family so well.

Brenna was more relaxed than Cole had ever seen her. He had expected she'd be nervous and shy and around his family, but if anything, she was less reserved around them than she was around him.

The image in front of him blurred into another one that he saw just as clearly: Brenna sitting on the porch swing with his mother, her body ripe with his child. Brenna, her arms outstretched, encouraging a little girl with chubby toddler legs to walk toward her, her eyes alight with the laughter he had just heard.

"That seems like a real fine girl," Jack said, breaking Cole's reverie.

"Yeah," Cole agreed.

"First girl you brought back here since that Susan person."

"Yeah." A month ago Cole probably would have still bristled at his ex-fiancée being referred to as "that Susan person." That he no longer even cared what his family had thought of her told him how far he had come. Susan had accused him of being a farm boy at heart. He guessed she was right.

"Mean something special?"

Cole hadn't tried to keep his feelings for Brenna a secret, but he hadn't realized he was quite so transparent, either. Not until he had caught his grandmother's knowing wink during dinner. "I'm hoping."

Jack laughed. "Skittish, is she?"

"Big time."

Jack cupped his hand around the back of Cole's neck. "It may take a bit more work than just hoping."

It was Cole's turn to laugh. "Yeah. But when the lady is skittish, you just have to take it slow."

"And sometimes you just have to get her used to being close. Don't be going too slow, son. Your mother is counting on some more grandchildren." He let go of Cole. "But don't you be tellin' her I said so."

Cole laughed and followed his dad through the gate in front of the house and up the walk to the porch. Taking in the pile of stems next to Brenna's feet, he said, "It's good to see you're earning your keep."

Brenna flashed him a smile. "I'm working on getting into your grandmother's good graces so I'm on her pie list."

Cole sat down next to Brenna and leaned across her knees. He looked up at Grandmom, giving her a beseeching smile. "You wouldn't give her my piece of pie—the one you saved for me? Would you?"

"Depends. She's offered to weed the garden."

"Weed?" Cole placed his palm on Brenna's forehead. "I think she spent too much time in the sun this afternoon. Nobody would agree to weed when they could go fishing."

Norah stood up. "I think we've all heard that one before. Brenna, you're all set with your room, aren't you?" When Brenna nodded, she added, "Is there anything else I can get for you?"

"No. Thanks. Everything has been wonderful."

"Well, I'm going to call it a day. 'Night."

A chorus of "good-nights" followed her through the door.

"Me, too," Jack said. He paused at the porch step and took one of Brenna's hands in both of his. "I'm real happy to have you in our home."

Brenna met his eyes, which were as warm as his work-hardened hands. She almost thought she heard the word *family* instead of *home*. "Thank you."

Grandmom stood and followed him into the house. She paused just inside the screen door. "There are *two* pieces of pie."

"I knew it." Cole pulled Brenna to her feet. He smacked his lips. "Grandmom's pie at bedtime. Almost the best thing in the world."

At the age of ten, he had been sure nothing would surpass apple pie at bedtime. Now that he was thirty something, he could think of a number of things. At the top of the list was having Brenna James pressed close to him with nothing but heat separating them.

His body responded to his sensual promise to himself, and with effort he channeled his thoughts back to the companionable conversation between Brenna and Grandmom.

They dished up the pie and two large glasses of milk. Grandmom sat down with them. The conversation gradually turned to matters dealing with the ranch, and Brenna excused herself. Cole squeezed her hand as she left the kitchen, but continued to give Grandmom his attention. Worry was in her voice, and though Brenna would have preferred his company, she didn't begrudge his choosing to spend the time with his grandmother.

After she showered, she sat for a long time in the dark, looking out the window, listening to the companionable sound of crickets chirping, watching the moon and bright stars. She finally lay down and drifted off to sleep, more content and at peace with herself than she remembered being in a long time. She woke to the sound of something pattering against the screen.

A clandestine sound, full of invitation. She got out of bed and looked out. Cole stood in the yard, his silhouette looking unnaturally large in the moonlight. She smiled and waved at him.

He put his fingers to his lips, and motioned for her to join him. She nodded, and quickly dressed.

A few robins called, and the sky was black except for a strip of gray at the horizon. When she stepped outside a few minutes later, the scent of dew permeated the air.

"Good morning," Cole whispered, drawing her into his arms and giving her a thorough kiss. "Ready to go see my pond at sunrise?"

"Yes."

"I don't just want to watch the sun come up," he said. The need in his eyes made it impossible to misunderstand what he meant, especially after he added, "I intend to make love with you."

"I know," she said, heat flowing suddenly through her.

"Ah, Brenna," he said, giving her another kiss. "If you only knew how long I've waited for this."

He picked up a folded plaid blanket from the picnic table near the back door and led her out of the yard.

The path to the pond was illuminated by the setting moon. The water was mirror-smooth, reflecting the pale predawn sky. Near the fallen log where she and Cole had sat on the previous afternoon, he spread out the blanket. Sitting down, he took off his sneakers, and Brenna followed suit. They stretched out, and by unspoken mutual consent didn't touch each other. Cole rested his chin on folded hands. The lonely call of an owl echoed across the pond.

As the sky became lighter, Brenna's senses heightened. Coupled with her anticipation was her awareness of the pond and its inhabitants. The secret sounds of night became her own, and its peace became hers as well. With the soft flutter of huge wings, the blue heron settled on the shallow end of the pond, silhouetted against the pale gray-gold sky.

In the distance a rooster crowed, and Brenna's attention shifted from the pond to the horizon. It wasn't going to be a spectacular sunrise, because not a single cloud filled the sky—just the promise of another hot sunny day.

"Herons are the most magnificent birds," Cole whispered.

The big bird gracefully waded into the pond.

"I wonder where his mate is?" Brenna asked.

"She's probably sitting on a nest somewhere."

Cole brushed a kiss at her forehead, then trailed his lips down the side of her face. "I'm glad I'm here with you." He kissed her lightly and drew back just far enough to look in her eyes. They were smoky. He waited, as if he knew she wanted to kiss him just as much as he wanted her to.

He brushed his hand down her hair. "Do you know this is where I'd planned to seduce you?"

"Did you?" Her voice was no more than a whisper.

His fingers slid to her nape. "That's why I brought you here, fair lady. To the ranch. To the pond. So you could see who I was."

"A farm boy?"

After a second's hesitation, he nodded. "I used to hate thinking so."

"And now?"

His mouth hovered closer. "And now...I want to make love to you the way I've been dreaming since the first time I saw you."

"At the bar?" Her lips touched his cheek.

"At my office. The day you came to give your deposition." He drew back just enough to sear her face with a warm, intimate glance. "The most unlawyerly thoughts I've ever had."

"If anyone had ever told me then I'd been here with you now. Like this. And liking it—"

"You like it?" His lips trailed from her chin up the line of her jaw to the soft shell of her ear.

"I...love it."

She lifted her face the scant inch to touch his lips with her own, her excitement growing. Alone. They were alone at last. Fulfilling a fantasy she hadn't known he'd had. Just the two of them and a golden sunrise.

She held perfectly still and closed her eyes, content for this instant to feel the soft caress of his lips touching hers. Wrapping her arms around his neck, she turned slightly and brought herself more closely within his embrace. He sighed, and she parted her lips, wanting the sweet invasion of his mouth.

Cole rolled on his back, pulling Brenna astride with her legs on either side of him. He pulled her head down, giving her the deep kiss she wanted as he pulled her soft cotton knit shirt out of the waistband of her jeans and slid his palms up her back. He already knew she was braless, but the confirmation under his hard palm spanning her back sent heat surging through his veins and pooling hotly at his groin.

"Ah, Brenna," he murmured pressing kisses over her cheeks, her jaw, her eyes, before returning to her mouth. "We've finally made it, haven't we?"

She brought her palms on either side of his face and lifted her own far enough away to meet his eyes. "I want you," she whispered. "I'm beginning to think I've wanted you forever."

Her confession made loving her an urgent thing that could wait no longer. He lifted his head to capture her mouth in a long kiss. He skimmed his hands down her back, then up her sides, lingering at the swell of her breasts. They curved fully from her sides, skin silkier yet than any he had touched. The urge to look at her became even stronger than his desire to touch her, and he pulled her arms through her shirtsleeves, breaking the kiss only long enough to pull the shirt over her head.

He kissed her again, cherishing her mouth the way he imagined cherishing her body. He pulled back far enough to look at her, and his breath caught. Full. Round. Lovely. Ivory skin and tightly puckered, deep rose nipples.

"Oh, Brenna," he whispered, his eyes meeting hers.

Bathed within his silent approval, Brenna shivered, not from the almost cool morning air, but from the invisible tightening of her body. When his warm hands cupped her, she shivered again. "I've dreamed so long of being alone with you just like this."

He raised his head until his mouth touched hers, his fingers gently kneading the flesh of her full breasts, his thumbs at last lightly grazing across her nipples. Brenna's breath hitched. Her glance dropped to his hands touching her, his skin dark against hers. He teased the nipples again, loving the sounds she made, loving the way she pressed her pelvis against him, loving the way her feminine body looked beneath his hands.

She pulled his open shirt out of his waistband, and flowed back into his arms. The touch of his chest against her was wonderful, and she wound her fingers through his hair. The heaven of skin touching skin, unbroken from their mouths to their jeans soon became another form of torture. Cole shifted, rolling her to her side, cupping her derriere and pulling her against him.

He couldn't resist teasing her. He hooked a finger under her waistband behind the zipper. "Want to wait another couple of days?"

Boldly, she cupped his sex, hidden by his jeans, thrusting into her hand. Brenna trembled, savoring his blatant need. She traced a finger down the center of his chest, opened her eyes and smiled sweetly. "I can stand it if you can."

His answer was a groan as he ground himself into her teasing palm. His lips sought the valley between her breasts, and he nuzzled her velvet skin, lost in the sensation of her soft breast at his cheek. He traced a path with his tongue to the tip of her breast.

"Beautiful, so beautiful," he murmured the instant before pulling her breast gently into his mouth, just as the first rays of the sun burst from the horizon.

The sudden light streaming across them was no more intense than Brenna's response to his touch. Warmth shattered through her, pulsing, surging ever downward. Over and over she pressed her lips across his sunlit head in soft kisses. His gentle tonguing of her breast changed to more insistent sucking, and the ache inside Brenna intensified again. He nuzzled her other breast and gave it the same complete loving. She fumbled at his zipper. She wanted him naked. Now. Even so, her fingers trembled at the snap of his jeans.

Cole reluctantly left her breast, on fire from her artless response to him. He wanted to help her with the fastening to his jeans but he loved watching her free him from the denim. The snap popped open, and she sighed as she lowered the zipper. Impatiently she shoved his jeans and shorts over his hips. Her hands lightly tracing down his thighs and dancing across his stomach were absolutely the most erotic thing he had ever seen or felt.

A single drop from him appeared and glistened in the sunlight, which she caught with her fingertip and smoothed over his velvet skin, making him shimmer like polished amber. The achingly light pressure of her cool fingers against his hot skin caused him to jerk, then press himself more urgently into her hand, silently telling her he loved her touch. Cole tore his gaze away from her loving ministrations and unfastened her jeans. He lifted her hips away from the blanket and pulled her jeans over her bare feet, then finished kicking off his own.

Her body was dappled in sunlight and shade, but the most beautiful shadow fell at the apex of her thighs. She parted her legs for his hand. Trembling beneath the onslaught of sensation, she ached for his intimate caress. When his fingers at last reached their destination, she whispered, "Yes...oh, Cole...yes."

He wrapped her inside his arms, capturing her mouth in a kiss, wholly exploring it with the promise of completion. Brenna slid her hands up his back, absorbed in all his textures. The sleekness of his hair. The warmth of his body covering hers. The incredible sensation of his hair-roughened skin teasing each of her nerve endings into wonderfully alive pleasure points. Her breasts flattened into his chest, but she wanted even closer.

He kissed her, cherishing her lips as he cherished the vestibule of her womanhood, seeking the depths of her mouth as he sought the depths of her body.

"Please," she whispered.

"Please, what?" Cole's eyes reflected the same deep need that his loving hands called forth from her.

She had never wanted anything as much as she wanted to be one with him. She licked her lips and feathered her hands down his back. "Please love me. Now."

Cole rolled away from her, and for a split second Brenna was terrified he'd leave her in this aching vulnerability. When she saw the flat foil wrapped package he had pulled from the pocket of his jeans, she held out her hand.

"Let me." She took the package from him, opened it, and lovingly fitted its contents to his hard length. She smiled at him, urging him closer for what she suspected would be her last lucid thought. "Thank you," she whispered.

Her extra attention to make him feel desirable at the moment of sheathing was as brand-new as the day. He caught her mouth in a deep kiss, his fingers gently urging the bud of her femininity to again throb for him. She sighed into his mouth and her hands urged him closer, yet closer still. An initial tiny tightening of her flesh when he touched her told him she hadn't been this close to any man in a long, long time. It shouldn't have mattered, but the knowledge pleased him, excited him.

Brenna's soft exclamation was lost under his purring groan as he held both of them perfectly still, caught in an endless moment of exquisite beauty. Cole opened his eyes and gazed down at her, her face bathed in clear sunlight, her lips swollen from his kisses, her eyes dark with passion. For him.

She smiled and raised her hand to caress his cheek. He turned his head just enough to press a kiss into her palm.

Their eyes locked, he began to move, and she met him in a sensuous counter-dance. Their tempo increased and Brenna felt the first waves of her release begin to pulse from her depths. This had never happened within a man's embrace, nor with this kind of intensity.

She wanted to open herself even wider to Cole's loving invasion of her body, in awe that it was possible for one person to give this much pleasure to another. Her eyes held fast with his, and she could not have looked away if she had wanted to. Nothing was as important as Cole moving within her, the only reality the surging rhythms of ecstasy bubbling from her core. One by one they burst through, each shattering with its completeness, each more intense than the previous one. The cry on her lips was Cole's name, the man she held passionately with her gaze and her body was Cole.

The surging sweetness of Brenna pulsing around him was an irresistible lure to him, pulling him more deeply within her velvet softness. Cole abandoned himself to the timeless rhythms of her body. Beautiful. Brenna. Beloved. His climax burst through him, as dazzling as sunlight sparkling in a profusion of diamond lights over a blue pond.

Chapter 17

Brenna snuggled closer to Cole, her satisfaction complete. He held her securely within the crook of his arm, his breathing so even she assumed he was asleep. She raised her eyes to the firm outline of his jaw, then propped herself up on one elbow to study him more closely. She found his eyes wide open and as bright as the morning. His expression reflected a satisfaction as great as her own.

"Your loving is the most wonderful gift I've ever had," he said, tracing a finger down the side of her face and neck, then following the contours of her collarbone.

His statement both pleased and shocked her, answering her unspoken question. She knew how heart-shattering it had been for her. That he might have found it equally moving...

"Yours, too. I've never..." Her voice faded as the words she sought escaped her.

He grinned, lifted his head to kiss her temple, and pressed her head back against his chest. "You've never?"

She didn't know how to tell him that his touch made her fantasies pale beneath reality. His confession demanded she be equally forthright. "You're the most wonderful thing that ever happened to me."

Cole smoothed his hand over her hair. "I'm glad." He slanted her a teasing glance. "Maybe it's the place."

She tilted her head against his arm and smiled at him. "Think so?"

He caressed her with the flat surface of his hand from neck to waist, his fingers returning to curl around her breast, his palm accepting its weight. "We'll have to do some research to find out for sure."

"What kind of research?" Brenna began her own exploration within the swirls of hair covering his chest.

Cole rolled her off his shoulder and touched her nipple with his tongue, making it glisten, then softly blew on it until it puckered into a hard knot. "We'll probably have to try making love again right here, just to see if the results are the same."

Brenna's breath caught in her throat as little separate shocks flickered to her core that had been wholly satisfied the moment before. "And if it is?"

He smiled. "Then we'll have to expand the scope of our study. Try a motel on the way home."

She arched into him, offering him her other breast. "And then?"

He took the offering of her silken skin, sucking deeply until the nipple on his tongue was as hard as its twin. Her question was forgotten, and the only thing that remained was to warm himself within the sunlight that was Brenna. His caresses became more urgent as his body responded to the memory of her sensual heat. Though he would have denied its possibility an hour before, he wanted her more now than he ever had.

"Brenna?" His voice was hoarse with the need that tightened his body.

She understood the question behind his ragged breathing. Her eyes rose to his, her expression full of wonder. "I didn't expect to want you again." Her hands traveled down his body. "Like this." She stroked the inside of his thighs. "So soon."

"Kiss me, Brenna," he commanded softly, rolling her onto her back. "Open your sweet mouth, and kiss me."

His words inflamed her, and in that moment she would have died rather than deny his sensuous request. She pulled his head down, her open mouth inviting his exploration. All thought fled, and her skin became a shimmering surface aching for his touch.

She pulled him close, needing him with an intensity that was almost frightening. Scooping her into his arms, he spread her legs with his knees, then held himself rigid, not...quite...touching her. She met his gaze, aching for him in a way she hadn't thought possible. His pupils grew very black, and he lowered his body the fractional inch required to complete contact. It felt good. So good.

He groaned, then sheathed himself within her, easing the awful ache. Almost at once, they both began to move, the rhythm escalating.

His rhythm broke for a fraction of a heartbeat as he brought Brenna more deeply within his arms. This is what she'd been dreaming of and hadn't known it. This is what she'd needed her whole life and hadn't known it. She wrapped her arms around him, fiercely, as though he might be wrenched from her embrace. She'd die if that happened.

Icy fear rose to the surface, and her conscience rose for one last stab at her. *How could you do this to him?*

As if sensing she wasn't quite with him, he captured her mouth, an invasion of heat, sweetness, and unbearable pleasure that banished conscious thought and brought her right back with him. He held on to her even more tightly. She gloried in the fierce pressure of Cole's embrace and wrapped her legs around his, pulling him even closer. Each thrust brought her piercing pleasure until she wanted to be lost forever within the sensual tide of ecstasy that was Cole.

The top of their wanton climb thundered over them. Cole collapsed on top of Brenna, too exhausted for the moment to do anything except gasp for deep clearing breaths. Brenna's breathing was no less labored, but she made no move to ease herself from beneath his body.

He smoothed her love-dampened hair away from her face and pressed his lips all over her face in soft caresses. She smiled, and Cole wanted to see that particular smile again and again for the rest of his life.

Cole didn't want to move. Never had making love felt this good. Not the first time, or even the second, when he knew how good it would feel. Not ever. Briefly, he wondered what it was. A difference in physiology? Maybe. But he'd made love with enough different women without it ever remotely feeling like this to doubt it. Or was it as simple as being in love with her? If so, he'd never been in love with Susan.

He finally raised himself on his elbows to look at Brenna. Her skin glowed. Her dark hair caught the sunshine, radiating color he hadn't noticed before, gold and red and coppery glints. She opened her eyes and his breath caught. Her normally clear eyes were smoky, serene. She smiled and reached to trace the outline of his brow with her fingers.

He turned his face and kissed her hand, wanting to tell her he loved her. Remembering the way she'd run every time he pushed her, he remained silent.

Making the deliberate choice to lighten the intensity of the moment, he grinned. "So much for the first part of our research."

"I forgot what you said the second part was supposed to be." She rested her fingers lightly against the pulse beating at the base of his neck.

He planted a hard kiss on her mouth. "Make love in a new location." He stood up and offered his hand, then led her toward the water.

"In the pond?" Her tone was dubious.

"Nope. This is simple skinny-dipping with a boy from Nebraska." The look he gave her was as fun-filled as his voice. "Ever been skinny-dipping with a boy from Nebraska, Brenna?"

"No."

"Good." He led her across sun-warmed stones that jutted into the pond. "Then this is a first." He released her hand and made a shallow dive into the water and surfaced a moment later with a shout of exhilaration. His invitation was irresistible, and Brenna followed him into the water. It was a cool counterpoint to her flushed body, and instead of cooling her desire, offered her sensitive body a whole new plane of sensuous delights that kept her intensely aware of her sexuality.

She and Cole frolicked in the water like a couple of kids, though she had never felt less like a child. When Cole held her in his arms a few minutes later, he was clearly as aroused as she, but he made no move to deepen their embrace from love play into something more.

They climbed out of the water and lay back down on the blanket, simply holding hands and letting their bodies dry in the warm sun. Brenna angled her face toward the sun, and a smile of contentment spread over her face. If a genie had appeared, she knew exactly what she would ask for. To let this moment extend for the rest of her life. Her conscience made a feeble struggle to be heard, but she firmly banished it. There would be time to listen later. Just not now.

They arrived back at the house an hour later, ravenous and teasing each other about the exercise that led to that state of hunger. Brenna almost hoped the hour would be late and everyone would be off with the many tasks of running the ranch. She wasn't ready to face anyone, just yet. However, Grandmom, Norah, and Jack were just sitting down to breakfast as they came through the door.

"Beautiful morning, isn't it," Cole announced, giving both his mother and grandmother a kiss before sitting down between them. "I'd forgotten how great being up in time to see the sunrise is."

"Did you enjoy it, too?" Norah asked.

"I loved it," Brenna answered, accepting the serving dishes to bacon, eggs, and raisin toast, helping herself, and passing them one by one to Jack.

"Still want to go out and check that fence along the east ridge?" Cole asked his dad.

"The help would be great, but I figured you'd want to show Brenna around."

"Don't worry about me," she said, catching Grandmom's glance. "I have a date with a hoe."

"I was teasing—" Grandmom said.

"I know," Brenna interrupted. "But I wasn't. It's a gorgeous garden, and I want to know your secrets for getting it to grow like that."

"Wrong," Cole teased. "She wants that last piece of pie we didn't eat last night."

Brenna met his eyes across the table. Accepting his light banter in the presence of the amused attention of his family was easier than she had thought it would be. "Well..."

Cole mockingly shook his finger at Grandmom. "If she eats my piece of pie while Dad and I are out—"

"I'll just have to make another one, won't I?" Grandmom finished.

"I'm sort of in favor of a chocolate cake," Jack said.

Cole flashed his dad a dirty look that was returned in kind until they both laughed. "Okay. If that's what Dad wants, I guess I can stand it." He glanced back at Brenna, his eyes full of sensual promise. "Just expect retribution if you eat my pie. On second thought, I probably should stick around to keep an eye on it."

"Probably." Brenna knew just what kind of punishment he had in mind, and she couldn't wait. She was tempted to tell him he would just have to take the shirt off her back, but the only answer she gave him in front of his parents and grandmother was a silky smile that he answered with a wink.

"Good idea, son," Jack said. "Might as well help with the weeding. We can check the fence later."

Brenna and Cole followed Grandmom outside after breakfast, where she donned an old-fashioned calico bonnet with a wide brim that shaded her face. Brenna stared at her, again caught in memories of following Nonna down a long row of green beans. The calico bonnet was a reminder of times gone by. Times more leisurely than the hectic pace that filled Brenna's days.

She and Cole and Grandmom moved down the rows of vegetables, making short work of the few weeds that dared make an appearance in the well-tended garden. Cole shared his childhood memories, surprising Brenna when he was able to coax a few from her.

Her best memories were from her grandparents' farm, and at one time she had thought she'd never recall them without feeling a profound sense of melancholy. Today she remembered happier times. Riding in a wheelbarrow with her grandfather pushing. Collecting worms so they could go fishing. Counting snails in the bottom of the brook.

For the first time in years she also remembered good times with her parents. Learning to swim in the ocean with her father in Hawaii. Playing softball with her mother and brother in West Germany. Watching an eclipse with her father. Sitting on his lap and listening to baseball games. Helping him water fledgling tomato plants.

Where had it all gone so wrong? She had no answers for that and found herself left with bittersweet memories. With effort she brought her attention back to Cole and Grandmom.

He was teasing her about the bright empty seed packages stapled to stakes at the end of each row. "Not a chance that you'll pick corn and think you have peas."

"Not me," Grandmom returned. "But mighty helpful for a young man who used to help me in the garden."

Cole straightened and looped his arms over his hoe. "You're not going to tell Brenna about the time I pulled up all the corn seedlings, are you?"

Brenna chuckled, easily imagining him doing just that.

"I wouldn't, but since you brought it up—"

"That was before I could read," Cole said to Brenna.

She caught his glance, wondered for a second if his simple statement had any hidden messages, but his eyes revealed nothing more than the pleasure of memories shared with his grandmother.

"And he couldn't tell the difference between corn plants and grass, either," Grandmom added.

Brenna laughed. As she came to the end of the row, she paused to look at the empty package. Most of the others she had recognized from the words alone. This one she didn't. She stared at the package, unable to identify the plants even by the picture, then recited the letters in her mind, unable to get them to form a word she knew. S-P-I-N-A-C-H. Brenna began hoeing around the plants.

"I do love fresh spinach," Grandmom said. "Though I never acquired a taste for eating it raw."

Brenna glanced again at the sign. "I love spinach salad." She glanced back at the small plants, which suddenly looked more familiar. "Cooked is good, too."

A few minutes later Grandmom left Brenna alone with Cole to finish up the weeding.

"She works too hard," Cole said when the back porch door closed behind her.

"I think it's what keeps her young." Brenna stopped at the end of the row of radishes.

"What keeps you young?" he teased. "Is that what you need to keep you young? A garden?"

Brenna smiled. "It wouldn't hurt. I'm not sure I'd be this neat, though. I always wanted one of those wild-looking English cottage gardens that look overgrown and lush and beautiful."

"Kind of tough to have in an apartment."

"Yeah."

"I have room for a garden like that," he said. "Maybe that's what my place needs."

Brenna looked up, squinting against the sunshine behind him. "With the way you *love* weeding, I don't think that's a good idea, Cole. You'd end up with a yard full of thistles."

He stepped across a row of lettuce and a row of beets, bent to her, lifting her face, and kissed her. Thoroughly. "I thought maybe you'd like to help me with a garden. Now that you're not working nights all the time, we'll have time to get you out to my house."

The implied promise made Brenna's breath hitch.

From the back porch, Grandmom called, "Lemonade, anyone?"

Cole's gaze swept over Brenna's face one last time before he stepped around her, answering his grandmother. "That's what I like about you, Grandmom. You always know just what I want."

Her answer was lost beneath another taunting onslaught from Brenna's conscience. Gardens and spending time at this house and this visit to his childhood home and making love with him. Each one of those had taken the relationship to a new level. It was all consummately alluring to her. She wanted this. Lord, how she wanted it.

"Brenna!" Cole held up his glass of lemonade. "I'm gonna check on my dad. Want to come?"

Her emotions in turmoil, she shook her head. "You go on ahead. I promised I'd finish this, and we're almost done."

"I'll be back in a bit." He waved and headed across the yard.

Grandmom came back down the steps with another glass of lemonade in her hands. "This one is for you."

Brenna laid her hoe down and stood up. Grandmom sat down on the bottom step, and Brenna joined her.

"This is a special, special place."

"Most young folks think a farm is a boring place. Cole's fiancée never thought much of it when he brought her here. She couldn't wait to leave."

Cole's fiancée.

Surprise held Brenna speechless.

She should have guessed he would have been engaged, maybe even more than once, maybe even married at some point. She frowned, trying to remember if he'd ever mentioned it. His only reference had been vague—a woman he had brought here a long time ago.

In as casual a tone as she could muster, Brenna asked, "When was that?"

Grandmom thought a moment. "A couple of years ago, I guess. Maybe even three. It was about the time he went to work for that big law firm of his." She glanced at Brenna. "Anyway, that young lady didn't like the ranch, and we all wondered what you'd be like when he told us he was bringing you home."

Reminded of the acceptance and sense of homecoming she'd felt last night, Brenna wondered if Cole's unmentioned fiancée had been given the same welcome. Brenna would bet Cole's parents trusted Cole's judgment enough to give anyone the warmth and hospitality they had given her. A flare of jealousy surprised her and made her intensely curious about the kind of woman Cole had asked to marry him.

Choosing more neutral ground, Brenna said, "What's not to like? Maybe a farm isn't for everyone, but some of my best memories come from my grandparents' farm in Pennsylvania."

Accepting the change in subject, Grandmom asked about the farm and soon had Brenna relating anecdotes about her visits there. They eventually got back to weeding, the conversation flowing comfortably between them. They finished just before lunchtime. Jack and Cole returned, and Norah, who had spent the morning in the office, helped prepare lunch. They ate on the front porch and made plans for the Fourth of July celebration on Friday.

Grandmom wanted to go into Scottsbluff to see the fireworks, and Cole said they absolutely had to have watermelon or the holiday would be canceled. After lunch Cole again disappeared with his father to finish the repair on the combine. Norah returned to the office. Brenna helped Grandmom wash and dry the dishes, enjoying the older woman's easy companionship.

"Did you make all the doilies I've seen on the furniture?" Brenna asked, putting the last of the glasses in the cupboard.

"Most of them. Norah made a few and one or two are from my mother."

"They're beautiful. Learning to crochet is something I've always wanted, but never taken the time to do."

"If you like the doilies in the living room, you'd love some that my husband's mother made. Tiniest little stitches you ever did see."

Brenna followed Grandmom to her bedroom where she opened a cedar trunk that was full of handmade linens, some dating back to the Civil War era. The stories Grandmom told about each piece were magic to Brenna. As she fingered the old quilts and coverlets, she felt a connection that transcended time.

"This is really beautiful," she said when Grandmom laid a white batiste christening gown across Brenna's lap. The aroma of the cedar chest and starch filled the air, which Brenna liked as much as she liked the texture of the fine stitches.

Their conversation gradually turned from the past to the present, and Brenna confessed that knots were all she had ever been able to make.

"It's not that hard." Grandmom pulled a skein of thick yarn out of a basket setting on the floor and sorted through a group of crochet hooks until she found the one she wanted. She demonstrated making a slip knot, then a chain, then the stitches required to make a granny square. The two of them laughed over Brenna's efforts.

"I don't know about this," she said skeptically, after producing a lopsided rectangle.

"You're doing fine," Grandmom said. "I've got an instruction book here someplace that has pretty good diagrams." She stood up and went to a bookshelf, leafing through a group of magazines until she found the one she wanted.

"I couldn't impose like that," Brenna said.

"Sure you can," Grandmom said. "The diagrams are easy. And you can borrow this as long as you want."

"Thank you," Brenna said, "but..."

Oh, God, not again, she thought. When had the deceptions gotten to be so difficult to carry off? When had the glib half-truths she had told for years suddenly begun to sound exactly like what they were—lies?

Grandmom sat back down next to Brenna. "There was once a young girl," she said. "Her mother died when she was twelve. And this girl had six younger brothers and sisters she had to care for. And she had a father who thought school was overrated, and certainly not something a girl needed. So, even before her mother died, she didn't have much schooling. Afterward, she quit. She read well enough to get by—barely. Like you, she left home when she was very young.''

''You?''

Grandmom nodded. ''Like you, she needed to read much better than she did to make her way in the world.''

Ice replaced the blood flowing through Brenna. ''How did you know?'' she whispered.

Chapter 18

Grandmom took both of Brenna's hands in hers. "I watched you, my dear."

"Oh, God," Brenna muttered.

"Cole doesn't know..."

Brenna shook her head, equally astounded and alarmed this woman had seen through the deceptions. Not only seen through them, but challenged her as well.

"How did the two of you meet?" Grandmom asked. "He never did say."

Brenna glanced away. Remembering his shock over her being a dropout, she wondered what he had told his family about her. Too easily she imagined the kind of woman Cole was probably accustomed to dating. Doctors and lawyers and MBA executives.

Brenna cleared her throat. "He was the attorney representing a man who sued me."

"Oh, my. You two certainly would have had some differences to overcome."

The surprise in Grandmom's voice made Brenna smile. "That's putting it mildly." She met the older woman's gaze. "I didn't intend to deceive him. I really didn't."

"That's often the case with lies of omission."

The statement might have been a sharp accusation or a reprimand at the least. Instead, it was merely a mild statement of fact, uttered without the slightest rancor. The lack of accusation made Brenna feel worse, compelling her to explain.

"At first, I thought we'd go out just once or twice, and that would be the end of it. I didn't expect to enjoy his company so much." She ducked her head, then looked up. "He makes me feel so good. And he listens to me, you know? Really listens like what I think matters."

Grandmom nodded as though she understood.

Brenna plunged on. "I kept getting in deeper, and my lies of omission...I know they're going to cause trouble. I just can't stand the idea of telling him anything that would..."

"Be the end of it," Grandmom finished, compassion in her voice.

"Yeah." Brenna swallowed the lump in her throat.

"You're right. He'll be angry," Grandmom mused. "Not so much about the reading, but about the deceit."

"I know." Her plan to delay telling him until she had mastered reading had at its core an unforgivable flaw—a deliberate lie.

Grandmom patted her hand. "I guess it all comes down to whether you trust him."

Brenna stared at Cole's grandmother. She hadn't thought of it in so stark a light. If she had been asked whether she trusted Cole, she would have said yes without hesitation. And yet, in this...did she trust him?

"Okay, where is everybody?" came Cole's baritone voice from the living room.

"Up here," Grandmom called back.

His footsteps thundered up the stairs, giving Brenna scant time to pull herself together. He appeared in the doorway. When Brenna caught his eye, he winked. She returned his smile, comparing this carefree, boyish side of his personality to the stern man she had first met. Both aspects of the man drew her.

Did she trust him to understand her illiteracy? More importantly, would he forgive her deceptions? Brenna wished the answer was either a simple yes or no. Nothing else in her attraction to Cole was simple, and this was no exception.

"Do you still need to go to the grocery store, Grandmom?" he asked.

"If you want that watermelon."

His smile broadened to a grin. "Oh, I thought I'd go steal that from McCracken's farm."

"And come back home with buckshot in your—"

"I'm sure you have me confused with someone else," he interrupted.

"I'm sure not," she retorted. "Though it was a relief when you decided to give up a life of crime in favor of the law."

Cole planted his hands on his hips. "Actually, I planned to graduate from stealing watermelons to robbing banks."

"In some circles, that might be a more highly rated career choice than being a lawyer," Brenna teased.

"You..." He pointed a finger at her. "You've obviously been spending too much time with my grandmother. We're going to have to do something about that."

She nodded. "Bringing her back to Denver might be good."

Grandmom chuckled. "Just what a young man needs in his bachelor pad. A meddling old woman."

"You're not old. I might even be able to fix you up with a date," Cole assured her.

"As though I need your help," she said tartly.

Cole laughed. "Give me ten minutes to shower. You're coming to the store with us, right, Brenna?"

She grinned. "Of course. After all that nonsense you told us at lunch about picking out the perfect watermelon, I wouldn't miss it."

A few minutes later Brenna piled into the pickup with Cole and Grandmom. Brenna's bare legs brushed next to Cole's denim-clad ones, and it was impossible for her not to remember her reaction to taking off his jeans hours earlier. Cole held her hand between changing gears and pointing out things he considered interesting.

"The real purpose of this outing," Cole announced in a tour-guide voice after they pulled onto the highway, "is to show our eminent world traveler, Miss Brenna James, the famous landmark Chimney Rock." He stopped talking, and after an instant of silence made a rolling motion with his free hand. Brenna and Grandmom looked at one another and, smiling, shrugged almost in unison. "You're supposed to ask me why it's a famous landmark," he prompted.

"Ah," was Grandmom's response.

Brenna grinned. "Okay, Mr. Tour Guide, I'll bite. Why is it famous?"

"I'm glad you asked that," Cole said. He pointed through the windshield where the tall outline of Chimney Rock jutted into the sky. "Every time I see it, I wonder what it must have been like, following a wagon train on the Oregon Trail, and waiting for this landmark to appear on the horizon."

"It's famous because you wonder about it?" Brenna teased.

Cole squeezed her knee, his hand lingering an all-too-brief moment on her thigh. "It's famous because it's the first significant landmark for the wagon trains after they left Independence."

"I think I knew that."

"She thinks she knew that," Cole echoed. He turned off the highway, then parked the pickup in front of one of the numerous markers found along the Oregon Trail route. "What a tour guide doesn't need is harassment." He cut the engine and stretched his arm along the seat back and pulled Brenna closer to him. "I suppose you're going to tell me that you've seen point-of-interest signs all over the world."

"As a matter of fact, I have," she agreed, as her mind urged her, taunted her. *Tell him. I dare you. Tell him that you couldn't read this sign if your life depended upon it.*

She looked at the sign, then at Grandmom, half expecting her to announce to Cole that she—Brenna—couldn't read.

"Some tour guide, refusing to read these signs for the poor foreign tourists who look at the words and see gibberish," Brenna said, her lips curved in a smile she didn't feel, easy casualness filling her voice. She glanced at him again. "The last time I was on vacation with my parents was in Europe. I remember very clearly that tour guides were responsible for all points of interest, not the tourists."

Cole grinned and gave Brenna a casual swipe over the top of her head. "You're asking for trouble, ma'am."

She poked him in the side with her elbow. "I wouldn't want to put you out of work, Mr. Tour Guide, sir."

He dropped a kiss on her cheek and put the truck back into gear. "This tour guide says, 'Onward, ho!' And, besides, I hated these things when I was a kid. I'm never going to make my kids suffer the way my parents made me suffer.''

Grandmom snorted. Cole burst into laughter, and Brenna joined in, shaking with relief.

Brenna was positive Cole would feel her trembling as he pulled the truck back onto the highway. She clasped her hands together and forced herself to participate in the easy banter between him and his grandmother.

She was the worst kind of coward, and she hated being one. Did she trust him? Not to pity her. Not to lose interest in her. Not to think she was stupid. Obviously not, or she would have told him by now.

She avoided Grandmom's gaze, dreading the censure she suspected she would see there, knowing she deserved it.

''Brenna, is there anything special you'd like for our Fourth of July feast?'' Grandmom asked.

Brenna faced Cole's grandmother and found exactly what her voice reflected. Concern. Friendship.

''No,'' Brenna said, then cleared the huskiness from her voice. ''Thank you.'' Disdain, censure, hostility. Those would have been easier to bear.

At the grocery store, Brenna found herself participating in his non-sensical method of determining which watermelons were the ripest, the sweetest. She even found herself agreeing that the best kind of watermelons were those stolen from some poor farmer's patch. Through it all, she wondered if, like Alice, she had fallen down a rabbit-hole to some strange, wonderful place. This man who played silly games with his grandmother could not be the same harsh lawyer she remembered from her first meeting with him.

''What's left on the list?'' Cole asked Grandmom, pushing the cart down the aisle, putting things not on the list into the basket. Peanuts. Pretzels. Oreo cookies.

''Important things,'' she responded, eyeing his additions. ''Flour. Milk.''

''Milk,'' Cole said, drawing Brenna close. ''You know I used to get up at four in the morning to milk the cow before I went to school. Now they buy it from the store. Can you believe it?''

''And you trudged through the snow to catch the bus, I bet.''

He shook his head solemnly. "This was before buses. I walked miles."

Brenna laughed. "You're quite well preserved for such an old—"

"Watch it," he warned. "If you say mean things, I may not invite you to my campfire."

"What campfire is this?" she asked.

"One down next to the lake. We can't roast marshmallows without a fire." He winked, and Brenna imagined that marshmallows weren't the only thing he planned to roast.

Brenna noticed he added staples to the basket that weren't on the list. And besides getting things he liked for himself, he casually added the kind of tobacco his dad used in his pipe, a bag of chocolate candies like the ones in a dish on his mother's desk, a bottle of peach-flavored seltzer Grandmom had mentioned she liked. At the checkout counter, he kept Grandmom so preoccupied that he had the groceries paid for before she was able to take the cash out of her wallet. This was a side of him Brenna hadn't imagined, a side she liked.

Since sunrise this morning, she had experienced the most fulfillment she had ever known, and she had seen the return of her oldest companion—fear of discovery.

All with people she'd like to know and love for the rest of her life, if that were her choice to make.

In her heart of hearts, she wished it was.

"There's something I have to tell you," Brenna said to Cole two days later, when they were about a hundred miles from Denver.

They each had been increasingly silent during the long drive. Each exit off the interstate represented a crossroads to her. At each one, her conscience mocked her deceit. She had to tell him and get it over with.

"My turn first," Cole said, clearing his throat. His glance left the highway for a moment as he met her gaze. "I haven't been honest or fair with you."

His statement echoed exactly what she had intended to say to him.

His gaze left the highway again, and he took her hand. "You and me... We have something good going, don't you think?"

Brenna nodded and ran her tongue over lips that felt dry, chapped. She didn't dare speculate about where this was going.

Cole's attention returned to the long, straight expanse of highway that stretched in front of them. "I let you believe that I quit from Jones, Markham and Simmons." He cleared his throat. "It didn't happen quite like that. I was given a choice between resigning or being fired."

She didn't know what she had been expecting him to say. This wasn't it. Clearly, she remembered he had told her he left the firm shortly after her case was finished. "Because of me?"

"The situation with you and Harvey Bates was the final straw on a very large pile." Cole gave her hand a reassuring squeeze. "One of the first things you learn after getting out of law school is how to build cases on what you want to present, how to control your own agenda, how to get a judge and jury to see what you want them to see. When you're part of a big firm, you learn how to use the system to acquire cases that are good for the firm. Financially. Prestige-wise."

"Harvey Bates was prestigious?" Brenna asked, confused.

"Hell, no. If a case has prestige, the partners handle it. But clients like Bates are the bread and butter of a firm. He spends several thousand dollars with the firm every year. That's what associates are for. To take the dregs the partners don't want to handle, or don't have time to handle."

"Harvey Bates."

Cole nodded. "Among others." He glanced back at her. "I've been thinking about this a lot. I told Zach MacKenzie the other day that I'd tolerate nothing less than the whole truth. And then I didn't have the guts to give you what I demanded of others." A wry smile lifted the corner of his mouth. "Not exactly a high point for me. That's the first thing."

"There's more?" *The whole truth.* The words echoed in her mind, and her heart sank.

"Have you ever been seriously involved with someone? To the point of thinking about marriage?"

Again, he completely surprised her. She hadn't anticipated the question, and she answered honestly, "Once. I was—"

Cole pressed a finger against her mouth. "I'm not asking you to tell me about it, fair lady." A brief smile slashed across his face.

"Unless this guy is still around. In which case I'll be forced to challenge him to a duel at sunrise."

Brenna shook her head, smiling at the image he so easily painted in her head.

"Good. What's in the past for you is none of my business." His hand lifted again, and he caressed her cheek with the back of his fingers. "I was, too. Once. Serious, as in engaged."

Oh, God. She didn't want to know about his past. She didn't want to know they had gotten this serious. The skeletons rattling in his closet were benign in comparison to the monsters in hers. Through dry lips, she said, "The Susan person."

Cole chuckled. "I should have guessed Grandmom would have told you."

"How did you know?"

"That's how Grandmom always refers to her. They didn't get along."

"You don't have to tell me about her."

"I want to."

"I don't—"

"I want you to know, Brenna. This has been eating at me for days, and I want to get it behind me." He gave her a quick glance. "I met her just after I passed the bar. She was working for a Big Eight firm."

"Big Eight?"

"One of the largest CPA firms in the country. She's a CPA, very bright, very ambitious. We had lots of interests in common. Or so I thought at the time. We planned to have it all. Vacations in Aspen and Hawaii, Christmases in Acapulco. She accepted a position in Chicago, and I planned to go with her. We even rented a great apartment—a penthouse in an elegant old building that had been renovated."

Brenna schooled her expression into one of polite interest as his words ate away at her. His voice held the reminiscence of fond memories. Though the lifestyle Cole described wasn't one she had ever wanted, she hated the dreams he had built with someone else, hated knowing those dreams made her jealous.

"I had quit my job, put my house up for sale, and she had already moved."

"What happened?"

"I got an offer on my house—for the price I was asking. And I couldn't sign the papers. Susan told me I'd never stopped being a farm boy."

"I'm sorry," Brenna said.

"I'm not." Cole's big hands flexed over the top of the steering wheel before he let his fingers loosely curl around it again. "I was then, but I'm not anymore." He glanced at Brenna. "I resented the hell out of her accusations. I'm an attorney, and I like being one. But the ranch is just as much a part of who I am. You know?"

"I know," Brenna agreed softly. "But that's part of you, too, isn't it? Vacations in exotic locales and—"

"At the time, I wanted it."

"And now?" She was torturing herself for asking, but she had to know.

"I like working in a city. I discovered what made me happiest, though, was to live in the country. Penthouse apartments, hell, they're fine." He gave Brenna a quick look, a genuine wide smile filling his face. "I just couldn't figure out where to keep a Shop-Vac and a radial-arm saw in one."

"No place for your toys, huh?" she teased, the ache in her heart easing at his confession.

"Tools, fair lady, not toys." He clasped her hand within his again. "Now. Your turn. Michael told me your dad is coming for a visit. Is that what's bothering you?"

"Some." *Tell him.* This was a time for confessions. He had given her an opening. A big one. Her throat squeezed closed against the words that would drive him from her life.

Cole squeezed her hand. "You can come stay with me if you want."

"That's a tempting offer. Only, I promised myself I wouldn't run away—" Sudden realization choked her voice. She had promised herself she wouldn't run away from her father anymore. Yet she was running away from the inevitable with Cole.

"Hell of a thing, dads are sometimes," Cole said. "And there isn't anything wrong with running, sometimes. Listening to you and Zach MacKenzie made me realize how lucky I am. Zach's father told him he deserved what's happened to him."

"And Zach believes him?"

"Damned if I know. Probably. Zach checked himself into a treatment hospital last week."

Brenna heard a tinge of anger creep into Cole's voice. "That makes you mad?"

"The timing is lousy. The hell of it is that I admire what he's done. It takes guts to admit you've got a problem, then deal with it. In some ways he reminds me of you."

"Another person in an impossible mess, huh?" She let go of Cole's hand and wrapped both of hers around herself, chilled to the bone, knowing she had to give up the deceptions, unable to say the words aloud.

Cole shook his head. "A person who faces things head-on when the going gets tough. I'm not sure I'd have the courage to choose the path he's taken."

"He's a nice guy," Brenna said. "I hope things work out for him." *Tell him, you coward. Just tell him.*

"He's done his part," Cole said. "All I have to do is mine. Which reminds me. Did the guy who owns Score talk to you about filing for unemployment?"

The balance of the drive into Denver focused increasingly on the matters at hand for the upcoming week. Brenna's search for a new job and filing for unemployment. Cole's schedule, which included a couple of court appearances. Moments before they arrived back at Michael and Jane's apartment, Cole offered again to have Brenna come stay with him while her father visited.

She wanted to accept. Doing so would be the coward's way out. And sooner or later, she was determined to stop being a coward.

Chapter 19

"Dad arrived night before last," Michael told Brenna at breakfast the following morning. His announcement was a reality check that instantly faded the rosy images left from her trip with Cole.

She set down her cup on the counter with such force that hot coffee sloshed over the rim. She glanced around the kitchen as if she expected her father to materialize. "I didn't think he was coming until next week."

"He sure surprised the hell out of us," Michael said with a rueful smile. "Told me it was your idea that he spend the Fourth with us."

"How nice," she said, sure of no such thing. Grabbing a clean dishcloth from the drawer, she wiped up the coffee off the counter.

"Of course, he managed to get business in, too," Michael added. "He was here in Denver until last night. We took him down to the Springs, and he'll be back late tomorrow or maybe the day after." Michael shook his head, a look of disgust marring his features.

"What aren't you telling me?"

"He says he wants to spend time with us. Then, over the weekend when we have time off, he's busy with other things." A trace of irritation filled Michael's voice. "He says he wants to spend time with Teddy, then invites Jane and me to the Denver Country Club for dinner and says he'll pay for a sitter."

To Brenna, that sounded exactly like the Colonel. Appearances were everything. Children were to be seen and not heard, and she knew from personal experience that it was better to not even be seen. She decided if she was lucky—very lucky—she might be able to avoid seeing her father altogether. She had unpleasant memories of every visit she had with him over the last ten years. She felt a pang of guilt, knowing that she had been so concerned with her own troubles, she had ignored the fact that things had probably been no better for her brother.

"I'm sorry, Michael."

"Me, too," he returned, his frown easing. "I just keep hoping he'll change. After he retired, I thought things might be different."

"What's that old saying about a leopard and its spots?"

"A rose by any other name," he said.

"Still stinks," Brenna finished.

Michael laughed. "That's a very disrespectful tone, miss."

"*Sir* to you, young man." Brenna sat down at the table next to him. "Seriously, I am sorry you had a rough weekend. I'm not sorry I missed it, but—"

"You're willing to make it up?" Michael asked, a glint in his eye.

"Uh...no. Not even for a very large bribe, which I could use."

"I'm too poor to bribe you. You're the rich one."

"Uh-huh," Brenna agreed. "That's why my wages—excuse me, my *ex*-wages—are being garnished, and the very reason I gave up a nice condo to live in the lap of luxury with you."

"Brenna." Michael waited until she looked at him before he continued. "You have money."

"Not me. I used the last of my savings to pay for John Miller's inept services."

"Remember a couple of weeks ago when all those old photographs and things came from Dad? There was a passbook with that stuff." At her even more puzzled frown, Michael added, "You know. The one that had a picture of Mom with it."

"It wouldn't have any money in it. Not after all this time."

"I bet it does."

Five minutes later, she found the passbook in the back of her closet where she had stuffed it in a box with old pictures and other papers. Sitting down on the bed, she simply held the book, remembering back to the night she had left home.

Brenna stared, unseeing, afraid to open the book and afraid not to, and so full of regret she hadn't told her mother that she loved her before she died.

"Well, open it," Michael urged.

She shook her head. "I'm scared to." She held it toward him. "You do it."

Michael took the passbook and sat down next to Brenna. "Look at this," he said, resting his finger under the first column. "Mom opened this account a week after you were born." He slid his finger down the column. "Every birthday. Christmas. A lot of times in between." Michael closed the book and pressed into her hand. "There's a lot of money in here, Brennie. Eight thousand dollars. Plus interest for the last eleven years."

"Another few dollars."

Michael shook his head. "It's been compounding a long time. I bet it's doubled."

"Enough to pay off the judgment," she breathed. If Michael was right, this was an answer to her prayers.

"Call them," Michael urged.

Her telephone call to the bank confirmed the account was open. Michael's hunch was verified—the balance was more than fifteen thousand dollars. The bank had a branch in Denver, and the customer service representative on the phone told Brenna they would be happy to see her any time. She hung up the telephone, at once stunned and ecstatic.

Michael gave her a hug. "Happy?"

Brenna nodded, though a sense of disbelief kept her wary. "Do you think Dad knew what this was?"

Michael shrugged. "Who knows?"

"I can't imagine he would have given this to me if he had known."

"It's your money, Brenna. The key to your independence."

"Yeah."

"He can't hurt you any more unless you let him, Brennie."

"I know," she replied, her response automatic. In her head, she knew he was right. In her heart…she wished she had Michael's conviction.

But fifteen thousand dollars! The sum seemed a fortune to her. Like ice breaking up in a spring thaw, ideas and plans and dreams rushed through her.

"I'm going to school," she announced. "Right after I get this judgment paid off. And I need a good lawyer." She jumped up, feeling like a little kid who wanted everything…and right now. She gave her brother a quick hug. "Fortunately, I happen to know one."

She called Cole's office, and when his secretary picked up the phone, asked Cole to fit her into his schedule for a half hour some time during the day. Myra told her the only free time in his schedule was mid-morning.

"Fine," Brenna told her. "I'll be there."

If she thought Brenna's request for an appointment was odd, she didn't say so. Cole called ten minutes later wanting to know what was on her mind.

"A surprise," she told him. "I'll see you at your office."

When she arrived an hour and a half later, he ushered her right past his secretary almost before she had a chance to say hello.

Shutting the door firmly behind him, Cole gathered Brenna close and thoroughly kissed her. "God, I'm glad to see you," he murmured between kisses. "Do you know how much I missed you?"

Brenna couldn't resist teasing him. "You just saw me twelve hours ago."

"I don't care," Cole said. "I'm having withdrawal pains."

Brenna arched her eyebrows. "Care to show me where you hurt, Counselor?"

Cole groaned. "You're tempting, fair lady."

"Good. I have a proposition for you."

He waggled his eyebrows. "This is getting better and better."

"I want to hire you," she said.

"Hire me?" He loosened his arms enough to look down at her. "Why?"

"Oh, Cole. An answer to my prayers. Look at this." She stepped out of his arms, took the passbook out of her purse, and handed it to him. "I called the bank, and with the interest since the last deposit, I have more than enough to pay off the judgment."

"That's great, honey, but—"

"Don't you see? I can pay off Harvey Bates. I can be finished with this. And I want you to handle it for me."

A slow grin lit Cole's face. "That would be just about a perfect end to this mess, wouldn't it?" He held out his hand. "Give me a dollar, Brenna."

"A dollar?"

He nodded.

She dug a dollar out of her purse and handed it to him.

"My retainer," he said, taking it from her and taking a kiss, too. "I'll collect the rest later."

"Are you sure I can afford your fee?" she asked.

He kissed her again. "Oh, yeah. You brought the judgment with you?"

"Right here," she said, handing him a file folder full of papers.

He riffled through them, found the sheets he was looking for, then sat down behind the desk. Brenna sat down to watch him as he rapidly scanned through the pages, jotting a couple of notes. After a quick perusal of the rest of the folder, he looked up. "Are you serious about this, Brenna?"

She nodded. "I want this behind me. The sooner, the better."

Cole picked up the telephone and dialed a number. A second later he identified himself, then asked for Roger Markham. Obviously on hold, he put a hand over the receiver and met Brenna's glance, his own eyes suddenly serious as a judge's.

"Do you trust me, fair lady?" Cole asked.

"Yes," Brenna answered without a second's hesitation.

"Good." Another moment passed before he spoke into the telephone receiver. "Roger," Cole said. "I'm representing Brenna James. She would like to make a deal to pay off the judgment with Harvey Bates.... Yes, you heard me right.... When? Any time today would be fine.... Of course, I'm serious.... Then let me explain it, Roger. She's willing to deal, but it needs to be today. If you want to spend time jacking around, then I'll recommend she countersue Mr. Bates for harassment, negligence, and anything else I can dig up.... I appreciate your fitting me in. Two-thirty will be fine.... Yes.... See you then."

Cole grinned hugely when he hung up the telephone, and Brenna breathed a sigh, unaware until that moment she had been holding her breath. He crossed the room and opened the door. "Myra, I need you for a second."

"Sure thing, boss." She appeared in the doorway, a stenographer's pad in hand before Cole sat back down behind the desk.

"First, reschedule my appointments today for the balance of the week." He handed her the file folder. "Then, I need to dictate a release for this, which I need to have typed and finished by one-thirty."

Over the next hour Brenna watched Cole take charge of the situation with skill that she admired and that told her just how rotten a job John Miller had done for her. When Myra brought in the typed release, Cole went over it again, his brow furrowed, this time reading it aloud.

Just as she was about to decide he knew she couldn't read, he looked up and caught her watching him.

"Sorry," he said. "Old habits die hard. I always read these things out loud. I should have outgrown it by now, but sometimes it's the only way I can tell if I've left something important out." A fleeting grin crossed his features. "It's driven every secretary I've ever had crazy."

"I heard that," Myra called from the outer office. "I am not crazy."

Cole chuckled. "Except Myra." He raised his voice. "Not crazy, just loony."

"Ha, ha," came her response.

One more reprieve, Brenna thought. One she didn't deserve. "It's okay," she said. "I'm just curious why you didn't put a dollar amount in."

"That's part two of our plan." He stood up and pulled Brenna to her feet. "We're not going to give them all your money, fair lady." He led her out of the office. "C'mon. We need lunch, and we need to get some of your money out of the bank."

At two-thirty precisely, they stepped off the elevator and walked through the glass doors at the law offices of Jones, Markham and Simmons. She could hardly believe she was really here, but she knew

Cole was right. Strike while Roger Markham and Harvey Bates were still trying to figure out what was going on.

She and Cole waited a scant minute before the receptionist ushered them into the conference room where she had met with Cole and Harvey Bates all those months ago.

At the doorway she paused. Harvey Bates sat at the end of the table, looking much as he had the last time she saw him. She had never been afraid of the man, but she hated the power he had wielded over her, hated feeling like the victim she had become. She lifted her chin and walked into the room.

Cole pulled out a chair for her and greeted a slightly built, impeccably dressed man who followed them into the room.

"Roger, you're looking well."

"Miss James," he said with a slight nod to his head without acknowledging Cole's greeting. "You both know Mr. Bates."

Brenna's glance shifted to him. His mouth lifted in a smile that did nothing to erase the petulant look from his face.

"I knew sooner or later you'd ask your daddy for the money," he said.

Cole sat down next to Brenna. "Let's get to this, shall we? How much do you want to settle this today?"

Roger Markham frowned. "Why the entire amount, of course."

Cole smiled. It was an expression Brenna recognized—his civilized, cold, court smile. "Roger, Roger. This is me you're talking to. Not some poor slob who couldn't find his rear with both hands and a mirror. I know you don't expect Miss James to hand over nine thousand dollars."

"Since it's daddy's money, why do you care?" Bates asked.

Brenna met his gaze and curiosity overrode her vow to ignore him. "I'd love to know, Harvey, just why it is that you think my father has money, and if he did, why you think he'd give me a dime of it."

"Keeping track of the great Colonel James has been, shall we say, an interest of mine."

His expression changed, and Brenna had the sense of something inside him cracking.

"'Competence isn't enough. Excellence isn't enough. Perfection is the only acceptable goal,'" he quoted, his gaze returning to Brenna.

Chills crawled over her skin. She remembered those words well, knew their intonation. They had made up the opening of just about every lecture she had ever heard from her father. She remembered much of the rest of it, too. Competence wasn't enough to keep good men from dying. Neither was excellence. Only perfection. In the execution of a plan, only perfection was acceptable. As a daughter, she hadn't been perfect, and she had wanted him to love her anyway.

Bates appeared not to be aware of Cole or Roger Markham. "Do you know what your father's 'perfection' cost me?" His voice became hoarse with emotion. "A leg, my dear girl. You accused me of not having patience. You were wrong. I waited a long time, and when I met you, it was an answer to a thirty-year-old prayer. You told me to go to hell, and I can tell you I've been there. Eleven months of serving under a man who ignored the realities of guerrilla warfare in favor of perfection. Men died. Men were mutilated. And that bastard got a promotion!" Bates took a deep breath and wiped his forehead with a handkerchief. "At last I had a way to hurt him, if only a little. Nine thousand dollars is a drop in the bucket of what the grand Colonel James owes me."

Brenna's gaze dropped to her hands clasped tightly in her lap. She didn't know how Bates knew she was Colonel James's daughter. Maybe they had talked about it once, but she couldn't remember. She didn't care how he knew. Explained for her at last was the animosity Bates held for her.

She glanced him and murmured, "I'm sorry."

"You're sorry!" he snarled. "Not half as sorry as I'd like to make you!"

Cole surged out of his chair. "Bates—"

"Miss James. Cole," Roger Markham interrupted. He stood, and for a small man, exuded self-confidence and determination Brenna hadn't noticed before. "Mr. Bates and I will be gone for a few minutes. You'll wait?"

"Of course," Cole said as Roger ushered Harvey Bates from the room.

Cole took her hand as they watched the two men through the glass partition.

"I didn't know, Brenna," Cole said in a low voice. "I knew this was grudge match for Bates, but I swear to you, I didn't know why."

"Me, neither," she said, watching Bates and Markham talk. Bates waved his arms a couple of times, then turned and strode down the hallway, leaning heavily on his cane, his limp pronounced.

Brenna wanted to hate him for what he had put her through. At the moment, all she felt was pity.

Roger Markham returned to the conference room.

"I believe we were discussing an amount for the settlement," he said, ignoring the events that had just transpired, his expression giving no indication what he thought, if anything.

Cole nodded. "That's right." He held out his hand, and Brenna placed in his palm four groups of hundred dollars bills that had been separated into thousand-dollar increments. "Miss James is willing to settle this right now for four thousand dollars."

Just as Cole had predicted when they talked over lunch, Roger Markham couldn't take his eyes off the cash. He shook his head as though he didn't believe what he was seeing. "I've got to talk with Mr. Bates about this," he said. "Do you mind waiting for a few more minutes?"

He left without waiting for an answer and returned within five minutes. "Mr. Bates says the full nine thousand is the very least he'll consider."

Brenna's confidence wavered, but Cole had told her to expect this, as well.

Cole stacked the four groups of bills on top of one another. "Then we don't have anything to talk about after all." He stood up and handed Brenna the money.

"Eight thousand," Markham said.

"Four thousand, five hundred."

Markham shook his head. "That's his best offer."

"That's too bad, and not good enough."

"Seven thousand, then," Markham said.

"Make it five and you've got a deal," Cole said.

Roger shook his head. "I come down two thousand and you come up one."

Cole smiled one of his cold smiles. "I'm a reasonable man, Roger. Five five."

Markham's glance shifted to Brenna, then he nodded. "I'll get the agreement drawn up."

"There's no need." Cole sat back down and opened his portfolio. He penned in the dollar amount in the places he had left blank and handed the agreements to Roger. "I think you'll see this covers all the basics."

Roger pursed his lips as he handed the agreement back to Cole. "Sign it and I'll take it into Mr. Bates."

Cole took a pen out of his pocket and handed it to Brenna. She signed her name and gave him back the four thousand dollars plus fifteen hundred more.

He smiled at her. "We're almost done." Handing the signed agreements to Roger with the money, he said, "We'll need a receipt for the cash, Roger."

"But, of course."

Two hours ago Brenna had been furious with the idea of giving Harvey Bates any of her money, even though she wanted the judgment paid off. He didn't need the money—she did. But, giving it to him also marked a new beginning. And now that it was done, now that she knew about Bates's ties to her father, the anger had drained away. In its place was sadness for an embittered man.

A few minutes later, Roger returned with a receipt and the signed agreements. Cole separated out their copies and shook Roger's hand.

By the time they reached the elevator, she felt as thought she was walking on air. She stood sedately in front of the doors, waiting for the car to come, hanging on every bit of willpower she had ever possessed. The doors opened, and she and Cole entered the empty car. Cole pressed the button for the first floor.

When the car began to move, Brenna let out a whoop. Cole laughed, caught her in his arms, and lifted her off the floor.

"I'm free," she cried, throwing her arms around his neck. "I'm free!" She kissed him soundly. "Thank you. I couldn't have gone in there alone. I couldn't have—"

"You could, Brenna. But I'm glad I was here to help." He kissed her. "We have only the small matter of my fee to settle."

She grinned against his mouth. "Just what did you have in mind, Counselor?"

"Spend the night with me."

Sudden shyness caught up with her, but she nodded.

"I still have to get about six dozen other things done today," he said.

"Me, too," she agreed, though at the moment she couldn't remember what a single one was.

"Is eight o'clock too late?"

"No." Then she remembered. She was scheduled to get together with Nancy for another tutoring session at six. "Eight is fine."

A day of new beginnings. A day to trust him with the truth.

Chapter 20

When Brenna got back to the apartment after her tutoring session with Nancy, she found Cole sitting on the front stoop with Teddy and Michael. In a matter of minutes she gathered up her things, and after a quick goodbye to her brother, they were in the Jeep on their way to Cole's house.

He had fastened the canvas top on the Jeep, enveloping them inside their own private world.

"Still on cloud nine?" Cole asked, picking up her hand in his right hand, glancing at her briefly, his eyes gleaming in the dim light.

"Having Harvey Bates paid off feels good," Brenna responded. "I kept thinking of that old song about owing my soul to the company store. And I don't anymore."

Cole grinned. "I can relate." He kissed the back of her fingertips without taking his eyes off the road. "Nervous about coming home with me?"

"Scared to death." She glanced at him from the corner of her eye.

"You don't sound it."

"Don't let that fool you. I'm terrified." She pressed the back of her hand against her forehead in mock horror.

"So this is what terrified looks like. I always wondered."

She watched him as they drove, not caring whether they were on their way to a mansion or a sleeping bag under a pine tree and a sky full of stars. Being with him was all she cared about, all she wanted.

The drive took a bit more than a half hour, but to Brenna it seemed shorter. The graveled driveway was long and led to a two-story house that was shrouded in darkness. Even in the dark, she could see it was large with no other houses nearby—a far cry from the Cherry Creek townhome or the Lodo loft she had once envisioned him having.

Cole got out of the Jeep, came around to her side, gave her a chaste kiss so full of tenderness and promise, it made her heart ache. She cupped his cheek with her hand. Without saying a word, he looked at her, his eyes gleaming in the moonlight. He pressed another kiss into her palm, then guided her toward the house. They mounted shallow stairs to a wide porch. After unlocking the front door, he led her through the house without turning on lights.

"Are you a cat or something?" she whispered. "Prowling through the house in the dark?"

"Nope," he replied, lifting her in his arms. "I've just been thinking I didn't know how I was going to get along without having you in my bed. I hated taking you back to Michael's last night."

He kissed her. No chaste kiss, this one.

"If I turn the lights on, you're going to want a tour." He took her mouth in another kiss, this one deeper. She wound her arms around him. "And, fair lady, I don't want us to get distracted."

If he had asked her, she would have told him what was important to her. And it wasn't his house, curious though she was. He swept her off her feet and carried her up the stairs as though she weighed nothing, went through a wide doorway, and set her feet on the floor at the edge of the bed.

"Do you know what I've been thinking about today?" Cole asked.

Brenna shook her head as he began unbuttoning her blouse.

"I was thinking I've never made love to you in a bed." He pushed the blouse off her shoulders, letting it fall to the floor. "In my bed." He traced a path of liquid fire with his tongue from her shoulder to her neck. "I was thinking I'm glad you don't have a job at night any more. Having you with me at night—that's what I want." He flashed her an apologetic smile. "I know that sounds selfish."

"I...want that, too."

Pulling her into his arms, he unfastened the clasp of her bra and slid the straps down her arms. "I was thinking how happy I am for you that you've got the Harvey Bates mess behind you." He pulled back a fraction to let the bra drop to the floor between them. "I was thinking I'd go crazy if I had to wait another minute to hold you like this." Drawing her close again, he captured her mouth with his own.

At the touch of her breasts against the fabric of his shirt, Brenna was consumed with the kind of wanting he described—on fire from his words, on fire from his touch. She wrapped her arms around his neck and let herself sink into the moment. She drew closer, needing his touch more than air.

His lips trailed across her face, and she tipped her head back offering him access to her neck. As he gently caught the skin of her neck between his teeth, his hands slid lower, cupping her breasts for a too-brief, aching moment. Then he slid his palms down her back, under the waistband of her skirt and panties, pushing both down her legs until they fell to the floor.

With a groan, Cole gathered her back into his arms, fully absorbing the feeling of her naked body pressed against his clothed one. She fit him so perfectly. When she stood on tiptoe, arching her body against his, she took his breath away.

"I love you," he whispered against the satin skin of her neck. "I love you," he whispered as he lowered her onto the bed. "I love you," he whispered as he covered her body with his.

Those three words lit her soul like a comet streaking its blazing trail across the night sky. Unexpected. Breathtakingly beautiful. She pulled his head down, giving him a deep, searching kiss, tears slipping from under her closed eyelids. Sweet heaven, she wanted it to be true. More than anything she wanted to admit to him his feelings were returned. Fully. Her throat constricted, and the words went no further than the edge of her mind.

She showed him she returned his love in the only way she knew how. With hands that trembled, she helped him take off his shirt, spreading her fingers through the hair on his chest to the sensitive skin beneath. Lightly, she raked her nails across the front of his slacks, and her breath hitched when she felt his involuntary throb.

With a sigh of impatience, she unfastened the waistband of his trousers and unzipped the fly, teasing them both by not touching him.

A heavy, empty throb deep within urged her to hurry. She pushed the pants down his hips, laughing softly as they caught not only on his legs, but hers.

"Shoes," Cole muttered between biting kisses across her face and neck.

"Sorry, but I refuse to make love with a man wearing shoes," she said. "They have to go."

He joined her soft laugh, kicking off the shoes. "We might have to try that sometime as part of our research."

"Sounds pretty kinky to me." She helped free his legs of the slacks and encountered his socks. She slid those off his feet and threw them across the floor. "Socks are definitely out."

He pulled her back into his arms. "Better, my Brenna. Just you and me. Skin to skin." He pinned her beneath him, kneading the soft fullness of her breasts, finding the liquid softness at the juncture of her thighs. She lifted her hips into his hand, an invitation that was irresistible to him.

He brought himself closer, easing his painfully aroused flesh closer until he touched her softness. She melted over him, and he groaned, rubbing against her without giving her the culmination they both wanted. She wrapped her legs around his, urging him to complete his possession of her.

"Please love me," she whispered against his ear.

"I am," he said, giving her what she wanted. "I do. Ah, Brenna...I...do."

Cole felt Brenna shift her body until they were fitted together intimately, fully. She opened her eyes, luminous in the moonlight with tears and unspoken longing. Her half smile tore at him as he sensed she was as complete within his embrace as he was in hers. He caught her mouth in a kiss and held her there, at the crest of their shimmering peak until it became too much to bear. Together, they surged over the top in a wild rush of sensation that left them gasping for breath.

The moments that followed were languid, peaceful. Brenna knew she wasn't asleep, but she didn't feel fully awake either. Simply, the moment absorbed her. Cole's heated, sated body curled around hers, and within his embrace she felt safe, treasured, accepted. Precious feelings that made her press kisses against his temple, his cheek. One moment stretched into another, and at some point, she fell asleep.

When Brenna woke at sunrise, she found that sometime during the night Cole had covered them with a sheet. He lay with her back pulled against his chest, spoon style, his warm arm wrapped around her waist. She lightly brushed her hand over his arm, then smiled as he pressed a kiss against her shoulder. Even in sleep, his actions were loving.

Snuggled within the security of Cole's embrace, she examined the room and found it to be as masculine and unique as the man. Cream walls, an entire wall of built-in shelves that were filled with books, stereo equipment, and a television. Above them, suspended from a vaulted ceiling, a fan revolved. A skylight revealed a brilliant blue sky. A west-facing sliding glass door to a balcony had a magnificent view of Long's Peak.

Quietly, Brenna slipped out of bed and went to the door. She fell in love instantly with the view and knew she would find the mountain as fascinating when shrouded in winter snow as she did now. Below the balcony was a huge yard. Trees that would someday shade the house and provide privacy from the road had been planted on the south side of the yard. Brenna picked up Cole's shirt and slipped it on as she left the bedroom.

Last night she only had time for an impression of spaciousness as Cole brought her through the house. Cream walls throughout the house were set off by dark blue and dark brown accents. Everywhere, Cole's interest in sailing was apparent, from paintings and reproductions of nineteenth-century ships to the glass-covered wooden wheel that made up the coffee table. With a last satisfied glance at the living room, she went to the kitchen. She found the coffee and the coffee maker, and brewed a pot.

Then she went outside, strolling across the yard to the fenced vegetable garden that was as full of weeds as Cole had told her it would be. She resisted the urge to start a job that she knew she wouldn't have time to finish this morning.

Brenna turned back around to face the house. Her dream, come to life.

A spacious two-story house with a wide porch and a swing. Wide-open spaces big enough for children and dogs. Starched priscillas at the window.

Her breath caught, and tears filled her eyes.

Cole's home.

Her dream.

Unbidden comparisons between this house and all the houses she had lived in as a child filed one by one through her mind. Cole's home had a permanence she longed for. He had planted trees that took years to grow, to watch, to appreciate. Her mother had planted tomatoes, and two different years they had been transferred before they could be harvested. Cole had filled the flower beds with perennials—irises, shasta daisies, and poppies that would bloom for years. Her mother had kept two pots filled with petunias. Everywhere Brenna looked indicated this was a place where roots had been sunk...deeply. That felt as comfortable and terrifying as Cole himself did.

Cole awoke with a start, then swore under his breath at the time on the clock. He was out of bed and halfway across the room when his glance lit on Brenna's clothes strewn carelessly across the floor. The aching intensity of their lovemaking flooded him with a clarity that instantly aroused him.

"Brenna," he called. When she didn't answer, he went to the open door of the bedroom and called down the stairwell. Turning around, through the sliding glass door, he caught sight of her outside. He went to the door intending to tell her good-morning, but his voice trailed into a whisper when he saw her expression.

Even from the bedroom, he could see the wet tracks of tears on her face. She stood with her arms wrapped around her waist as she looked at the house. Then she turned away and dropped her head, her posture as full of defeat as it had been the day she had walked out of his office all those months ago.

Her tears were a punch in the gut. He didn't know their source, but only one thing mattered. Making her feel better.

Grabbing a robe off the hook on the bathroom door, Cole bounded down the stairs.

He threw open the kitchen door and stepped onto the porch. "Brenna, are you okay?"

She turned around just in time to see him come down the steps and across the lawn to her, concern etched on his face.

"Yes," she said, reaching to touch his cheek.

"No, you're not," he said gruffly. "You're crying. What's wrong?"

She wiped her eyes with the sleeves of the shirt she had borrowed from him. "You didn't want a wonderful apartment in Chicago," she said, her voice sounding vaguely accusing.

"I didn't," he agreed, wondering what had prompted that statement. "That was part of the problem."

"And Christmases in a tropical paradise?"

"I didn't want them, either. If that makes me dull, then I'm dull."

"You're not dull."

He smiled, even as he watched more tears trickle down her cheeks. "I'm glad you think so, Brenna."

"I love you," she whispered, her voice carrying a note of anguish he didn't understand. "I love you," she repeated, as if the realization surprised her.

Cole wrapped a hand around the back of her neck and pulled her against him. "Loving me isn't supposed to make you unhappy."

"It doesn't."

"Then why the tears?"

"I've never wanted anything so much or been so scared I can't have it," she answered truthfully.

Cole's laugh was soft, and he wrapped his arm around her shoulder as they walked toward the house. "I'm all yours, fair lady, for as long as you want."

Inside the house, Brenna turned into his arms, holding him close with all her strength. *For as long as she wanted.* Forever was what she wanted.

Cole smoothed his hand across the back of her head. "If we don't get a move on, I'm going to miss a court appearance this morning."

At the rueful tone in his voice, Brenna lifted her head and smiled through her tears. "All mine, huh? Or until it's time to go to work?" She aimed a playful swat at his backside, which he easily deflected.

"All yours," he repeated, picking her up and lifting her over his shoulder.

"Looks like I've got you, too," she said, pulling up the hem of his robe to pinch his bare bottom.

He laughed. "Two can play that game, sweetheart." He retaliated in kind, then let his big, warm palm linger on her skin, his long fingers skimming the back of her thighs.

They took a shower together, laughing and playing and appeasing the hunger they aroused in one another. Later, she lotioned her arms and legs while watching him shave. As he dressed, the playful man was gradually lost beneath a more austere facade. He kept touching her as they passed one another. She wanted nothing more than to have a lifetime of mornings with him just like this one.

Cole promised Brenna that he would call her just as soon as he got out of court. His lingering kiss and softly spoken "I love you" left no doubt in her mind that she was important to him.

Teddy greeted her with an enthusiastic hug when she stepped inside. Seconds later, Jane emerged from the bedroom, ready to leave for class. She took one look at Brenna and hugged her, as well.

"You're glowing," Jane said simply. "I think he is a good man— good for you."

Brenna couldn't have agreed more. Cole was good for her. She toyed with the idea of leaving everything alone, of hoping she would learn to read quickly enough to make the lack a moot point. Even as the thought came to her, she discarded it. Cole had been honest with her, and he deserved no less. And he loved her. She had to believe that somehow that would make things okay, that he would understand.

"Your father is in Fort Carson today," Jane said. "Michael and Teddy plan to go pick him up when he calls later."

"That's nice," Brenna responded absently, her thoughts still centered on Cole.

"Perhaps you would like to go with them."

She shook her head. "Not a good idea."

Jane got along well with the Colonel, a fact that always amazed Brenna, especially after she figured out that Jane assumed everyone got along with him as well as she did.

"It's been a good visit," Jane volunteered. "You know how stern your father can be, but I think he is enjoying himself."

"We're going to go see airplanes with Grandpa," Teddy said, pulling on Brenna's hand to get her attention.

"That sounds like fun," Brenna responded.

"Do you want to come?" he asked.

"I have other things to do today." Standing in line at the unemployment office held far more appeal than spending time with her father. No matter how neutral the territory, he always managed to find a way to make her feel defensive and on edge.

And face it, she told herself. She had plenty to make her feel on edge without adding her father to the mix. Yesterday she had promised herself the next time she saw Cole she would tell him she couldn't read. Well, she had spent a good part of yesterday with him, and she hadn't mentioned it. Not anything remotely close to it.

Jane left for class. Brenna set out crayons and a tablet of drawing paper for Teddy. She doodled with him, wondering how to tell Cole she could not read.

Her mental rehearsal took a dozen different forms, and none of it sounded right to her. *You know that lawsuit. Well, that happened because I couldn't read a bank statement. I really did think I had several thousand dollars in the account. You find bank statements confusing, too? No, that isn't what I mean.*

You remember that night you wanted to play Scrabble. Well, that's a little difficult. I couldn't spell the word Scrabble if you paid me.

She couldn't imagine boldly saying to Cole, "I can't read."

"I know that, Auntie Brennie," Teddy said,

She glanced at her nephew, unaware she had spoken aloud until Teddy responded.

"But you're learning. Just like me."

"Yes," Brenna said. "Just like you."

"I can help you."

"I know you can." She tousled Teddy's head, praying she would find the same matter-of-fact acceptance in Cole.

He called just as she and Teddy finished having lunch. "Will you be free by late afternoon?"

"I should be," she answered. "I have just one house to clean this afternoon, and it's a small one. I should be done by four-thirty or so."

"That's great. I intended to feed you dinner last night, and I missed it. We have to try again tonight. Maybe a picnic supper. What do you think?"

"That sounds like fun."

"I can't wait to see you," Cole said, his voice caressing. "You're hell on my libido and I have a problem only you can fix."

Warmth slid down Brenna's spine, and she wrapped the telephone cord around her finger. "You seem to have a one-track mind, Counselor."

"True." An instant of silence followed. "What about you, fair lady?"

"The same track."

"I love you, Brenna James. I need to get a few things together. I'll be in touch in a little while and we'll do something special tonight."

Michael arrived home a few minutes later. As Jane had, he invited her to go with him and Teddy to pick up the Colonel. After Brenna told him she had other obligations, he said, "Are you sure, sis? It's been a long time since you've spent any time with him."

"I'll have that chance later. He's going to be here a couple of more days, isn't he?"

"Yeah. I just hate to see things keeping going like they are between you two."

"It's the natural order of things," Brenna said without a trace of humor.

"He's not going to change," Michael said.

She felt her hands clench into fists. "He can accept me as I am or he can—"

Michael took one of her hands and uncurled her palm. "I don't mean to upset you. I was just hoping that some time with him might ease things between you."

"That's a nice thought, Michael. I think my best bet is to stay away from him. If we can get through one visit together without a fight, maybe that will be the beginning of better things." She smiled at her brother. "Besides, I have a date."

Michael grinned. "It's no contest then."

He left with Teddy a few minutes later. Less than a minute later, the doorbell rang, and Brenna answered it, assuming Michael had forgotten his keys or something else. The last thing she expected to see was a delivery from a florist shop—a beautiful bouquet of yellow roses, more brilliant than sunshine. She knew they had to be from Cole.

Brenna took the roses into her bedroom, inhaling their fragrance, and set them on the dresser. She pulled the small card out of its envelope, and groaned in frustration. "Dear Brenna" she recognized. The bold scrawl of the rest of the longhand was completely indecipherable to her. Symbol after symbol blurred together, and she could make out only the most rudimentary words. *A. The. Of. I love you, Brenna.*

Carefully, she set the card aside. She would give it to Cole later, she decided. She called his office to thank him for the flowers. Myra, his secretary, told Brenna he was gone for the day. She hung up the telephone, suddenly apprehensive, sure that Cole had said he would call.

She left for her housecleaning job a few minutes later, reassuring herself that she had nothing to worry about. He had said he would be in touch, and he would. If Cole was anything, he was a man of his word.

Chapter 21

Cole glanced at his watch and wondered if Brenna had received the flowers yet. Every time her soft "I love you" feathered through his memory, he wanted to shout his elation, wanted to hold her close, wanted to cherish her in all the ways she deserved to be cherished.

On the card he had written, "Grandmom once told me yellow is the color of love and faith. I gave you mine during our golden sunrise. Meet me at the pavilion in Washington Park at six o'clock for a picnic supper. Brenna, I love you. Cole."

He had contacted one of the upscale markets in Cherry Creek to put together the picnic supper. Linens instead of paper napkins. Cold jumbo shrimp instead of hot dogs. Hearts of palm instead of potato chips.

The discipline Cole had forced on himself for years eluded him. Often, Brenna slipped through the cracks of his concentration. She had been happy this morning. He knew it. Her vibrant, warm smile was a marked contrast to the controlled, emotionless person she had been last spring.

Just before noon, Myra appeared at the door of his office, immediately catching his attention when she called him by name instead of calling him boss. "Andrew Mathias is on the line."

Cole frowned, wondering why the district attorney for Zach MacKenzie's case would be calling him. He didn't have any appointments scheduled with the man.

"Do you want the file?"

Cole shook his head and reached for the phone. "Hello, Andrew."

"Cole," the other man responded over the line. "I wanted to let you know that I think you've got a problem."

Cole took off his glasses, appreciating Andrew's getting to the point immediately instead of beating around the usual pleasantries.

"I know your guy is in rehab." He paused.

Cole wondered if it was for effect, or if the man thought he might not know. "It isn't something we tried to hide," Cole responded. "We knew you'd probably find out."

"I've got two more witnesses that will testify as to his drinking problem."

"Either of these witnesses see Mr. MacKenzie the night of the accident?" Cole asked.

"One of them."

Cole swung his chair away from the desk, and he stared through the window, where a steady stream of traffic passed. The attorney on the other end of the line was silent, and Cole recognized the tactic for what it was. He, too, liked using silence to up the ante.

"Do these witnesses have names?" Cole asked.

"It's part of the discovery you're entitled to. Do you want me to fax them to you?

"Yes."

"Ready to talk a deal?"

"My client has entered a plea of not guilty. Nothing has changed."

"I'll tell you what. You talk to my witnesses. Then call me. My office is open to a deal."

Cole knew better than to tell the D.A. he wasn't interested. Bluff or real, the call accomplished what Drew Mathias had intended. Cole felt as though he had just found himself in the middle of a field with an ornery range bull breathing down his neck.

"I'll talk to your witnesses," he said.

"And I'll *talk* to you in a couple of days," Mathias said, breaking the connection.

Cole set the receiver back in the cradle, at once annoyed and suspicious of what Mathias could have that made him so sure they could plea-bargain the case. All he could do was wait until the fax came with the names. A scant five minutes later, the telephone rang in the outer office, followed by the distinctive whine of the fax machine when the line connected.

He surged out of his chair and went into the outer office where he watched the paper slowly feed through the fax machine.

"Problems?" Myra asked.

"As you damn well knew when you came to my door a minute ago."

"Ah, well, just so long as you don't shoot the messenger."

Her dry tone made Cole look at her, and he managed a smile, responding, "Not likely—all that workman's comp paperwork would be a pain."

The transmission finished, and Cole took the fax out of the machine. The two names on the D.A.'s sheet weren't ones Cole had come across before. He checked his calendar one last time—no appointments until his date with Brenna tonight, which gave him time to track down both persons. Mathias thought he had a bombshell, and Cole needed to know if he did.

When he left the office, telling Myra that he would be gone for the balance of the day.

The first witness turned out to be Pamela's brother. Cole figured any family of Zach's ex-fiancée would pretty much see things the way she did, especially a protective older brother. Cole was one of those brothers himself and knew he'd feel pretty much the same way about anyone who hurt his sister.

By the time he tracked down the second witness, a young woman, at a trailer court at the north end of the metro area, it was late afternoon. She came to the door, a pair of toddlers clinging to her legs. Hoisting one of the kids on her hip, she came outside when Cole identified himself.

The first thing he asked her was why she hadn't been on the original witness list.

She ducked her head. "I was scared," she finally admitted. "A guy from that all-night gas station on the corner called the cops—I know he did, because I asked him."

"When was that?"

"That night," she said, patting her child's head as he stood at her knee solemnly watching Cole. "Right when it happened."

"But you didn't stay."

She shook her head. "What could I do? I mean, I don't know first aid. And the one man was so badly hurt—"

"The one who died?"

She nodded. "And I needed to get home to my kids."

"What about the other driver?"

She looked up at Cole. "Oh, I remember him real well. He kept saying it was all his fault. And he staggered around like he was drunk, yelling and carrying on."

Cole figured shock, more than being drunk, could have been at the root of Zach's behavior.

"Do you think he was impaired?"

"Drunk?"

Cole nodded.

"Yes."

"Are you sure?"

She stared beyond Cole's shoulder a moment, then said, "Yeah. He staggered when he got out of the car—"

"Was he injured?"

"Not that I could see." She met Cole's gaze. "He didn't look hurt, okay? He looked...drunk. He acted drunk."

If it walks like a drunk, talks like a drunk, it must be a drunk, Cole thought, following her line of reasoning.

"After waiting—why come forward now?" Cole asked.

She met his gaze briefly, the glanced down at her children. "It could have been me—or my kids—instead of that man. I had to do something."

In the quick conversation that followed he learned she worked nights as a desk clerk at a big hotel, that she had been divorced for a year, and that she was genuinely convinced of the truth of her beliefs. She was likeable and credible, and had no personal link to the case.

Cole thanked the woman for her time and headed back into town. Stopping at a convenience store, he called Myra. When his own recording came on, he glanced at his watch and discovered the time

was well after five. Time to pick up the basket for his picnic supper
with Brenna.

Cole pushed aside the afternoon's complications and the pall they
had put on his mood. Time to focus on the evening ahead with
Brenna, he thought. He intended to make it romantic and memorable.

On the way to the market, he stopped on impulse at the Tattered
Cover and bought a book of Shakespeare's sonnets. Old-fashioned,
traditional, and a memento of a memorable day, he thought. He
grinned, imagining how she might tell their grandchildren someday
how she had been wooed with yellow roses, poems of love, and a
romantic picnic. Cole picked up the picnic basket, and by six o'clock
he was waiting for Brenna under the wide branches of an elm tree
near the pavilion at Washington Park.

The moment Brenna returned home, she called Cole's office again,
hoping he had checked in. He hadn't, but she left a message with his
secretary. Then Brenna called Cole's house. He didn't answer there,
either.

She was positive he had not said where they would go for dinner,
or what time he would pick her up. But he had promised they would
do something special.

She went through her closet twice, trying to decide what to wear.
Finally, she chose a pale aqua sundress that reminded her of the color
of the pond at the ranch just before sunrise.

She fidgeted as she waited, impatient to have the moment she told
him she could not read behind her. He would either understand, or
he wouldn't. She hoped with all her heart that he would. He had sent
her flowers, not just any flowers—but roses. And he had told her that
he loved her. Surely, those things counted for something.

The minutes dragged by, becoming one hour, then another. She
fretted. Why hadn't he called?

Still later she decided the interview that Myra told her about must
have taken longer than he had anticipated. Urging her vivid imagination to take a rest, she took the card that accompanied the roses
from her pocket, smoothing her fingers over the words. "He loves
you, Brenna," she said out loud. "And, it's going to be okay."

Brave words. She worried anyway.

* * *

By the time seven o'clock rolled around, Cole had to admit to himself that Brenna wasn't coming. He glanced again at his watch, the slow passage of time gnawing at him. Where was she? Had she misunderstood the place? Had she even received the flowers so she knew to come? Was she okay?

After fifteen more minutes passed, Cole gathered up the picnic, neatly packing the food back into the wicker basket with the napkins. He tucked the book of sonnets into the side of the basket and put everything into the Jeep. There, he waited ten minutes more, watching each person who came down the path, positive the next would be Brenna.

Myra had been after him to install a cellular telephone in his car, and he now wished he had done so months ago. A simple telephone call would confirm whether she was on the way. As it was, he had no choice but drive to the apartment and hope he didn't miss her on the way. Even so, he drove slowly, half expecting to see her hurrying down the sidewalk.

At the apartment, Cole got out of the Jeep and strode to the door, worried that something had happened to her. He rang the bell, then paced the narrow width of the front stoop.

When Brenna came to the door, the worry he saw in her expression was a mirror of his own feelings.

"Where have you been?" he asked, his voice harsher than he intended, reflecting his frustration and disappointment. "I waited, but—"

"Waited?" she echoed. "But I've been waiting."

"What do you mean you've been waiting? You were supposed to meet me." He stepped through the open door and the screen slammed behind him.

"Where?"

The constriction around his chest eased. "I should have figured you didn't get the flowers." He stepped close and brushed a soft kiss over her trembling mouth. "I had a wonderful picnic all planned for us, but if you didn't get the flowers, you wouldn't have known to come."

"The yellow roses are beautiful, Cole."

"You got them?"

"Yes. They're beautiful."

"Then the card must have been missing."

Brenna reached in her pocket and pulled out the card. She stared at it a moment, and when she looked up at him, her eyes were bright with unshed tears.

"No," she said finally, her voice husky. "The card came with it."

"Then you were late getting home and you couldn't get hold of me," Cole said, trying to find a logical explanation, sensing that she was on the verge of crying. "It's okay, fair lady. We can still have our picnic."

"You don't understand," she said.

He took her hand. "Then explain it," he said, bewildered by the conflicting emotions that chased across her face. The Brenna he knew was direct. No evasions, no omissions, no matter the cost to herself.

A hysterical bubble of laughter escaped her lips. She held the card out to Cole. "I—"

He glanced at the note, saw his instructions to meet him were clear. "Brenna?"

"I didn't know I was supposed to meet you."

Cole frowned. "But it says—"

"I can't..." She closed her eyes and tears squeezed out beneath the lids.

"Brenna, what's happened? Something with your father?"

She shook her head.

"What then?"

"I thought you'd call me."

"What does that have to do with this? I wrote you a note instead."

She nodded, her gaze diverted. He lifted her chin with his finger, and instead of meeting his gaze, hers slid past his shoulder. More puzzled than ever, Cole watched her. She had always been direct with him—it was one of the qualities he most admired about her.

"Brenna? Has something happened since this morning?"

"No," she whispered.

"No." Her evasiveness set off terrible warning bells that rang through his head. The tenuous hold he'd had on his temper since talking with the D.A. hours ago began to evaporate. All the day's frustrations piled one on another. He stepped away from her, raking his hands through his hair.

"Let me see if I've got this straight so far. You got my flowers.

You got my note. You weren't home late from work. And nothing has happened since this morning. But you're upset, and you didn't come to meet me."

She stared at the floor a long moment, then lifted her gaze to him. The anguish Cole saw there slipped past his frustration and made him reach for her. Just as he would have touched her, she stepped back.

"Fair lady, we can't solve this unless you tell me what's going on."

She swallowed convulsively and wrapped her arms around herself as if to ward off a chill. The silence stretched tautly between them.

"Maybe I should go," he said. "If you're not ready to talk, I guess the least I can do is give you some time." Gently, he touched her cheek with the side of his finger and turned around. He was halfway to the door when her anguished whisper reached him.

"I can't read."

Cole stopped midstride and shook his head. *I can't read.* Slowly, he turned around to look at her. She stood motionless where he had left her. The card from his flowers was gripped tightly in her hand. Suddenly, her fist opened, and the rumpled card fluttered to the floor. He felt an absurd desire to pick it up and smooth out all the wrinkles.

"What did you say?"

Another long moment passed, one that reminded him of the interminable time it took her to answer questions at the trial.

"I can't read," she said, finally, her voice devoid of emotion.

A dozen incidents sped through Cole's mind, each one reinforcing an inescapable conclusion. Brenna knew how to read. She was one of the most articulate people he had ever met. Of course, she could read. He knew she could.

She held out her hand. "I can't. Cole, honestly, I can't."

"I don't know why you would tell me such a thing," he said.

She watched his expression close into the granite hardness of the man she had first known, watched the metallic glitter appear in his gold-flecked eyes.

"It's the truth," she said, unable to hold his gaze, dropping her own again to the floor.

"The truth?" Cole closed the gap between them and lifted her face with his hand. "The truth, Brenna, is not this. The Brenna James I know looks me in the eye when she tells the truth. No evasions."

Her eyes closed, tears seeped beneath the lids. Cole waited until she opened them again.

"No omissions."

She shook her head, and again her glance skittered away.

"No deceptions." He let go of her and walked toward the door. "The truth? When you're ready to tell me what really is going on, Brenna, call me."

"I am telling you the truth."

He stopped in the doorway without turning around. "I don't think so," he said. "When I turn around you'll look away again." He braced an arm against the doorjamb. "If you want to call things off between us, all you need to do is say so. This kind of charade doesn't accomplish anything."

He opened the screen door and walked through it. The door closed behind him, and he went down the walk without looking back. The finality of the door closing resounded through Brenna's mind with the crack of gunfire. The sound echoed around her, and she finally covered her ears.

She didn't know how long she stood in the middle of the room, tears sliding like slow rain down her face and neck. Each choice she had made during the course of her life marched through her mind, each mistake magnified, each opportunity missed. The only man she had ever been in love with had just walked out the door. And she had no one—*no one*—to blame but herself.

The realization shattered her. One by one, her internal defenses fell, starkly baring all that she had failed to become.

The sun slipped behind the buildings across the street, and she watched the long shadows creep toward her until they touched her feet. Shadows, she thought. How very appropriate. One corner of her mind began working with perfect clarity, unlike the rest of her, which felt numb.

She had stood in shadows always. In Michael's shadow, which she hadn't resented Michael for. In shadows of her own making. She alone was responsible, even if she had once thought she had the best of reasons—wanting to be accepted for herself without competing with her brother. A choice, a stupid choice, that she had never imagined would cost her so much.

In shadows there were no illusions, no golden sunshine, no

warmth. Tomorrow she would begin to think about the future. To-night—she swallowed and turned toward her room. Tonight she would endure, because there was no other choice.

She undressed, letting her clothes fall where they would, and slid into bed where she wrapped herself into a cocoon of misery.

Hours later, within the fog of a restless dream, she felt arms around her, wanted them to belong to Cole, knew that they belonged to her brother. She took Michael's hand and tried to speak.

"Shh," he whispered. "Sleep."

"It hurts so much," she cried.

"I know. We'll talk about it in the morning."

"I love him," she said as he pulled the covers around her shoulders.

"I know."

"I ruined it, Michael."

He smoothed his hand over her head and sat on the edge of the bed. "Go back to sleep, Brennie. Things will be better in the morning."

She drifted back into a fitful sleep where her half-truths and evasions and deceptions chased her.

The Brenna James I know looks me in the eye when she tells the truth.

"What do you mean my own daughter is too tired to come tell me hello?" came her father's too-real voice.

Hi, dad. Are you ready to see my school papers?

"I think she's coming down with the flu. She said something about a beastly headache and the sniffles."

Heartache, Michael. Not headache.

"Do I have to go to bed, Daddy?"

Jane's lilting voice answered, "Come along, Teddy. I'll read you a bedtime story."

Read this sign about Chimney Rock, Brenna.

It's too heavy to be a bedtime story, Cole. I can't.

"The apartment seems pretty small. I imagine you'll be glad to have the space back when Brenna moves."

"She's been a lot of help, Dad."

Read the card accompanying these flowers, Ms. James. Show the court you can read.

I can't. I want to. But, I can't.

Dreams and voices haunted her as she slept, and those same dreams and voices haunted her after she awoke.

And she had no one to blame but herself.

Chapter 22

"**Y**ou look like hell, boss," Myra said to Cole the following morning, when she arrived a few minutes before eight. "Have you been here long?"

Cole swung his feet off the desk and pinched the bridge of his nose between his thumb and index finger. "Since about six."

"Couldn't sleep, hmm."

"Yeah."

"Did you find the D.A.'s witnesses?"

"Yeah. One of them will give a jury plenty to chew on."

"You had one message from last night that came in after you checked in," Myra said, handing him the pink slip of paper. "Brenna called late—just before five."

"She mentioned she had called," Cole said. Everything about the conversation was burned into his memory.

"She sounded really disappointed when I told her you had gone for the day. Keeping your secret was hard. How was the picnic?"

"It wasn't." Cole put his glasses back on and picked up a pencil. "I'd appreciate getting that brief on the Collins case from you as soon as possible, Myra."

"Cole—"

The only time she called him by name was when she was worried about him or when things weren't going so well. Grateful as he was for the support, Cole didn't want to talk about Brenna. He wasn't sure he could without losing his temper or bawling like a baby.

"Not now, Myra." Cole looked up at his secretary. They had shared a lot over the last year. Cole had listened when her husband ran off with a woman half his age. Cole had sat with her at the hospital when her son was injured in a car accident. She had listened when he and Susan broke up. Most of all, Cole admired her loyalty for leaving a lucrative job when he went out on his own. But he wasn't ready to talk about Brenna.

"Boss..."

"Later, okay?" he said, his tone softening.

She smiled. "Later. And I've got a bottle of Scotch, if it's that kind of talk."

Myra closed the door behind her, and Cole swiveled his chair around where he stared unseeingly out the window. *I can't read.*

Cole had never imagined three words could affect him so profoundly. An illiterate person was a migrant farmworker, or a kid running with one of the inner-city gangs, or a junkie. It wasn't Brenna—it couldn't be Brenna who was bright, and brave, and loyal. It couldn't be.

He picked up the telephone and dialed Brenna's number. Michael, not Brenna, answered the telephone.

Bluntly, Cole asked how she was.

"There's a lot of ways I could answer that," Michael answered in the same vein. "Is she hurting? Damn straight. Am I mad about that? Yes. Is there one damn thing I can do to help her through this? No."

Cole closed his eyes.

"She's survived hurdles almost as big as your breaking her heart."

"She deserves more than that."

"She deserves the best," Michael said. "I like you, Cole. Until yesterday, I thought you were good for her."

"Can she read?"

The silence stretched over the line, and in the background, Cole could hear a radio playing.

"That's for her to tell you," Michael said, finally.

"She told me she couldn't," Cole answered.

"Then you have your answer."

"It makes no sense."

"Did you know she's moving out?" Michael asked.

"When?" The change of subject surprised Cole nearly as much as the announcement.

"Saturday."

"When did she decide that?" Had it been only yesterday morning they had ridden into town together, making plans?

"I was hoping you could tell me. She sprang that on me this morning on her way out."

Out where? Cole wondered. "Damn."

"Yeah." Michael cleared his throat. "The ball is in your court. She's holding herself together by a thread. Our dad is visiting, which is never good for her."

"He's already here?" So much for his intention to be a buffer between Brenna and her father.

"In or out. It's up to you." Michael paused again. "If you come back—"

"If I come back," Cole interrupted. "It will be for keeps. You won't see me otherwise."

"Fair enough," Michael said, breaking the connection.

Cole stared blindly at the papers strewn in front of him, hearing Brenna's anguished voice echo through his mind. *I can't read.* The statement haunted him, and Cole carefully examined each incident he could remember having anything to do with reading.

Brenna took Teddy to the library once or twice a week. In fact, Cole was pretty sure today was her day to do story hour again. If she did story hour, she read. So why had she said she could not?

Her admission that she had not finished school challenged Cole's every attitude about high-school dropouts. And Brenna fit none of them. She could hold her own in any situation, contributing when appropriate, asking the right questions to keep the conversation moving. She was articulate. She was curious. All the things Cole had observed led him to the same conclusion. She might be a dropout, but she sure as hell could read. He didn't understand her reasons for saying she couldn't.

There had to be some other reason for her not meeting him last night. Only what?

Unable to concentrate, he pushed his chair away from the desk and stood up. He felt as though he had all the pieces of a complex puzzle, pieces that were turned facedown so he couldn't see anything but the individual shapes to assemble the whole. Pieces that, alone, made no sense.

Cole pulled his jacket from the back of his chair and strode out of his office, telling Myra he didn't know when he would be back. If she was at the library reading, it was simple. She knew how to read and something else was going on with her.

After Cole parked the Jeep, he sat in front of the library a few moments more, drumming his fingers against the steering wheel. A confrontation with Brenna was the last thing he wanted, but he had to know.

He was positive she read. She was confident with the kids, holding the book and sharing it, with a comfort level that would be impossible if she wasn't thoroughly familiar with the story. She held the children's interest with nothing more than the power of her voice. To do that, she had to read.

Didn't she?

Cole left the Jeep and strode across the parking lot and through the front door of the library. He went down the stairs to the children's section. The children were gathered around the story-hour corner, and Cole could hear Brenna's voice weaving the story around them. At the moment, Cole was tempted to go back up the stairs. He had proven what he needed to.

He was no closer to understanding why she would tell him that she could not read. People who loved each other and trusted each other didn't lie. Period.

Instead of leaving, Cole found himself peering around the corner until he could see her. Brenna sat in front of the children, her legs crossed, a book with brilliant pictures held in front of her. Her voice drew him as it drew the children, but unlike the children he couldn't have repeated a single word she said.

Cole was shocked at how pale she was. She looked worse than he felt. Her eyes were on the children, not on the book. She didn't glance at it at all except to turn the pages, holding the book so each child could see the illustrations.

Brenna was just halfway through the story of the *Little Red Hen* when she became aware of someone else joining the children. She lifted her eyes expecting to find a child shyly standing at the back of the group. Instead she found her gaze focused on a pair of crisply pressed trousers.

Her hands grew suddenly clammy. Knowing who she would see didn't keep her gaze from climbing the length of his body until she met Cole's eyes. All the hardness she had first known in him was present this morning, his features chiseled into a somber mask, his eyes dark, hooded, expressionless.

She dropped her gaze. Her voice died away and the book fell heedlessly to the floor. Wearily, she picked up the book from the floor. She opened it, but she couldn't have said if she had stopped telling the story on page 1 or if she had finished.

Dear Lord, why was he here now?

The children turned around to look at Cole, then glanced back to Brenna.

Finally, she said, "I've lost my place. Where were we?"

"The little red hen needs help harvesting her wheat," said Teddy.

"Oh, yes." Brenna paged through the book until she found the illustrations for that part of the story. Somehow, she had to ignore Cole long enough to finish this. She wanted to flee, wanted to demand that he leave, knew neither one was possible.

Brenna continued with the narration, only half aware of what she was saying. When she glanced back at Cole, he was watching her with an intensity she found unnerving. She finished the story without knowing how. She only knew that she wasn't ready to talk to Cole.

He remained standing where he was after the story ended and the children got up and gradually left. After the last child said goodbye, Brenna sat a moment longer, her head bent.

"Hi, Cole," Teddy said.

Brenna watched him tip his head way up and smile.

"Hi," Cole responded. His gaze left Brenna and focused on Teddy. "Would you mind sitting down here and reading for a few minutes? I need to talk to Brenna."

"I think she needs to talk to you, too," Teddy said, his voice serious. "Last night she cried." He pointed to a table across the room. "I'll be over there. Okay, Auntie?"

Brenna nodded.

"Come on, Brenna," Cole said, coming a couple of steps closer. "We've got to talk."

As she had only scant weeks earlier, she wanted to tell him they had nothing to talk about. Instead, she stood and followed Cole up the stairs and through the wide front doors of the library. After the relative cool from the air conditioner inside, the air outside was hot. She watched Cole loosen his tie and unbutton the top button of his shirt as he led her to a bench underneath a couple of mature spruce trees.

He sat down next to her, leaned his elbows on his knees, and stared through his loosely clasped hands. "I don't understand," he said a few moments later. "You tell me that you can't read. And yet you're here. If reading stories during story hour isn't reading, Brenna, I don't know what is."

"I wasn't reading," she replied, still not looking at him directly. "I pick stories I know already. I pace the story according to the pictures. That's all."

Cole thought about that for a moment. Though it sounded a little far-fetched to him, her explanation seemed reasonable. More, her voice had a ring of truth he hadn't heard in it last night.

She lifted her gaze to his. "Is that the problem, Cole? That you don't believe me?" Her voice caught. "That you think...I'm lying?"

"I don't know what I believe." He straightened and glanced at her. "Your being here ought to prove that you read."

"I told you the truth."

"When?" he asked, pinning her with a hard glance. "The night you told me you hadn't finished school, but conveniently neglected to tell me you're illiterate? That first night at the bar? The day you told me about the year when your mother and grandmother died? All the weeks in between? Tell me, Brenna, just when did you tell me the truth?" He surged to his feet and thrust his hands into his pants pockets.

"It was all the truth," she answered, meeting his gaze. "All of it... It just wasn't the complete truth."

"Lies by omission," he muttered.

"You're right," she said, standing up. "I know I hurt you, Cole. I never meant to."

"That doesn't help a hell of a lot at the moment," he said.

"Do you think I wanted this?" she whispered. Emotion closed her throat and her eyes burned. She wrapped her arms around her waist and turned away from him. "At first, it didn't matter. I didn't ever expect to see you again, much less fall in love with you. And then..." She paused and took a deep breath. "Did you know that I told John Miller I couldn't read?"

Cole shook his head.

"I thought he'd protect me. I thought he had to know, and that was what I paid him for. Only he decided I was stupid. I trusted him." Her glance lifted to Cole's. "I didn't want to trust you."

"But?" he prompted.

"I did." Her voice fell again to a whisper, but she held his gaze. "And then it was too late. I didn't want...things...between us to end. And I knew it would the minute I told you. So I kept putting it off, hoping I'd figure out a way. And I kept thinking, how do I tell him? A dozen different times I've wanted to, and I just couldn't make myself say the words that would send you out of my life." She took a deep breath. "I don't expect you to understand that."

She glanced away. Never had she looked more vulnerable. He yearned to reach for her. But he didn't.

Her chin quivered, then firmed, and she looked back at him. "After you brought me home yesterday, I knew I couldn't put this off any longer. It wasn't being fair to you or to me." She took the crumpled card that had accompanied his flowers out of her pocket and held it out to him. "Don't you think I'd give my life to know what this says?"

Brenna dropped the card in his palm and walked away. Cole watched her, all his convictions shattered. He had been so sure he knew how to dispassionately discover one way or the other whether Brenna could read. Life was messier than law, though, and he had just discovered nothing could be less simple.

"Cole?"

He raised his head to look at her poised at the entry to the library. "I'm sorry I hurt you." Then she pulled open the door and disappeared into the building.

He raised his face to the heat of the bright sunshine, then dropped his head and opened up his palm. He smoothed the crumpled sheet of paper, hearing her voice echo in his mind. *Don't you think I'd give my life to know what this says?* Never had he heard her so anguished. And he just stood there, so sure he was right, discovering that he had wounded her in ways he was just beginning to comprehend.

As for himself, his head pounded and his heart ached. Literally. With every breath he took. Sometime later he found himself in the parking lot in front of his office, shocked that he didn't remember getting into the Jeep or driving across town.

He got out of the vehicle and went inside, automatically acknowledging Myra as he went through the outer office. At his desk, he stared at the folders littered over the surface and tried to marshal his thoughts into some sort of order.

Some minutes passed before he remembered the one call he had to make—to Zach, letting him know about the prosecution's new witnesses.

Ten minutes later when he had Zach on the line, Cole asked how he was doing.

"Fine," came Zach's response over the line. "Cut to the chase, Counselor. I know you didn't call for that."

"You're right," Cole admitted, succinctly relating his conversations with the D.A. and, subsequently, the two witnesses. He finished with, "The D.A. told me to call him back after I had interviewed them. He's pretty damn sure we're going to want to plea-bargain this."

"I could get nailed at the trial. Be found guilty."

"You could," Cole agreed. "Or you could be acquitted."

A moment of silence stretched across the line, then Zach asked, "Are you positive—one hundred percent positive—we can win this?"

"Life doesn't come with that kind of guarantee," Cole said.

"I'll be looking at some hard time if we lose."

"Yes."

"And we could lose."

Cole propped an elbow on the desk, tunneling his fingers into his hair when he rested his head on his hand. This was a case he believed in, dammit. And he was on the verge of urging his client to toss in the towel. How many ways would he lose today?

"Cole?" Zach prompted him a second later.

"Yeah." Cole cleared his throat. "We could lose. And if we do, you're the one who pays the price."

"See what the man is willing to offer," Zach said. "Then bargain it down as far as you can."

The directive didn't surprise Cole though he supposed it should have. "You're sure?"

"I'm sure."

"I don't think he's going to agree to any suspended sentences."

"I'm not expecting him to," Zach returned. "Bargain it. Do the best you can."

"Are you admitting to driving while under the influence?" Cole asked.

"I'm admitting I was irresponsible," Zach said. "Like I told you before, driving while you're angry isn't any smarter than driving drunk. If I hadn't been so mad...it might have turned out differently." He cleared his throat. "Call me back and let me know what the damage is."

After Zach hung up, Cole sat staring at the phone, wondering if he had a tenth of Zach's personal integrity or grit. A moment later, he called the D.A. Within another hour, they had struck a deal. An involuntary manslaughter charge with a two-year sentence, the first year in prison, the balance in a halfway house. And the D.A. agreed to schedule the appearance in front of the judge after Zach finished his thirty-day stint at Maizer's.

It wasn't the end to the case Cole had wanted. It didn't seem fair. How was it fair that a man like Zach MacKenzie went to jail and a man like Harvey Bates got away scot-free?

The question of fairness haunted Cole long after he went home, long after he spent the evening digging postholes for the fence he'd started months ago. His grandmother had been fond of telling him that fair was a weather report, not a promise from God or his parents. Inevitably his thoughts drifted back to Brenna. The total *un*fairness of her situation ate at him. He began to dissect every conversation he could remember. Through them all, she had shown inquisitiveness and intelligence. *Enough to compensate for not reading? Enough to have functioned in spite of not reading?*

All of her expressions haunted him, as well, from her complete seriousness to her smile as the first rhythms of ecstasy pulsed through her, from her tears the other morning, to her joy when he took her sailing.

Over the next days, Cole worked by rote. No longer in the intense cycle of preparing for Zach's trial, Cole found himself unable to concentrate. A dozen times a day, his thoughts strayed to Brenna. The more he thought about her, the more edgy and angry he became. Gradually, his anger became more sharply focused, and he realized he wasn't mad at her because she couldn't read. He was mad because she had lied to him.

Or had she?

The night they had gone to the theater, he clearly remembered her saying, *Aren't you more than the sum of your job? Is what you do to earn a living the most important piece?*

Like his grandmother, Brenna was wise. Her jobs weren't what he thought about when he was with her.

He tried to imagine what she must have gone through trying to decide how to tell him she was illiterate. Especially if she loved him. He had pursued her, even though she had been reluctant to see him. And look what it had cost them both.

By Friday afternoon, Cole was restless and tense, knowing he had put off calling her long enough. When he finally dialed her house, he wasn't even sure what he would say to her if she answered. Instead he reached her sister-in-law, Jane, who told him Brenna was out and not expected back until late. Did he want to leave a message? He didn't.

He loved her, and she deserved to be told that face-to-face.

His eyes burned. He had walked away from her rather than listen. He had judged her rather than understand. He had run away rather than cherish her. He hadn't faced the plain, unadorned truth when she gave it to him. No. evasions. No omissions.

No deceptions.

Chapter 23

Saturday morning Brenna awoke early. Sitting up in bed, she pulled aside the curtain to gaze outside. The world beyond her window was washed in the shades of gray that came an hour or so before the sunrise. Letting the curtain fall back into place, she rolled onto her back, and stared at the ceiling.

Another day of survival.

This one would be busier than most, since she was moving into her own place again. A scant three days ago, she had recruited Nancy to go apartment-hunting with her, and they found a place that fit Brenna's budget. Since it was immediately available, Brenna saw no reason to put off moving.

Reestablishing her independence ought to have been a red-letter day. Instead, she felt like she was running, something she had vowed never to do again. The Colonel's visit had intensified the feeling. Somehow when he was around she always felt like the bungling six-year-old who had never once lived up to his expectations. So far, she had managed to avoid being alone with him and she had been able to steer their few conversations toward Teddy's or Michael's and Jane's activities.

The Colonel was staying at the Marriott downtown, but Brenna

knew he would be by shortly after seven to meet Michael for breakfast and a game of golf. Weekend mornings had always begun at
seven, and she would bet he hadn't changed that routine, though he
had been retired from the service for several years now.

Unable to sleep, Brenna finally got out of bed. Only the cat, Penelope, was awake, and she wound her way through Brenna's legs.
She picked up the cat and petted it a moment before making coffee.
While the coffee brewed, she went to take a shower. When she came
back to the kitchen a few minutes later, her father was striding up
the walk, carrying a paper under his arm. Brenna went to the door
and let him in.

"Hello, Dad," she said, managing a civil smile.

"Brenna," he acknowledged, stepping over the threshold without
touching her.

Unbidden came the images of Cole's mother and father and grandmother each hugging him when he came into the room, even after
they had been there for a couple of days. Brenna doubted her father
had hugged anyone, even Teddy.

He didn't smile, and she had the urge to look away. Her mother
had once said his gray eyes were like her own. Brenna had always
hated looking at his eyes. Surely hers weren't hard like his, cold like
his.

Preceding him into the kitchen, she poured them both a cup of
coffee. He sat down at one of the kitchen chairs and snapped out the
newspaper. She always had the feeling he used the newspaper as a
shield, but she was equally sure he was aware of her watching him.

"You're right on time," she said, glancing at the clock. Seven-
fifteen.

"Old habits die hard."

She sat down across from him, noting he wore his casual slacks
and golf shirt like a uniform, all crisply pressed as though he might
be asked to stand for inspection. Brenna resisted the urge to check
her fingernails for dirt. Instead, she wrapped her cold hands around
the warm ceramic surface of the mug.

The silence stretched between them, uncomfortable and taut and
reminding Brenna why she had done her level best to avoid being
alone with him. A moment later, he folded the paper and set it on
the table, then took a sip of his coffee.

He inclined his head slightly, studying her. "Have you found a job yet?"

Brenna took another sip of her own coffee and shook her head. How like him to get straight to whatever point he wanted to make. No small talk, no setting the other person at ease.

"I'm in no hurry to find one," she said. "I have enough house-cleaning customers to keep the wolf from the door."

"You can't expect to clean houses for the rest of your life."

"I don't." She glanced at him. "I've decided to go back to school." Her decision had been one of the small steps to grow into the person she wanted to become. She had already contacted Adult Ed to find out the requirements to earn her GED.

The Colonel folded his arms across his chest. "It's a little late for that, isn't it?"

"Better late than never."

"What makes you think you'll do any better in school now than you ever did?" he asked.

Brenna met his gaze over the top of her cup. "Now I want to."

"Just what do you plan to study?" he asked.

She shrugged. "I don't know. I haven't thought that far ahead."

"That sounds to me like the same problem you've always had," he said. "I suppose you haven't really enrolled yet, either."

"Not yet, I've just—"

"You're looking for yet another way to avoid your responsibilities. Getting a job—a well-paid job is the important thing here. It's high time you started pulling your own weight."

Brenna set her cup on the table and folded her hands to keep them from trembling. "I am pulling my own weight," she said, struggling to keep her voice even. "And I have been since I was fifteen years old. I'm not asking for any help."

"Not now. But you always get around to it sooner or later."

Brenna gave her father a level stare, remembering too well where their conversations inevitably led. "Just how many times in the last ten years have I asked you for help?" When he didn't immediately answer, she repeated, "How many times?"

He stared at her, his eyes clear and hard.

"Not once," she answered for him.

"And how many times have you asked Michael for help?" he

countered. "It takes a lot of nerve to sponge off your brother, expecting him to pick up the pieces."

"I didn't run to him," Brenna replied, her temper beginning to fray. "He offered. He knew I needed help, and he offered. There's a difference." Her hands clenched into fists beneath the table. "And as for support—you've confused emotional support with financial support."

"Only weak people need either one."

Brenna sighed. Whether she agreed with him was immaterial. Their differences would never change, and hoping for something more was futile. She stood up to leave. "I've got a lot to do this morning. I'll talk to you later."

"I haven't dismissed you," he said.

Brenna stopped at the kitchen doorway. "I'm not a child to be dismissed."

"You've never stopped being a child," he said, his voice harsh. "In all the ways that matter, you never matured into an adult. When things get tough, you turn into a pansy. And why your brother puts up with—"

"Maybe he loves me."

"Something you take advantage of every chance you get."

"I've never taken advantage of Michael." Brenna felt her discipline slip, the calm mask behind which she hid her temper dissolve. She had to leave now before they both said things they would regret. At that she winced. She might have regrets. She doubted her father had a single one.

"You've been doing just that for months, without earning enough money to help him out."

She folded her arms across her chest, feeling compelled to defend herself though every ounce of logic told her to do so was tilting at windmills.

"That's not true." Without realizing, she extended a hand to her father. "What's really the problem here? I'm moving out, and that proves I can support myself again. I'm getting my life back together, and I don't intend to make the same mistakes I've made before. I want to go to school. All the things you've said time and again I had to do. Okay. I'm doing them." She touched her chest with her hand. "For me. Not for you. Not for anyone else. For me."

"That's the way it's always been for you, Brenna. You don't think of anyone else. You broke your mother's heart when you ran away from home. And now." He turned in his chair. "Michael told me you spent the money she saved for you. You just couldn't wait to throw it—"

"That money was a godsend," she retorted. "It got me out of the bottom of a hole I would have spent the next ten years in."

Brenna felt movement behind her, and glanced over her shoulder. Michael stood there, dressed only in jeans, his dark hair sleep-tousled.

"Yesterday you told me the money didn't matter," Michael said. "That you didn't care how she spent it."

"You stay out of this!" the Colonel ordered. "She's been wasting her time, her talent, and taking the easy way out for years."

Cole approached the door of the apartment, the sound of angry voices carrying through the open window of the kitchen. Though he had never heard the voice, he recognized it at once. Clear, decisive. Each word enunciated with clipped precision. Brenna's father.

Brenna's voice, when it came a second later, was calm in comparison to her father's, and filled with sarcasm. "That's right, Dad," she said. "My life has been real easy."

Cole knew as surely as the sun blazed in the morning sky he had arrived just in time. Right, he mocked himself. If you had been in time, she wouldn't be in there facing this alone. If you had been in time, she wouldn't even be here.

Cole knocked on the door as the scalding voices continued to pour from the kitchen.

"You've shirked from every challenge you've ever faced," the Colonel said. "It's high time you planned instead of running off on some harebrained scheme."

Teddy, still in pajamas, opened the screen door. "Hi, Cole."

Cole touched the boy's hair. "Hi."

"I know what I want," Brenna said.

"They're having a fight," Teddy said to Cole, his glance straying to the kitchen.

Cole picked up the child and stepped into the apartment. "That they are. Why don't you go back to your room and play. Okay?"

"School?" the Colonel scoffed. "This is just another whim. You're going to school, but you haven't applied."

Teddy looked up at Cole. "Do you want to come with me?"

He shook his head. "I'm going to stay and help Brenna."

"Dad," Michael said, "C'mon, arguing won't accomplish anything."

Teddy smiled at Cole. "She'll like that. She's been real sad."

Teddy's reply went through Cole like a knife. He set the boy down. "I know. Now scoot."

"Michael, stay out of it," the Colonel said.

"Like hell," Michael responded. "For years, I've watched you belittle every single thing she ever tried to do. Not once did you tell her you were proud of her. And you know what I hated most about that? I was the stick you used to beat her up with."

Cole moved to the kitchen doorway, unnoticed by the three people inside. Michael's broad back hid Brenna from his view.

"I just wanted her to live up to her potential," the Colonel shouted. "Which she never did. She could have done anything you did if she had just once tried."

"That's always been your bottom line, Dad," Brenna said. "Take a good look at me. I'm not Michael. I'm me. Michael is my brother, and I love him, but I'm not like him. I'm not a genius. Not gifted. And *not* worthless. And I don't have to stand here and listen to you rant at me."

She brushed past Michael and collided with Cole.

He put his hands on her arms to steady her. "Hi."

What little color was left in her face drained away, leaving only a faint line around her lips. Michael glanced over his shoulder, his expression nearly as stunned as Brenna's. Behind Michael, Cole could see Brenna's father, his expression full of irritation and derision.

"Who the hell are you?" the Colonel demanded.

Cole offered the man his hand. "Cole Cassidy. You must be Colonel James. I've heard a lot about you."

Cole was positive only sheer reflex made the Colonel take his hand. When he released it, Cole glanced back down at Brenna who watched him with wide, pain-filled eyes.

Casually as he could muster, Cole said, "I hear you're moving today. Need any help?"

Brenna stared at him. She expected to blink and find him gone. She closed her eyes. When she opened them a moment later, Cole was still there, his hand gently holding her arm. Being with him the other day at the library was the most painful moment she had ever endured. Knowing Cole could hurt her so deeply almost made the pain her father inflicted a preferable choice. Only Cole, no one else, only Cole could break her heart.

He held out his other hand to her. Slowly her eyes lifted from Cole's hand. A hand that knew her intimately, a hand that was warm and strong, a hand that had never given her anything but comfort and pleasure. Cole's mouth was deeply bracketed by creases, and though his expression was grim, she recognized the plea in his eyes asking her to trust him. In that blinding instant, she knew he would not deliberately hurt her.

She placed her hand within Cole's. His fingers wrapped around hers, offering her warmth and reassurance.

He took a backward step toward the door and she followed him.

"Running again?" the Colonel taunted.

Brenna turned around to stare at her father as a stunning realization crystallized for her. "Yes. I am. Sometimes it's the only way to keep myself safe."

She turned her back on her father and led Cole toward the door.

"You're not finished here," the Colonel said.

Cole glanced over his shoulder then turned around to face Brenna's father. "Oh, but she is."

The Colonel leveled a stare that Cole knew was meant to intimidate. "Just who the hell do you think you are?"

"Your future son-in-law," Cole said. "And we might as well get one thing straight right now. If you ever, *ever,* want to be welcome in our home, you'll give Brenna the respect due her." Cole looked down at Brenna, felt the fine trembling of her body where it brushed against his. His voice gentle, he asked, "Have you had breakfast yet?"

She shook her head without looking at him.

He tipped his head toward her. "Would you like to have breakfast with me?"

"Yes," she replied, meeting his gaze, her eyes clear and direct.

Cole offered Michael his right hand. "I told you if I came back it was for keeps. We'll call later." Cole paused, then turned to face Brenna's father, and after a second offered the man his hand. "When we meet again, sir, I hope it's under better circumstances."

This time the Colonel didn't accept the offered hand. Cole held his out a moment longer, meeting the man's eyes, recognizing the challenge. Cole turned away from the older man, winked at Michael, and walked with Brenna out the front door.

"Cassidy." The Colonel's voice followed them outside in an imperative command.

Cole wanted to ignore it. Instead, he turned around and faced the door, the figures inside shadowy beyond the screen.

"I'm not finished."

"That's where you're wrong."

"I can find you, boy, no matter who you are or what you do, I can ruin you."

"Damn your arrogance." Cole released Brenna's hand, his temper no longer in check. He climbed the two steps to the apartment door. Cole opened the door and held it there with his foot.

The Colonel might be used to operating in an environment where people were cowed by his belligerence. Its effect on Cole was to make him angrier than he had been since the day he had watched Harvey Bates subject Brenna to the same kind of aggression.

"First," Cole said, "don't ever threaten me. I won't be playing by your rules, and I can promise you I give as good as I get. Second, Brenna is a free agent who can go where she wants, when she wants. If she wants to come back in here, I won't stop her. Third, I'm in love with her, and I protect and cherish the people I love. Take that as a threat, Colonel, or a friendly warning. As far as I'm concerned, you can go to hell."

Cole removed his foot from the door and let it slam shut. Turning around, he found Brenna standing in the middle of the sidewalk, her expression stricken.

"Do you want to go back in there or come with me?" He knew his voice was too harsh, but he couldn't help it. Only after the words were out of his mouth did he recognize they sounded like an ultimatum.

"With you," she answered without a shred of hesitation or doubt.

Cole smiled and took her hand. Her own answering smile wasn't much, but she squeezed his hand. He helped her into the Jeep, then slid behind the steering wheel.

Brenna glanced at Cole when the vehicle pulled away from the curb. Her thoughts raced, but one overwhelming fact stayed with her. Cole had defended her. She hadn't expected to ever have his friendship again, much less his love.

Cole negotiated the Jeep through traffic, a pair of reflective sunglasses hiding his eyes. His expression was harsh, though, and she wondered what he was thinking.

Son-in-law. A thrill of anticipation shot through her. Somehow, things would be all right.

Absently her attention focused on the mountains that drew closer as Cole drove northwest and she understood he was taking her home. Afternoon thunderstorms would gather over the mountains later, but for now, there wasn't a cloud in the sky. Like life, Brenna thought. She and Cole had problems to solve. For the moment, though, their future seemed as clear as the summer sky.

She hadn't dared hope he would forgive her for deceiving him. Now that she had a second chance, she was determined to give Cole the kind of honesty he deserved. No evasions. No lies by omissions. No deceptions. Not even small ones.

By the time Cole exited the highway for the last lap toward home, he decided that he had been too heavy-handed with Brenna's father. She had things well in hand when he got there, and she had been winning her own battle. Once again, he should have held on to his temper.

Then, minutes later, he turned onto the road that led to his house, feeling as insecure as a teenager wanting to kiss a girl for the first time. He stared at the house as though he had never seen it before. He hadn't consciously planned to bring Brenna here, had focused only on going someplace where they could talk without being interrupted.

Now that he was here, he had no idea what to do next. He turned to Brenna, unsure of how she would feel about being here. He got out of the Jeep without looking at her and walked around to open the door for her.

His voice was gruff as he held out his hand. "I hope this is okay—coming here, I mean."

"It's fine." She placed her hand in his, and at her touch, he trembled.

She looked up at him suddenly, as if she knew just how unsure of himself he was. She gave him a slow smile. "I'm scared, too," she said.

"Ah, fair lady," he whispered. "C'mon."

Brenna followed Cole onto the porch, then into the kitchen. It was spotless except for a cup and plate in the sink. Cole didn't release her hand even when he opened the refrigerator and surveyed its meager contents.

"Do you want cereal or eggs?"

"I want to talk," she answered.

"Okay." He closed the refrigerator and led her through a pair of glass doors that separated the kitchen from the entryway. In the living room, he sat down on one end of a high-backed couch without releasing her hand. His eyes were full of so much hunger and regret, she nearly flinched.

Brenna sank down next to him. "I'm sorry. I should have—" she began.

"I'm sorry. I should have—" he said at the same moment.

Cole caught her face within his large hands. He gazed at her long seconds, watching her eyes dilate and grow smoky. He leaned forward and brushed his lips across hers in a caress of silent apology. Her lips trembled beneath his as she returned his chaste kiss.

Brenna held herself rigid, half frightened that she would wake up in a moment and discover this was yet another unfulfilled dream. But in her dreams, his lips weren't this soft. In her dreams, Cole's hands had never held her with such care. In her dreams, she didn't feel the erratic pounding of his heart beneath her hand.

Tears welled as she realized what she had nearly lost. She wrapped her arms around his neck, sighed and parted her lips, touching him with the tip of her tongue.

He returned her touch in kind, urging her closer, reveling in her taste that was the sweetest, the best he had ever known. The knowledge that he had nearly lost her made him tighten his arms around her until her breasts flattened into his chest. She pressed herself even closer, her fingers ice-cold against his neck, a marked contrast to the searing heat of her mouth, her renewed tears leaving his face as wet as her own.

"Oh, God, Brenna. I love you so much," he said between long, soul-rending kisses. "I didn't mean to hurt you."

"I know." She ran her fingers through his hair, traced the outline of his face, pressed her lips across his high cheekbones, then captured his mouth again in a kiss that was as necessary to her as air. "I didn't mean to hurt you, either."

He pulled her across his lap, looped her arms around his neck, and wrapped his own around her back. Holding her close, he rubbed his cheek against her hair. Nothing had ever felt so right, and he wanted to make damn sure she knew there was nothing more important than the two of them together. He wanted to take her upstairs and make long, sweet love to her until they were both mindless. But they had to talk.

"I wish...I had done things differently the other night." Cole closed his eyes against the remembered hurt of Brenna standing in the middle of the room with tears in her eyes.

"Don't," she whispered, pressing her hands against his mouth.

"But, if I had—"

"Things would have come apart some other time," she finished. "The fault—"

"I don't want any blaming here," he interrupted. "For either of us."

"But—"

"No. We can move past that. We *are* past that."

She brushed his hair off his forehead. "What do you suggest?"

"I don't know. I'm just scared to death of losing you."

"I know," she whispered around the lump in her throat.

He brushed her hair away from her face. "Marry me."

She met his gaze and tears filled her eyes.

"I love you, Brenna," he whispered. "Marry me."

She brought his hand to her mouth and kissed it. "I can't. I love you, but don't ask that of me. Not now."

"Brenna—"

"You'd be ashamed of me."

"Never."

"I know you don't believe me, but I can't—"

"Read?" he finished. "I believe you. I've thought about you all week. I know you were telling me the truth."

"I never finished school—"

"I'll take you in my life any way I can get you."

"It—marriage—will never work. Sooner or later, you'll be in the position of being ashamed to be—"

Cole stilled her words by pressing his fingers against her lips. "I've never known anyone I admire more. I wasn't angry because you couldn't read. I was angry because—"

"Because I lied to you."

"Ah, fair lady—"

"If I had been truthful..." Brenna swallowed and dropped her gaze from Cole's. "And...the truth is...I won't saddle you with an illiterate wife." She lifted her eyes. "I'm enrolled in a tutoring program, Cole, and I want to go back to school. I want to earn my GED."

"I'm glad," he said, "but I'd want you whether you—"

"Would you, Cole?" she whispered. "Honestly? I believe you love me." She touched his cheek. "But for you to believe in me, to respect me, I need to believe in *me,* I need to respect *me.* Do you understand?"

"I'm trying, fair lady."

"Your offer to marry me—"

"Stands," he said.

She smiled. "Ask me the day I've earned my GED. If you still want me then—if you still love me then, I'll marry you."

"That might take years."

She smiled. "I want to be your wife. That could be a pretty powerful inducement."

He grinned. "Does that mean I can give you a ring?"

"Like going steady?" she teased.

"More like promising to say yes when I ask you to marry me," he answered.

"No diamonds."

"Oh, there will be diamonds," he countered, offering his hand. "But if you insist, I can wait until you have your GED."

"What's this?" she asked, nodding toward his extended arm.

He leaned forward and kissed her. "When we shake hands on this, fair lady, we have a legal, binding contract that I'll hold you to."

Brenna glanced at his large callused hand, then raised her eyes to his. Her lips curved in a smile. "Are there any terms in this contract I should be aware of, Counselor?"

He grinned. "I thought I'd take you upstairs in a minute and demonstrate the terms I have in mind."

She placed her hand in his, trusting in him and the future that would be theirs. "Sounds like a good deal to me."

Eighteen months to the day later, Cole waited for Brenna at the end of a platform full of dignitaries passing out GED certificates. She stood with a group of other graduates, her head high. Cole had eyes only for her.

Overall, the months had sped by. Brenna had insisted on keeping her own apartment, and the only token of commitment she had accepted from him was his old high-school class ring, which she wore on a chain around her neck. He had never seen anyone work harder. She drove herself relentlessly. Along the way, Michael encouraged her and at the same time reminded her she didn't have to be perfect— all she had to do was her best and let the devil take the hindmost. That encouragement and support cemented his friendship with Cole. Recently she had begun to make plans for college, which he applauded.

Brenna's name was called, and Cole watched her stride across the platform. When she was handed her GED certificate, he took her picture and heard Teddy's and Michael's cheers from the audience.

She came toward him, her smile brilliant. He held out his hand and steadied her as she stepped off the platform. Then he kissed her, took her left hand in his, and slid a huge diamond solitaire on her finger.

"I hope you believe in short engagements, fair lady."

She laughed, looking so radiant she took his breath away.

"Grandmom already told me she's counting on a Valentine's Day wedding."

His eyebrows lifted. "That's three weeks away."

She smiled. "I know."
"Perfect."
And it was.

* * * * *

Dear Reader,

Several years ago I became a volunteer for literacy at my local library, never expecting this extraordinary experience would spawn the idea for a story. A memorable part of the training was being challenged to read English words written with Cyrillic characters. I found the process confusing and frustrating—exactly what being unable to read is like.

In 1993 the U.S. Department of Education released the results of the National Adult Literacy Survey, which found that between forty million and forty-four million adults in the United States are functionally illiterate (reading at third-grade level or less). The reasons are as varied as the number of nonreaders, who can be found in every sector of our society. The statistics are overwhelming, but behind each one is a person who has dreams and goals and aspirations similar to your own, including the student with whom I was paired—a person who became my friend.

Since the problem of adult illiteracy first garnered national attention about twenty years ago, a number of local, state and national organizations have been formed in the U.S. and Canada, all with the goal of reducing the illiteracy rate. If you want more information, contact your local library or your community's Literacy Resource Center (which can usually be found through the Department of Education) or any of the following organizations. Literacy Volunteers of America, Inc. or Laubach Literacy International.

Thank you, Karen Echols, for passing on the methods to teach reading. Thank you, Robin Owens and Lynn Eisaguierre, for your insights regarding the law profession. Thanks also to the Colorado Literacy Resource Center. Any mistakes are mine alone.

Take 2 bestselling love stories FREE

Plus get a FREE surprise gift!

Special Limited-Time Offer

Mail to Silhouette Reader Service™

3010 Walden Avenue
P.O. Box 1867
Buffalo, N.Y. 14240-1867

YES! Please send me 2 free Silhouette Intimate Moments® novels and my free surprise gift. Then send me 6 brand-new novels every month, which I will receive months before they appear in bookstores. Bill me at the low price of $3.57 each plus 25¢ delivery and applicable sales tax, if any.* That's the complete price, and a saving of over 10% off the cover prices—quite a bargain! I understand that accepting the books and gift places me under no obligation ever to buy any books. I can always return a shipment and cancel at any time. Even if I never buy another book from Silhouette, the 2 free books and the surprise gift are mine to keep forever.

245 SEN CH7Y

Name	(PLEASE PRINT)
Address	Apt. No.
City	State	Zip

UIM-98   ©1990 Harlequin Enterprises Limited

In **July 1998** comes

THE MACKENZIE FAMILY

by *New York Times* bestselling author

LINDA HOWARD

The dynasty continues with:

Mackenzie's Pleasure: Rescuing a pampered ambassador's daughter from her terrorist kidnappers was a piece of cake for navy SEAL Zane Mackenzie. It was only afterward, when they were alone together, that the real danger began....

Mackenzie's Magic: Talented trainer Maris Mackenzie was wanted for horse theft, but with no memory, she had little chance of proving her innocence or eluding the real villains. Her only hope for salvation? The stranger in her bed.

Available this July for the first time ever in a two-in-one trade-size edition. Fall in love with the Mackenzies for the first time—or all over again!

Available at your favorite retail outlet.

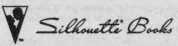

Silhouette Books

Look us up on-line at: http://www.romance.net   PSMACFMLY

International bestselling author

JOAN JOHNSTON

**continues her wildly popular Hawk's Way
miniseries with an all-new, longer-length novel**

THE SUBSTITUTE GROOM

HAWK'S WAY

August 1998

Jennifer Wright's hopes and dreams had rested on her summer wedding—until a single moment changed everything. Including the *groom*. Suddenly Jennifer agreed to marry her fiancé's best friend, a darkly handsome Texan she needed— and desperately wanted—almost against her will. But U.S. Air Force Major Colt Whitelaw had sacrificed too much to settle for a marriage of convenience, and that made hiding her passion all the more difficult. And hiding her biggest secret downright impossible…

**"Joan Johnston does contemporary Westerns
to perfection."** —*Publishers Weekly*

Available in August 1998
wherever Silhouette books are sold.

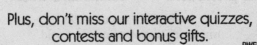

The World's Most Eligible Bachelors are about
to be named! And Silhouette Books brings
them to you in an all-new, original series....

World's Most
Eligible Bachelors

Twelve of the sexiest, most sought-after men share
every intimate detail of their lives in twelve never-
before-published novels by the genre's top authors.

Don't miss these unforgettable stories by:

Dixie Browning

Marie Ferrarella

Jackie Merritt

Tracy Sinclair

BJ James

Rachel Lee

Suzanne Carey

Gina Wilkins

VICTORIA PADE

Maggie Shayne

Anne McAllister

Susan Mallery

Look for one new book each month in the
World's Most Eligible Bachelors series beginning
September 1998 from Silhouette Books.

Silhouette®

Available at your favorite retail outlet.